ALSO BY RAY BRADBURY

THE TOYNBEE CONVECTOR

RAY BRADBURY

Simon & Schuster Paperbacks

New York   London   Toronto   Sydney   New Delhi

Simon & Schuster Paperbacks
An Imprint of Simon & Schuster, Inc.
1230 Avenue of the Americas
New York, NY 10020

First Simon & Schuster trade paperback edition July 2019

SIMON & SCHUSTER PAPERBACKS and colophon are
registered trademarks of Simon & Schuster, Inc.

For information about special discounts for bulk purchases, please
contact Simon & Schuster Special Sales at 1-866-506-1949 or
business@simonandschuster.com.

The Simon & Schuster Speakers Bureau can bring authors to your live event. For
more information or to book an event, contact the Simon & Schuster Speakers
Bureau at 1-866-248-3049 or visit our website at www.simonspeakers.com.

Interior design by Alexis Minieri

Manufactured in the United States of America

1   3   5   7   9   10   8   6   4   2

Library of Congress Cataloging-in-Publication Data is available.

ISBN 978-1-9821-0515-0
ISBN 978-1-9821-0519-8 (ebook)

And this one, with love,
to my granddaughters
Julia
and
Claire
and
Georgia
and
Mallory

CONTENTS

THE TOYNBEE CONVECTOR

"Good! Great! Bravo for me!"

Roger Shumway flung himself into the seat, buckled himself in, revved the rotor and drifted his Dragonfly Super-6 helicopter up to blow away on the summer sky, heading south toward La Jolla.

"How lucky can you get?"

For he was on his way to an incredible meeting.

The time traveler, after 100 years of silence, had agreed to be interviewed. He was, on this day, 130 years old. And this afternoon, at four o'clock sharp, Pacific time, was the anniversary of his one and only journey in time.

Lord, yes! One hundred years ago, Craig Bennett Stiles had waved, stepped into his *Immense Clock*, as he called it, and vanished from the present. He was and remained the only man in history to travel in time. And Shumway was the one and only reporter, after all these years, to be invited in for afternoon tea. And? The possible announcement of a second and final trip through time. The traveler had hinted at such a trip.

"Old man," said Shumway, "Mr. Craig Bennett Stiles—here I come!"

The Dragonfly, obedient to fevers, seized a wind and rode it down the coast.

———

The old man was there waiting for him on the roof of the Time Lamasery at the rim of the hang glider's cliff in La Jolla. The air swarmed with crimson, blue, and lemon kites from which young men shouted, while young women called to them from the land's edge.

Stiles, for all his 130 years, was not old. His face, blinking up at the helicopter, was the bright face of one of those hang-gliding Apollo fools who veered off as the helicopter sank down.

Shumway hovered his craft for a long moment, savoring the delay.

Below him was a face that had dreamed architectures, known incredible loves, blueprinted mysteries of seconds, hours, days, then dived in to swim upstream through the centuries. A sunburst face, celebrating its own birthday.

For on a single night, one hundred years ago, Craig Bennett Stiles, freshly returned from time, had reported by Telstar around the world to billions of viewers and told them their future.

"We made it!" he said. "We did it! The future is ours. We rebuilt the cities, freshened the small towns, cleaned the lakes and rivers, washed the air, saved the dolphins, increased the whales, stopped the wars, tossed the solar stations across space to light the world, colonized the moon, moved on to Mars, then Alpha Centauri. We cured cancer and stopped death. We did it—Oh Lord, much thanks—we did it. Oh, future's bright and beauteous spires, arise!"

He showed them pictures, he brought them samples, he gave them tapes and LP records, films and sound cassettes of his wondrous roundabout flight. The world went mad with joy. It ran to meet and make that future, fling up the cities of promise, save all and share with the beasts of land and sea.

The old man's welcoming shout came up the wind. Shumway shouted back and let the Dragonfly simmer down in its own summer weather.

Craig Bennett Stiles, 130 years old, strode forward briskly and, incredibly, helped the young reporter out of his craft, for Shumway was suddenly stunned and weak at this encounter.

"I can't believe I'm here," said Shumway.

"You are, and none too soon," laughed the time traveler. "Any day now, I may just fall apart and blow away. Lunch is waiting. Hike!"

A parade of one, Stiles marched off under the fluttering rotor shadows that made him seem a flickering newsreel of a future that had somehow passed.

Shumway, like a small dog after a great army, followed.

"What do you want to know?" asked the old man as they crossed the roof, double time.

"First," gasped Shumway, keeping up, "why have you broken silence after a hundred years? Second, why to *me*? Third, what's the big announcement you're going to make this afternoon at four o'clock, the very hour when your younger self is due to arrive from the past—when, for a brief moment, you will appear in two places, the paradox: the person you were, the man you are, fused in one glorious hour for us to celebrate?"

The old man laughed. "How you *do* go on!"

"Sorry." Shumway blushed. "I wrote that last night. Well. Those are the questions."

"You shall have your answers." The old man shook his elbow gently. "All in good—time."

"You must excuse my excitement," said Shumway. "After all, you *are* a mystery. You were famous, world-acclaimed. You went, saw the future, came back, told us, then went into seclusion.

Oh, sure; for a few weeks, you traveled the world in ticker-tape parades, showed yourself on TV, wrote one book, gifted us with one magnificent two-hour television film, then shut yourself away here. Yes, the time machine is on exhibit below, and crowds are allowed in each day at noon to see and touch. But you yourself have refused fame—"

"Not so." The old man led him along the roof. Below in the gardens, other helicopters were arriving now, bringing TV equipment from around the world to photograph the miracle in the sky, that moment when the time machine from the past would appear, shimmer, then wander off to visit other cities before it vanished into the past. "I have been busy, as an architect, helping build that very future I saw when, as a young man, I arrived in our golden tomorrow!"

They stood for a moment watching the preparations below. Vast tables were being set up for food and drink. Dignitaries would be arriving soon from every country of the world to thank—for a final time, perhaps—this fabled, this almost mythic traveler of the years.

"Come along," said the old man. "Would you like to come sit in the time machine? No one else ever has, you know. Would you like to be the first?"

No answer was necessary. The old man could see that the young man's eyes were bright and wet.

"There, there," said the old man. "Oh, dear me; there, there."

———

A glass elevator sank and took them below and let them out in a pure white basement at the center of which stood—

The incredible device.

"There." Stiles touched a button and the plastic shell that

had for one hundred years encased the time machine slid aside. The old man nodded. "Go. Sit."

Shumway moved slowly toward the machine.

Stiles touched another button and the machine lit up like a cavern of spider webs. It breathed in years and whispered forth remembrance. Ghosts were in its crystal veins. A great god spider had woven its tapestries in a single night. It was haunted and it was alive. Unseen tides came and went in its machinery. Suns burned and moons hid their seasons in it. Here, an autumn blew away in tatters; there, winters arrived in snows that drifted in spring blossoms to fall on summer fields.

The young man sat in the center of it all, unable to speak, gripping the armrests of the padded chair.

"Don't be afraid," said the old man gently. "I won't send you on a journey."

"I wouldn't mind," said Shumway.

The old man studied his face. "No, I can see you wouldn't. You look like me one hundred years ago this day. Damn if you aren't my honorary son."

The young man shut his eyes at this, and the lids glistened as the ghosts in the machine sighed all about him and promised him tomorrows.

"Well, what do you think of my *Toynbee Convector*?" said the old man briskly, to break the spell.

He cut the power. The young man opened his eyes.

"The *Toynbee Convector*? What—"

"More mysteries, eh? The great Toynbee, that fine historian who said any group, any face, any world that did not run to seize the future and shape it was doomed to dust away in the grave, in the past."

"Did he say *that*?"

"Or some such. He did. So, what better name for my

machine, eh? Toynbee, wherever you are, here's your future-seizing device!"

He grabbed the young man's elbow and steered him out of the machine.

"Enough of that. It's late. Almost time for the great arrival, eh? And the earth-shaking final announcement of that old time traveler Stiles! Jump!"

———

Back on the roof, they looked down on the gardens, which were now swarming with the famous and the near famous from across the world. The nearby roads were jammed; the skies were full of helicopters and hovering biplanes. The hang gliders had long since given up and now stood along the cliff rim like a mob of bright pterodactyls, wings folded, heads up, staring at the clouds, waiting.

"All this," the old man murmured, "my God, for *me.*"

The young man checked his watch.

"Ten minutes to four and counting. Almost time for the great arrival. Sorry; that's what I called it when I wrote you up a week ago for the *News.* That moment of arrival and departure, in the blink of an eye, when, by stepping across time, you changed the whole future of the world from night to day, dark to light. I've often wondered—"

"What?"

Shumway studied the sky. "When you went ahead in time, did *no one* see you arrive? Did anyone at *all* happen to look up, do you know, and see your device hover in the middle of the air, here and over Chicago a bit later, and then New York and Paris? *No one?*"

"Well," said the inventor of the *Toynbee Convector,* "I don't suppose anyone was *expecting* me! And if people saw, they surely did not know what in blazes they were looking at. I was careful, anyway, not to linger too long. I needed only time to photograph the rebuilt cities, the clean seas and rivers, the fresh, smog-free air, the unfortified nations, the saved and beloved whales. I moved quickly, photographed swiftly and ran back down the years home. Today, paradoxically, is different. Millions upon millions of mobs of eyes will be looking up with great expectations. They will glance, will they not, from the young fool burning in the sky to the old fool here, still glad for his triumph?"

"They will," said Shumway. "Oh, indeed, they *will!*"

A cork popped. Shumway turned from surveying the crowds on the nearby fields and the crowds of circling objects in the sky to see that Stiles had just opened a bottle of champagne.

"Our own private toast and our own private celebration."

They held their glasses up, waiting for the precise and proper moment to drink.

"Five minutes to four and counting. Why," said the young reporter, "did no one else ever travel in time?"

"I put a stop to it myself," said the old man, leaning over the roof, looking down at the crowds. "I realized how dangerous it was. I was reliable, of course, no danger. But, Lord, think of it— just *anyone* rolling about the bowling-alley time corridors ahead, knocking tenpins headlong, frightening natives, shocking citizens somewhere else, fiddling with Napoleon's life line behind or restoring Hitler's cousins ahead? No, no. And the government, of course, agreed—no, insisted—that we put the *Toynbee Convector* under sealed lock and key. Today, you were the first and the last to fingerprint its machinery. The guard has been heavy and constant, for tens of thousands of days, to prevent the machine's being stolen. What time do you have?"

Shumway glanced at his watch and took in his breath.

"One minute and counting down—"

He counted, the old man counted. They raised their champagne glasses.

"Nine, eight, seven—"

The crowds below were immensely silent. The sky whispered with expectation. The TV cameras swung up to scan and search.

"Six, five—"

They clinked their glasses.

"Four, three, two—"

They drank.

"One!"

They drank their champagne with a laugh. They looked to the sky. The golden air above the La Jolla coast line waited. The moment for the great arrival was here.

"Now!" cried the young reporter, like a magician giving orders.

"Now!" said Stiles, gravely quiet.

Nothing.

Five seconds passed.

The sky stood empty.

Ten seconds passed.

The heavens waited.

Twenty seconds passed.

Nothing.

At last, Shumway turned to stare and wonder at the old man by his side.

Stiles looked at him, shrugged and said:

"I lied."

"You what!?" cried Shumway.

The crowds below shifted uneasily.

"I lied," said the old man simply.

"No!"

"Oh, but yes," said the time traveler. "I never went anywhere.

I stayed but made it seem I went. There is no time machine—only something that *looks* like one."

"But why?" cried the young man, bewildered, holding to the rail at the edge of the roof. "Why?"

"I see that you have a tape-recording button on your lapel. Turn it on. Yes. There. I want everyone to hear this. Now."

The old man finished his champagne and then said:

"Because I was born and raised in a time, in the sixties, seventies, and eighties, when people had stopped believing in themselves. I saw that disbelief, the reason that no longer gave itself reasons to survive, and was moved, depressed and then angered by it.

"Everywhere, I saw and heard doubt. Everywhere, I learned destruction. Everywhere was professional despair, intellectual ennui, political cynicism. And what wasn't ennui and cynicism was rampant skepticism and incipient nihilism."

The old man stopped, having remembered something. He bent and from under a table brought forth a special bottle of red Burgundy with the label 1984 on it. This, as he talked, he began to open, gently plumbing the ancient cork.

"You name it, we had it. The economy was a snail. The world was a cesspool. Economics remained an insolvable mystery. Melancholy was the attitude. The impossibility of change was the vogue. End of the world was the slogan.

"Nothing was worth doing. Go to bed at night full of bad news at eleven, wake up in the morn to worse news at seven. Trudge through the day underwater. Drown at night in a tide of plagues and pestilence. Ah!"

For the cork had softly popped. The now-harmless 1984 vintage was ready for airing. The time traveler sniffed it and nodded.

"Not only the four horsemen of the Apocalypse rode the horizon to fling themselves on our cities but a fifth horseman, worse than all the rest, rode with them: Despair, wrapped in dark shrouds of defeat, crying only repetitions of past disasters, present failures, future cowardices.

"Bombarded by dark chaff and no bright seed, what sort of harvest was there for man in the latter part of the incredible twentieth century?

"Forgotten was the moon, forgotten the red landscapes of Mars, the great eye of Jupiter, the stunning rings of Saturn. We refused to be comforted. We wept at the grave of our child, and the child was *us*."

"Was that how it was," asked Shumway quietly, "one hundred years ago?"

"Yes." The time traveler held up the wine bottle as if it contained proof. He poured some into a glass, eyed it, inhaled, and went on. "You have seen the newsreels and read the books of that time. You know it all.

"Oh, of course, there were a few bright moments. When Salk delivered the world's children to life. Or the night when *Eagle* landed and that one great step for mankind trod the moon. But in the minds and out of the mouths of many, the fifth horseman was darkly cheered on. With high hopes, it sometimes seemed, of his winning. So all would be gloomily satisfied that their predictions of doom were right from day one. So the self-fulfilling prophecies were declared; we dug our graves and prepared to lie down in them."

"And you couldn't allow that?" said the young reporter.

"You know I couldn't."

"And so you built the *Toynbee Convector*—"

"Not all at once. It took years to brood on it."

The old man paused to swirl the dark wine, gaze at it and sip, eyes closed.

"Meanwhile, I drowned, I despaired, wept silently late nights thinking, What can I do to save us from ourselves? How to save my friends, my city, my stage, my country, the entire *world* from this obsession with doom? Well, it was in my library late one night that my hand, searching along shelves, touched at last on an old and beloved book by H. G. Wells. His time device called, ghostlike, down the years. I *heard!* I understood. I truly listened. Then I blueprinted. I built. I traveled, or so it *seemed.* The rest, as you know, is history."

The old time traveler drank his wine, opened his eyes.

"Good God," the young reporter whispered, shaking his head. "Oh, dear God. Oh, the wonder, the wonder—"

There was an immense ferment in the lower gardens now and in the fields beyond and on the roads and in the air. Millions were still waiting. Where was the great arrival?

"Well, now," said the old man, filling another glass with wine for the young reporter. "Aren't I something? I made the machines, built miniature cities, lakes, ponds, seas. Erected vast architectures against crystal-water skies, talked to dolphins, played with whales, faked tapes, mythologized films. Oh, it took years, years of sweating work and secret preparation before I announced my departure, left and came back with good news!"

They drank the rest of the vintage wine. There was a hum of voices. All of the people below were looking up at the roof.

The time traveler waved at them and turned.

"Quickly, now. It's up to you from here on. You have the tape, my voice on it, just freshly made. Here are three more tapes, with fuller data. Here's a film-cassette history of my whole inspired fraudulence. Here's a final manuscript. Take, take it all, hand it on. I nominate you as son to explain the father. Quickly!"

Hustled into the elevator once more, Shumway felt the world fall away beneath. He didn't know whether to laugh or cry, so gave, at last, a great hoot.

The old man, surprised, hooted with him, as they stepped out below and advanced upon the *Toynbee Convector.*

"You see the point, don't you, son? Life has *always* been lying to ourselves! As boys, young men, old men. As girls, maidens, women, to gently lie and prove the lie true. To weave dreams and put brains and ideas and flesh and the truly real beneath the dreams. Everything, finally, is a promise. What seems a lie is a ramshackle need, wishing to be born. Here. Thus and so."

He pressed the button that raised the plastic shield, pressed another that started the time machine humming, then shuffled quickly in to thrust himself into the *Convector's* seat.

"Throw the final switch, young man!"

"But—"

"You're thinking," here the old man laughed, "if the time machine is a fraud, it won't work, what's the use of throwing a switch, yes? Throw it, anyway. *This* time, it *will* work!"

Shumway turned, found the control switch, grabbed hold, then looked up at Craig Bennett Stiles.

"I don't understand. Where are you *going*?"

"Why, to be one with the ages, of course. To exist now, only in the deep past."

"How can that *be*?"

"Believe me, this time it will happen. Goodbye, dear, fine, nice young man."

"Goodbye."

"Now. Tell me my name."

"What?"

"Speak my name and throw the switch."

"Time traveler?"

"Yes! *Now!*"

The young man yanked the switch. The machine hummed, roared, blazed with power.

"Oh," said the old man, shutting his eyes. His mouth smiled gently. "Yes."

His head fell forward on his chest.

Shumway yelled, banged the switch off and leaped forward to tear at the straps binding the old man in his device.

In the midst of so doing, he stopped, felt the time traveler's wrist, put his fingers under the neck to test the pulse there and groaned. He began to weep.

The old man had, indeed, gone back in time, and its name was death. He was traveling in the past now, forever.

Shumway stepped back and turned the machine on again. If the old man were to travel, let the machine—symbolically, anyway—go with him. It made a sympathetic humming. The fire of it, the bright sun fire, burned in all of its spider grids and armatures and lighted the cheeks and the vast brow of the ancient traveler, whose head seemed to nod with the vibrations and whose smile, as he traveled into darkness, was the smile of a child much satisfied.

The reporter stood for a long moment more, wiping his cheeks with the backs of his hands. Then, leaving the machine on, he turned, crossed the room, pressed the button for the glass elevator and, while he was waiting, took the time traveler's tapes and cassettes from his jacket pockets and, one by one, shoved them into the incinerator trash flue set in the wall.

The elevator doors opened, he stepped in, the doors shut. The elevator hummed now, like yet another time device, taking him up into a stunned world, a waiting world, lifting him up into a bright continent, a future land, a wondrous and surviving planet. . . .

That one man with one lie had created.

TRAPDOOR

Clara Peck had lived in the old house for some ten years before she made the strange discovery. Halfway upstairs to the second floor, on the landing, in the ceiling—

The trapdoor.

"Well, my God!"

She stopped dead, midstairs, to glare at the surprise, daring it to be true.

"It can't be! How could I have been so blind? Good grief, there's an *attic* in my house!"

She had marched up and downstairs a thousand times on a thousand days and never *seen*.

"Damned old fool."

And she almost tripped going down, having forgotten what she had come up for in the first place.

Before lunch, she arrived to stand under the trapdoor again, like a tall, thin, nervous child with pale hair and cheeks, her too bright eyes darting, fixing, staring.

"Now I've discovered the damn thing, what do I *do* with it? Storage room up there, I bet. Well—"

And she went away, vaguely troubled, feeling her mind slipping off out of the sun.

"To hell with that, Clara Peck!" she said, vacuuming the parlor. "You're only fifty-seven. Not senile, yet, by God!"

But still, why hadn't she *noticed*?

It was the quality of silence, that was it. Her roof had never leaked, so no water had ever tapped the ceilings; the high beams had never shifted in any wind, and there were no mice. If the rain had whispered, or the beams groaned, or the mice danced in her attic, she would have glanced up and *found* the trapdoor.

But the house had stayed silent, and she had stayed blind.

"Bosh!" she cried, at supper. She finished the dishes, read until ten, went to bed early.

It was during that night that she heard the first, faint, Morse-code tapping, the first graffiti-scratching above, behind the blank ceiling's pale, lunar face.

Half-asleep, her lips whispered: Mouse?

And then it was dawn.

————

Going downstairs to fix breakfast, she fixed the trapdoor with her steady, small-girl's stare and felt her skinny fingers twitch to go fetch the stepladder.

"Hell," she muttered. "Why bother to look at an empty attic? Next week, maybe."

For about three days after that, the trapdoor vanished.

That is, she forgot to look at it. So it might as well not have been there.

But around midnight on the third night, she heard the mouse sounds or the whatever-they-were sounds drifting across

her bedroom ceiling like milkweed ghosts touching the lost sur-
faces of the moon.

From that odd thought she shifted to tumbleweeds or dan-
delion seeds or just plain dust shaken from an attic sill.

She thought of sleep, but the thought didn't take.

Lying flat in her bed, she watched the ceiling so fixedly she
felt she could x-ray whatever it was that cavorted behind the
plaster.

A flea circus? A tribe of gypsy mice in exodus from a neighbor's house? Several had been shrouded, recently, to look like
dark circus tents, so that pest-killers could toss in killer bombs
and run off to let the secret life in the places die.

That secret life had most probably packed its fur luggage
and fled. Clara Peck's boarding house attic, free meals, was their
new home away from home.

And yet. . . .

As she stared, the sounds began again. They shaped themselves in patterns across the wide ceiling's brow; long fingernails
that, scraping, wandered to this corner and that of the shut-away
chamber above.

Clara Peck held her breath.

The patterns increased. The soft prowlings began to cluster
toward an area above and beyond her bedroom door. It was as
if the tiny creatures, whatever they were, were nuzzling another
secret door, above, wanting out.

Slowly, Clara Peck sat up in bed, and slowly put her weight to
the floor, not wanting *it* to creak. Slowly she cracked her bedroom
door. She peered out into a hall flooded with cold light from a full
moon, which poured through the landing window to show her—

The trapdoor.

Now, as if summoned by her warmth, the sounds of the tiny
lost ghost feet above rushed to cluster and fret at the trapdoor
rim itself.

Christ! thought Clara Peck. They *hear* me. They want me to—

The trapdoor shuddered gently with the tiny rocking weights of whatever it was arustle there.

And more and more of the invisible spider feet or rodent feet of the blown curls of old and yellowed newspapers touched and rustled the wooden frame.

Louder, and still louder.

Clara was about to cry: Go! Git!

When the phone rang.

"Gah!" gasped Clara Peck.

She felt a ton of blood plunge like a broken weight down her frame to crush her toes.

"Gah!"

She ran to seize, lift and strangle the phone.

"Who!" she cried.

"Clara! It's Emma Crowley! What's *wrong?!*"

"My God!" shouted Clara. "You scared the hell out of me! Emma, why are you calling this late?"

There was a long silence as the woman across town found her own breath.

"It's silly, I couldn't sleep. I had this hunch—"

"Emma—"

"No, let me finish. All of a sudden I thought, Clara's not well, or Clara's hurt, or—"

Clara Peck sank to the edge of the bed, the weight of Emma's voice pulling her down. Eyes shut, she nodded.

"Clara," said Emma, a thousand miles off, "you—all *right?*"

"All right," said Clara, at last.

"Not sick? House ain't on fire?"

"No, no. No."

"Thank God. Silly me. Forgive?"

"Forgiven."

"Well, then . . . good night."

And Emma Crowley hung up.

Clara Peck sat looking at the receiver for a full minute, listening to the signal that said that someone had gone away, and then at last placed the phone blindly back in its cradle.

She went back out to look up at the trapdoor.

It was quiet. Only a pattern of leaves, from the window, flickered and tossed on its wooden frame.

Clara blinked at the trapdoor.

"Think you're *smart*, don't you?" she said.

There were no more prowls, dances, murmurs, or mouse-pavanes for the rest of that night.

———

The sounds returned, three nights later, and they were—larger.

"Not *mice*," said Clara Peck. "Good-sized *rats. Eh?*"

In answer, the ceiling above executed an intricate, cross-currenting ballet, without music. This toe dancing, of a most peculiar sort, continued until the moon sank. Then, as soon as the light failed, the house grew silent and only Clara Peck took up breathing and life, again.

By the end of the week, the patterns were more geometrical. The sounds echoed in every upstairs room; the sewing room, the old bedroom, and in the library where some former occupant had once turned pages and gazed over a sea of chestnut trees.

On the tenth night, all eyes and no face, with the sounds coming in drumbeats and weird syncopations, at three in the morning, Clara Peck flung her sweaty hand at the telephone to dial Emma Crowley:

"Clara! I *knew* you'd call!"

"Emma, it's three a.m. Aren't you surprised?"

"No, I been lying here thinking of you. I wanted to call, but felt a fool. Something *is* wrong, yes?"

"Emma, answer me this. If a house has an empty attic for years, and all of a sudden has an attic full of things, how come?"

"I didn't know you *had* an attic—"

"Who *did?* Listen, what started as mice then sounded like rats and now sounds like cats running around up there. What'll I do?"

"The telephone number of the Ratzaway Pest Team on Main Street is—wait. Here. MAIN seven-seven-nine-nine. You *sure* something's *in* your attic?"

"The whole damned high school track team."

"Who used to live in your house, Clara?"

"Who—?"

"I mean, it's been clean all this time, right, and now, well, *infested.* Anyone ever *die* there?"

"Die?"

"Sure, if someone died there, maybe you haven't got mice, at *all.*"

"You trying to tell me—ghosts?"

"Don't you believe—?"

"Ghosts, or so-called friends who try spooking me with them. Don't call again, Emma!"

"But, *you* called *me!*"

"Hang up, Emma!!"

Emma Crowley hung up.

In the hall at three fifteen in the cold morning, Clara Peck glided out, stood for a moment, then pointed up at the ceiling, as if to provoke it.

"Ghosts?" she whispered.

The trapdoor's hinges, lost in the night above, oiled themselves with wind.

Clara Peck turned slowly and went back, and thinking about every movement, got into bed.

She woke at four twenty in the morning because a wind shook the house.

Out in the hall, could it be?

She strained. She tuned her ears.

Very softly, very quietly, the trapdoor in the stairwell ceiling squealed.

And opened wide.

Can't be! she thought.

The door fell up, in, and down, with a thud.

Is! she thought.

I'll go make sure, she thought.

No!

She jumped, ran, locked the door, leaped back in bed.

"Hello, Ratzaway!" she heard herself call, muffled, under the covers.

———

Going downstairs, sleepless, at six in the morning, she kept her eyes straight ahead, so as not to see that dreadful ceiling.

Halfway down she glanced back, started, and laughed.

"Silly!" she cried.

For the trapdoor was not open at all.

It was shut.

"Ratzaway?" she said, into the telephone receiver, at seven thirty on a bright morning.

———

It was noon when the Ratzaway inspection truck stopped in front of Clara Peck's house.

In the way that Mr. Timmons, the young inspector, strolled with insolent disdain up the walk, Clara saw that he knew everything in the world about mice, termites, old maids, and odd late-night sounds. Moving, he glanced around at the world with that fine masculine hauteur of the bullfighter midring or the skydiver fresh from the sky, or the womanizer lighting his cigarette, back turned to the poor creature in the bed behind him. As he pressed her doorbell, he was God's messenger. When Clara opened the door she almost slammed it for the way his eyes peeled away her dress, her flesh, her thoughts. His smile was the alcoholic's smile. He was drunk on himself. There was only one thing to do:

"Don't just stand there!" she shouted. "Make yourself useful!" She spun around and marched away from his shocked face.

She glanced back to see if it had had the right effect. Very few women had ever talked this way to him. He was studying the door. Then, curious, he stepped in.

"This way!" said Clara.

She paraded through the hall, up the steps to the landing, where she had placed a metal stepladder. She thrust her hand up, pointing.

"There's the attic. See if you can make sense out of the damned noises up there. And don't overcharge me when you're done. Wipe your feet when you come down. I got to go shopping. Can I trust you not to steal me blind while I'm gone?"

With each blow, she could see him veer off balance. His face flushed. His eyes shone. Before he could speak, she marched back down the steps to shrug on a light coat.

"Do you know what mice sound like in attics?" she said, over her shoulder.

"I damn well do, lady," he said.

"Clean up your language. You know rats? These could be rats or bigger. What's bigger in an attic?"

"You got any raccoons around here?" he said.

"How'd they get *in*?"

"Don't you know your own house, lady? I—"

But here they both stopped.

For a sound had come from above.

It was a small itch of a sound at first. Then it scratched. Then it gave a thump like a heart.

Something moved in the attic.

Timmons blinked up at the shut trapdoor and snorted.

"Hey!"

Clara Peck nodded, satisfied, pulled on her gloves, adjusted her hat, watching.

"It sounds like—" drawled Mr. Timmons.

"Yes?"

"Did a sea captain ever live in this house?" he asked, at last.

The sound came again, louder. The whole house seemed to drift and whine with the weight which was shifted above.

"Sounds like cargo." Timmons shut his eyes to listen. "Cargo on a ship, sliding when the ship changes course." He broke into a laugh and opened his eyes.

"Good God," said Clara, and tried to imagine that.

"On the other hand," said Mr. Timmons, half-smiling up at that ceiling, "you got a greenhouse up there, or something? Sounds like plants growing. Or a yeast, maybe, big as a doghouse, getting out of hand. I heard of a man once, raised yeast in his cellar. It—"

The front screen door slammed.

Clara Peck, outside glaring in at his jokes, said:

"I'll be back in an hour. Jump!"

She heard his laughter follow her down the walk as she marched. She hesitated only once to look back.

The damn fool was standing at the foot of the ladder, looking up. Then he shrugged, gave a what-the-hell gesture with his hands, and—

Scrambled up the stepladder like a sailor.

———

When Clara Peck marched back an hour later, the Ratzaway truck still stood silent at the curb.

"Hell," she said to it. "Thought he'd be done by now. Strange man tromping around, swearing—"

She stopped and listened to the house.

Silence.

"Odd," she muttered.

"Mr. Timmons!?" she called.

And realizing she was still twenty feet from the open front door, she approached to call through the screen.

"Anyone *home?*"

She stepped through the door into a silence like the silence in the old days before the mice had begun to change to rats and the rats had danced themselves into something larger and darker on the upper attic decks. It was a silence that, if you breathed it in, smothered you.

She swayed at the bottom of the flight of stairs, gazing up, her groceries hugged like a dead child in her arms.

"Mr. Timmons—?"

But the entire house was still.

The portable ladder still stood waiting on the landing.

But the trapdoor was shut.

Well, he's *obviously* not up in there! she thought. He wouldn't climb and shut himself in. Damn fool's just gone away.

She turned to squint out at his truck abandoned in the bright noon's glare.

Truck's broke down, I imagine. He's gone for help.

She dumped her groceries in the kitchen and for the first time in years, not knowing why, lit a cigarette, smoked it, lit another, and made a loud lunch, banging skillets and running the can opener overtime.

The house listened to all this, and made no response.

By two o'clock the silence hung about her like a cloud of floor polish.

"Ratzaway," she said, as she dialed the phone.

The Pest Team owner arrived half an hour later, by motorcycle, to pick up the abandoned truck. Tipping his cap, he stepped in through the screen door to chat with Clara Peck and look at the empty rooms and weigh the silence.

"No sweat, ma'am," he said, at last. "Charlie's been on a few benders, lately. He'll show up to be fired, tomorrow. What was he *doing* here?"

With this, he glanced up the stairs at the stepladder.

"Oh," said Clara Peck, quickly, "he was just looking at— everything."

"I'll come, myself, tomorrow," said the owner.

And as he drove away into the afternoon, Clara Peck slowly moved up the stairs to lift her face toward the ceiling and watch the trapdoor.

"*He* didn't see you, *either*," she whispered.

Not a beam stirred, not a mouse danced, in the attic.

She stood like a statue, feeling the sunlight shift and lean through the front door.

Why? she wondered. Why did I lie?

Well, for one thing, the trapdoor's shut, isn't it?

And, I don't know why, she thought, but I won't want anyone going up that ladder, ever again. Isn't that silly? Isn't that strange?

———

She ate dinner early, listening.

She washed the dishes, alert.

She put herself to bed at ten o'clock, but in the old downstairs maid's room, for long years unused. Why she chose to lie in this downstairs room, she did not know, she simply did it, and lay there with aching ears, and the pulse moving in her neck and in her brow.

Rigid as a tomb carving under the sheet, she waited.

Around midnight, a wind passed, shook a pattern of leaves on her counterpane. Her eyes flicked wide.

The beams of the house trembled.

She lifted her head.

Something whispered ever so softly in the attic.

She sat up.

The sound grew louder, heavier, like a large but shapeless animal, prowling the attic dark.

She placed her feet on the floor and sat looking at them. The noise came again, far up, a scramble like rabbits' feet here, a thump like a large heart there.

She stepped out into the downstairs hall and stood bathed in a moonlight that was like a pure cool dawn filling the windows.

Holding the banister, she moved stealthily up the stairs. Reaching the landing, she touched the stepladder, then raised her eyes.

She blinked. Her heart jumped, then held still.

For as she watched, very slowly the trapdoor above her sank away. It opened, to show her a waiting square of darkness like a mine shaft going up, without end.

"I've had just about *enough*!" she cried.

She rushed down to the kitchen and came storming back up with hammer and nails, to climb the ladder in furious leaps.

"I don't believe any of this!" she cried. "No more, do you hear? *Stop!*"

At the top of the ladder she had to stretch up into the attic, into the solid darkness with one hand and arm. Which meant that her head had to poke halfway through.

"Now!" she said.

At that very instant, as her head shoved through and her fingers fumbled to find the trapdoor, a most startling, swift thing occurred.

As if something had seized her head, as if she were a cork pulled from a bottle, her entire body, her arms, her straight-down legs, were yanked up into the attic.

She vanished like a magician's handkerchief. Like a marionette whose strings are grabbed by an unseen force, she whistled up.

So swift was the motion that her bedroom slippers were left standing on the stepladder rungs.

After that, there was no gasp, no scream. Just a long breathing silence for about ten seconds.

Then, for no seen reason, the trapdoor slammed flat down shut.

———

Because of the quality of silence in the old house, the trapdoor was not noticed again. . . .

Until the new tenants had been in the house for about ten years.

ON THE ORIENT, NORTH

It was on the Orient Express heading north from Venice to Paris to Calais that the old woman noticed the ghastly passenger.

He was a traveler obviously dying of some dread disease.

He occupied compartment 22 on the third car back, and had his meals sent in and only at twilight did he rouse to come sit in the dining car surrounded by the false electric lights and the sound of crystal and women's laughter.

He arrived this night, moving with a terrible slowness to sit across the aisle from this woman of some years, her bosom like a fortress, her brow serene, her eyes with a kindness that had mellowed with time.

There was a black medical bag at her side, and a thermometer tucked in her mannish lapel pocket.

The ghastly man's paleness caused her left hand to crawl up along her lapel to touch the thermometer.

"Oh, dear," whispered Miss Minerva Halliday.

The maître d' was passing. She touched his elbow and nodded across the aisle.

"Pardon, but where is that poor man going?"

"Calais and London, madame. If God is willing."

And he hurried off.

Minerva Halliday, her appetite gone, stared across at that skeleton made of snow.

The man and the cutlery laid before him seemed one. The knives, forks, and spoons jingled with a silvery cold sound. He listened, fascinated, as if to the sound of his inner soul as the cutlery crept, touched, chimed; a tintinnabulation from another sphere. His hands lay in his lap like lonely pets, and when the train swerved around a long curve his body, mindless, swayed now this way, now that, toppling.

At which moment the train took a greater curve and knocked the silverware, chittering. A woman at a far table, laughing, cried out:

"I don't *believe* it!"

To which a man with a louder laugh shouted:

"Nor do *I*!"

This coincidence caused, in the ghastly passenger, a terrible melting. The doubting laughter had pierced his ears.

He visibly shrank. His eyes hollowed and one could almost imagine a cold vapor gasped from his mouth.

Miss Minerva Halliday, shocked, leaned forward and put out one hand. She heard herself whisper:

"*I* believe!"

The effect was instantaneous.

The ghastly passenger sat up. Color returned to his white cheeks. His eyes glowed with a rebirth of fire. His head swiveled and he stared across the aisle at this miraculous woman with words that cured.

Blushing furiously, the old nurse with the great warm bosom caught hold, rose, and hurried off.

Not five minutes later, Miss Minerva Halliday heard the maître d' hurrying along the corridor, tapping on doors, whispering. As he passed her open door, he glanced at her.

"Could it be that you are—"

"No," she guessed, "not a doctor. But a registered nurse. Is it that old man in the dining car?"

"Yes, yes! Please, madame, this way!"

The ghastly man had been carried back to his own compartment.

Reaching it, Miss Minerva Halliday peered within.

And there the strange man lay strewn, his eyes wilted shut, his mouth a bloodless wound, the only life in him the joggle of his head as the train swerved.

My God, she thought, he's *dead*!

Out loud she said, "I'll call if I need you."

The maître d' went away.

Miss Minerva Halliday quietly shut the sliding door and turned to examine the dead man—for surely he was dead. And yet. . . .

But at last she dared to reach out and to touch the wrists in which so much ice-water ran. She pulled back, as if her fingers had been burned by dry ice. Then she leaned forward to whisper into the pale man's face.

"Listen very carefully. *Yes?*"

For answer, she thought she heard the coldest throb of a single heartbeat.

She continued. "I do not know how I guess this. I know who you are, and what you are sick of—"

The train curved. His head lolled as if his neck had been broken.

"I'll tell you what you're dying from!" she whispered. "You suffer a disease—of *people*!"

His eyes popped wide, as if he had been shot through the heart. She said:

"The people on this train are killing you. *They* are your affliction."

Something like a breath stirred behind the shut wound of the man's mouth.

"Yesssss . . . ssss."

Her grip tightened on his wrist, probing for some pulse:

"You are from some middle European country, yes? Somewhere where the nights are long and when the wind blows, people *listen*? But now things have changed, and you have tried to escape by travel, but . . ."

Just then, a party of young, wine-filled tourists bustled along the outer corridor, firing off their laughter.

The ghastly passenger withered.

"How do . . . you . . ." he whispered, ". . . know . . . thissss?"

"I am a special nurse with a special memory. I saw, I met, someone like you when I was six—"

"Saw?" the pale man exhaled.

"In Ireland, near Killeshandra. My uncle's house, a hundred years old, full of rain and fog and there was walking on the roof late at night, and sounds in the hall as if the storm had come in, and then at last this shadow entered my room. It sat on my bed and the cold from his body made *me* cold. I remember and know it was no dream, for the shadow who came to sit on my bed and whisper . . . was much . . . like you."

Eyes shut, from the depths of his arctic soul, the old sick man mourned in response:

"And who . . . and *what* . . . am I?"

"You are not sick. And you are not dying . . . You *are*—"

The whistle on the Orient Express wailed a long way off.

"—a ghost," she said.

"Yesssss!" he cried.

It was a vast shout of need, recognition, assurance. He almost bolted upright.

"Yes!"

At which moment there arrived in the doorway a young

priest, eager to perform. Eyes bright, lips moist, one hand clutching his crucifix, he stared at the collapsed figure of the ghastly passenger and cried, "May I——?"

"Last rites?" The ancient passenger opened one eye like the lid on a silver box. "From you? No." His eye shifted to the nurse. *"Her!"*

"Sir!" cried the young priest.

He stepped back, seized his crucifix as if it were a parachute ripcord, spun, and scurried off.

Leaving the old nurse to sit examining her now even more strange patient until at last he said:

"How," he gasped, "can *you* nurse *me*?"

"Why——" she gave a small self-deprecating laugh. "We must *find* a way."

With yet another wail, the Orient Express encountered more mileages of night, fog, mist, and cut through it with a shriek.

"You are going to Calais?" she said.

"And beyond, to Dover, London, and perhaps a castle outside Edinburgh, where I will be safe——"

"That's almost impossible——" She might as well have shot him through the heart. "No, no, wait, wait!" she cried. "Impossible . . . without *me*! I will travel with you to Calais and across to Dover."

"But you do not *know* me!"

"Oh, but I dreamed you as a child, long before I met someone like you, in the mists and rains of Ireland. At age nine I searched the moors for the Baskerville Hound."

"Yes," said the ghastly passenger. "You are English and the English *believe*!"

"True. Better than Americans, who *doubt*. French? Cynics! English is best. There is hardly an old London house that does not have its sad lady of mists crying before dawn."

At which moment, the compartment door, shaken by a long curve of track, sprang wide. An onslaught of poisonous talk, of delirious chatter, of what could only be irreligious laughter poured in from the corridor. The ghastly passenger wilted.

Springing to her feet, Minerva Halliday slammed the door and turned to look with the familiarity of a lifetime of sleep-tossed encounters at her traveling companion.

"You, now," she asked, "who exactly are *you*?"

The ghastly passenger, seeing in her face the face of a sad child he might have encountered long ago, now described his life:

"I have 'lived' in one place outside Vienna for two hundred years. To survive, assaulted by atheists as well as true believers, I have hid in libraries in dust-filled stacks there to dine on myths and moundyard tales. I have taken midnight feasts of panic and terror from bolting horses, baying dogs, catapulting tomcats . . . crumbs shaken from tomb lids. As the years passed, my compatriots of the unseen world vanished one by one as castles tumbled or lords rented out their haunted gardens to women's clubs or bed-and-breakfast entrepreneurs. Evicted, we ghastly wanderers of the world have sunk in tar, bog, and fields of disbelief, doubt, scorn, or outright derision. With the populations and disbeliefs doubling by the day, all of my specter friends have fled. I am the last, trying to train across Europe to some safe, rain-drenched castle-keep where men are properly frightened by soots and smokes of wandering souls. England and Scotland for me!"

His voice faded into silence.

"And your name?" she said, at last.

"I *have* no name," he whispered. "A thousand fogs have visited my family plot. A thousand rains have drenched my tombstone. The chisel marks were erased by mist and water and sun. My name has vanished with the flowers and the grass and the marble dust." He opened his eyes.

"*Why* are you doing this?" he said. "*Helping* me?"

And at last she smiled, for she heard the right answer fall from her lips:

"I have never in my life had a *lark*."

"Lark!?"

"My life was that of a stuffed owl. I was not a nun, yet never married. Treating an invalid mother and a half-blind father, I gave myself to hospitals, tombstone beds, cries at night, and medicines that are not perfume to passing men. So, I am something of a ghost myself, yes? And now, tonight, sixty-six years on, I have at last found in you a patient, magnificently different, fresh, absolutely new. Oh, Lord, what a challenge. A race! I will pace you, to face people off the train, through the crowds in Paris, then the trip to the sea, off the train, onto the ferry! It will indeed be a—"

"Lark!" cried the ghastly passenger. Spasms of laughter shook him.

"Larks? Yes, *that* is what we are!"

"But," she said, "in Paris, do they not *eat* larks even while they roast priests?"

He shut his eyes and whispered, "Paris? Ah, yes."

The train wailed. The night passed.

And they arrived in Paris.

And even as they arrived, a boy, no more than six, ran past and froze. He stared at the ghastly passenger and the ghastly passenger shot back a remembrance of antarctic ice floes. The boy gave a cry and fled. The old nurse flung the door wide to peer out.

The boy was gibbering to his father at the far end of the corridor. The father charged along the corridor, crying:

"What goes *on* here? Who has frightened my—?"

The man stopped. Outside the door he now fixed his gaze on this ghastly passenger on the slowing braking Orient Express. He braked his own tongue. "—my son," he finished.

The ghastly passenger looked at him quietly with fog-gray eyes.

"I—" The Frenchman drew back, sucking his teeth in disbelief. "Forgive me!" He gasped. "Regrets!"

And turned to run, shove at his son. "Trouble-maker. Get!" Their door slammed.

"Paris!" echoed through the train.

"Hush and hurry!" advised Minerva Halliday as she bustled her ancient friend out onto a platform milling with bad tempers and misplaced luggage.

"I am *melting*!" cried the ghastly passenger.

"Not where *I'm* taking you!" She displayed a picnic hamper and flung him forth to the miracle of a single remaining taxicab. And they arrived under a stormy sky at the Père Lachaise cemetery. The great gates were swinging shut. The nurse waved a handful of francs. The gate froze.

Inside, they wandered at peace amongst ten thousand monuments. So much cold marble was there, and so many hidden souls, that the old nurse felt a sudden dizziness, a pain in one wrist, and a swift coldness on the left side of her face. She shook her head, refusing this. And they walked on among the stones.

"Where do we picnic?" he said.

"Anywhere," she said. "But carefully! For this is a *French* cemetery! Packed with cynics! *Armies* of egotists who burned people for their faith one year only to be burned for *their* faith the next! So, pick. Choose!" They walked. The ghastly passenger nodded. "This first stone. Beneath it: *nothing*. Death final, not a *whisper* of time. The *second* stone: a woman, a secret believer because she loved her husband and hoped to see him again in eternity . . . . a murmur of spirit here, the turning of a heart. *Better*. Now this third gravestone: a writer of thrillers for a French magazine. But he *loved* his nights, his fogs, his castles. *This* stone is a proper temperature, like a good wine. So here we shall sit, dear lady, as you decant the champagne and we wait to go back to the train."

She offered a glass, happily. "*Can* you drink?"

"One can try." He took it. "One can only try."

———

The ghastly passenger almost "died" as they left Paris. A group of intellectuals, fresh from seminars about Sartre's "nausea," and hot-air ballooning about Simone de Beauvoir, streamed through the corridors, leaving the air behind them boiled and empty.

The pale passenger became paler.

The second step beyond Paris, another invasion! A group of Germans surged aboard, loud in their disbelief of ancestral spirits, doubtful of politics, some even carrying books titled *Was God Ever Home?*

The Orient ghost sank deeper in his x-ray image bones.

"Oh, dear," cried Miss Minerva Halliday, and ran to her own compartment to plunge back and toss down a cascade of books.

"*Hamlet!*" she cried, "his father, yes? *A Christmas Carol. Four* ghosts! *Wuthering Heights.* Kathy *returns*, yes? To haunt the snows? Ah, *The Turn of the Screw*, and . . . *Rebecca!* Then—my favorite! *The Monkey's Paw! Which?*"

But the Orient ghost said not a Marley word. His eyes were locked, his mouth sewn with icicles.

"Wait!" she cried.

And opened the first book . . .

Where Hamlet stood on the castle wall and heard his ghost-of-a-father moan and so she said these words:

" 'Mark me . . . my hour is almost come . . . when I to sulphurous and tormenting flames . . . must render up myself . . .' "

And then she read:

"'I am thy father's spirit,/Doomed for a certain term to walk the night . . .'"

And again:

"'. . . If thou didst ever thy dear father love . . . O, God! . . . Revenge his foul and most unnatural murder . . .'"

And yet again:

"'. . . Murder most foul . . .'"

And the train ran in the night as she spoke the last words of Hamlet's father's ghost:

"'. . . Fare thee well at once . . .'"

"'. . . Adieu, adieu! Remember me.'"

And she repeated:

"'. . . remember me!'"

And the Orient ghost quivered. She pretended not to notice but seized a further book:

"'. . . Marley was dead, to begin with . . .'"

As the Orient train thundered across a twilight bridge above an unseen stream.

Her hands flew like birds over the books.

"'I am the Ghost of Christmas Past!'"

Then:

"'The Phantom Rickshaw glided from the mist and clop-clopped off into the fog—'"

And wasn't there the faintest echo of a horse's hooves behind, within the Orient ghost's mouth?

"'The beating beating beating, under the floorboards of the Old Man's Telltale Heart!'" she cried, softly.

And *there*! like the leap of a frog. The first faint pulse of the Orient ghost's heart in more than an hour.

The Germans down the corridor fired off a cannon of disbelief.

But *she* poured the medicine:

"'The Hound bayed out on the Moor—'"

And the echo of that bay, that most forlorn cry, came from her traveling companion's soul, wailed from his throat.

As the night grew on and the moon arose and a Woman in White crossed a landscape, as the old nurse said and told, and a bat that became a wolf that became a lizard scaled a wall on the ghastly passenger's brow.

And at last the train was silent with sleeping, and Miss Minerva Halliday let the last book drop with the thump of a body to the floor.

"*Requiescat in pace?*" whispered the Orient traveler, eyes shut.

"Yes." She smiled, nodding. "*Requiescat in pace.*" And they slept.

And at last they reached the sea.

———

And there was mist, which became fog, which became scatters of rain, like a proper drench of tears from a seamless sky.

Which made the ghastly passenger open, ungum his mouth, and murmur thanks for the haunted sky and the shore visited by phantoms of tide as the train slid into the shed where the mobbed exchange would be made, a full train becoming a full boat.

The Orient ghost stood well back, the last figure on a now self-haunted train.

"Wait," he cried, softly, piteously. "That boat! There's no place on it to hide! And the *customs!*"

But the customs men took one look at the pale face snowed under the dark cap and earmuffs, and swiftly flagged the wintry soul onto the ferry.

To be surrounded by dumb voices, ignorant elbows, layers of people shoving as the boat shuddered and moved and the nurse saw her fragile icicle melt yet again.

It was a mob of children shrieking by that made her say: "Quickly!"

And she all but lifted and carried the wicker man in the wake of the boys and girls.

"No," cried the old passenger. "The noise!"

"It's special!" The nurse hustled him through a door. "A medicine! Here!"

The old man stared around.

"Why," he murmured. "This is—a playroom."

And she steered him into the midst of all the screams and running.

"Children!" she called.

The children froze.

"Story-telling time!"

They were about to run again when she added, "*Ghost* story-telling time!"

She pointed casually to the ghastly passenger, whose pale moth fingers grasped the scarf about his icy throat.

"All fall *down!*" said the nurse.

The children plummeted with squeals to the floor. All about the Orient traveler, like Indians around a tepee, they stared up along his body to where blizzards ran odd temperatures in his gaping mouth.

He wavered. She quickly said:

"You *do* believe in ghosts, *yes?*"

"Oh, *yes!*" was the shout. "Yes!"

It was as if a ramrod had shot up his spine. The Orient traveler stiffened. The most brittle of tiny flinty sparks fired his eyes. Winter roses budded in his cheeks. And the more the children leaned, the taller he grew, and the warmer his complexion. With one icicle finger he pointed at their faces.

"I," he whispered, "I," a pause. "Shall tell you a frightful tale. About a *real* ghost!"

"Oh, *yes!*" cried the children.

And he began to talk and as the fever of his tongue conjured fogs, lured mists and invited rains, the children hugged and crowded close, a bed of charcoals on which he happily baked. And as he talked Nurse Halliday, backed off near the door, saw what he saw across the haunted sea, the ghost cliffs, the chalk cliffs, the safe cliffs of Dover and not so far beyond, waiting, the whispering towers, the murmuring castle deeps, where phantoms were as they had always been, with the still attics waiting. And staring, the old nurse felt her hand creep up her lapel toward her thermometer. She felt her own pulse. A brief darkness touched her eyes.

And then one child said: "Who *are* you?"

And gathering his gossamer shroud, the ghastly passenger whetted his imagination, and replied.

It was only the sound of the ferry landing whistle that cut short the long telling of midnight tales. And the parents poured in to seize their lost children, away from the Orient gentleman with the ghastly eyes whose gently raving mouth shivered their marrows as he whispered and whispered until the ferry nudged the dock and the last boy was dragged, protesting, away, leaving the old man and his nurse alone in the children's playroom as the ferry stopped shuddering its delicious shudders, as if it had listened, heard, and deliriously enjoyed the long-before-dawn tales.

At the gangplank, the Orient traveler said, with a touch of briskness, "No. I'll need no help going down. Watch!"

And he strode down the plank. And even as the children had been tonic for his color, height, and vocal cords, so the closer he came to England, pacing, the firmer his stride, and when he actually touched the dock, a small happy burst of sound erupted from his thin lips and the nurse, behind him, stopped frowning, and let him run toward the train.

And seeing him dash, like a child before her, she could only stand, riven with delight and something more than delight. And he ran and her heart ran with him and suddenly knew a stab of amazing pain, and a lid of darkness struck her and she swooned.

Hurrying, the ghastly passenger did not notice that the old nurse was not beside or behind him, so eagerly did he go.

At the train he gasped, "There!" safely grasping the compartment handle. Only then did he sense a loss, and turned.

Minerva Halliday was not there.

And yet, an instant later, she arrived, looking paler than before, but with an incredibly radiant smile. She wavered and almost fell. This time it was he who reached out.

"Dear lady," he said, "you have been so kind."

"But," she said, quietly, looking at him, waiting for him to truly see her, "I am not leaving."

"You . . . ?"

"I am going with you," she said.

"But your plans?"

"Have changed. Now, I have nowhere *else* to go."

She half-turned to look over her shoulder.

At the dock, a swiftly gathering crowd peered down at someone lying on the planks. Voices murmured and cried out. The word "doctor" was called several times.

The ghastly passenger looked at Minerva Halliday. Then he looked at the crowd and the object of the crowd's alarm lying on the dock: a medical thermometer lay broken under their feet. He looked back at Minerva Halliday, who still stared at the broken thermometer.

"Oh, my dear kind lady," he said, at last. "Come."

She looked into his face. "Larks?" she said.

He nodded and said, "Larks!"

And he helped her up into the train, which soon jolted and then dinned and whistled away along the tracks toward London and Edinburgh and moors and castles and dark nights and long years.

"I wonder who she was?" said the ghastly passenger looking back at the crowd on the dock.

"Oh, Lord," said the old nurse. "I never really knew."

And the train was gone.

It took a full twenty seconds for the tracks to stop trembling.

ONE NIGHT IN YOUR LIFE

He came into Green River, Iowa, on a really fine late spring morning, driving swiftly. His convertible Cadillac was hot in the direct sun outside the town, but then the green overhanging forests, the abundances of soft shade and whispering coolness slowed his car as he moved toward the town.

Thirty miles an hour, he thought, is fast enough.

Leaving Los Angeles, he had rocketed his car across burning country, between stone canyons and meteor rocks, places where you had to go fast because everything seemed fast and hard and clean.

But here, the very greenness of the air made a river through which no car could rush. You could only idle on the tide of leafy shadow, drifting on the sunlight-speckled concrete like a river barge on its way to a summer sea.

Looking up through the great trees was like lying at the bottom of a deep pool, letting the tide drift you.

He stopped for a hotdog at an outdoor stand on the edge of town.

"Lord," he whispered to himself, "I haven't been back through here in fifteen years. You forget how fast trees can grow!"

He turned back to his car, a tall man with a sunburnt, wry, thin face, and thinning dark hair.

Why am I driving to New York? he wondered. Why don't I just stay and drown myself here, in the grass.

He drove slowly through the old town. He saw a rusty train abandoned on an old side-spur track, its whistle long silent, its steam long gone. He watched the people moving in and out of stores and houses so slowly they were under a great sea of clean warm water. Moss was everywhere, so every motion came to rest on softness and silence. It was a barefoot Mark Twain town, a town where childhood lingered without anticipation and old age came without regret. He snorted gently at himself. Or so it seemed.

I'm glad Helen didn't come on this trip, he thought. He could hear her now:

"My God, this place is small. Good grief, look at those hicks. Hit the gas. Where in hell is New York?"

He shook his head, closed his eyes, and Helen was in Reno. He had phoned her last night.

"Getting divorced's not bad," she'd said, a thousand miles back in the heat. "It's Reno that's awful. Thank God for the swimming pool. Well, what are *you* up to?"

"Driving east in slow stages." That was a lie. He was rushing east like a shot bullet, to lose the past, to tear away as many things behind him as he could leave. "Driving's fun."

"Fun?" Helen protested. "When you could *fly*? Cars are so boring."

"Goodbye, Helen."

He drove out of town. He was supposed to be in New York in five days to talk over the play he didn't want to write for Broadway, in order to rush back to Hollywood in time to not enjoy finishing a screenplay, so that he could rush to Mexico City for a quick vacation next December. Sometimes, he mused,

I resemble those Mexican rockets dashing between the town buildings on a hot wire, bashing my head on one wall, turning, and zooming back to crash against another.

He found himself going seventy miles an hour suddenly, and cautioned it down to thirty-five, through rolling green noon country.

He took deep breaths of the clear air and pulled over to the side of the road. Far away, between immense trees, on the top of a meadow hill, he thought he saw, walking but motionless in the strange heat, a young woman, and then she was gone, and he wasn't certain she had been there at all.

It was one o'clock and the land was full of a great power-house humming. Darning needles flashed by the car windows, like prickles of heat before his eyes. Bees swarmed and the grass bent under a tender wind. He opened the car door and stepped out into the straight heat.

Here was a lonely path that sang beetle sounds at late noon to itself, and there was a cool, shadowed forest waiting fifty yards from the road, from which blew a good, tunnel-moist air. On all sides were rolling clover hills and an open sky. Standing there, he could feel the stone dissolve in his arms and his neck, and the iron go out of his cold stomach, and the tremor cease in his fingers.

And then, suddenly, still further away, going over a forest hill, through a small rift in the brush, he saw the young woman again, walking and walking into the warm distances, gone.

He locked the car door slowly. He struck off into the forest, idly, drawn steadily by a sound that was large enough to fill the universe, the sound of a river going somewhere and not caring; the most beautiful sound of all.

When he found the river it was dark and light and dark and light, flowing, and he undressed and swam in it and then lay out on the pebbled bank drying, feeling relaxed. He put his clothes back on, leisurely, and then it came to him, the old desire, the old dream, when he was seventeen years old. He had often confided and repeated it to a friend:

"I'd like to go walking some spring night—you know, one of those nights that are warm all night long. I'd like to walk. With a girl. Walk for an hour, to a place where you can barely hear or see anything. Climb a hill and sit. Look at the stars. I'd like to hold the girl's hand. I'd like to smell the grass and the wheat growing in the fields, and know I was in the center of the entire country, in the very center of the United States, and towns all around and highways away off, but nobody knowing we're right there on top of that hill, in the grass, watching the night.

"And just holding her hand would be good. Can you understand that? Do you know that holding someone's hand can be *the* thing? Such a thing that your hands move while not moving. You can remember a thing like that, rather than any other thing about a night, all your life. Just holding hands can mean more. I believe it. When everything is repeated, and over, and familiar, it's the first things rather than the last that count.

"So, for a long time," he had continued, "I'd like to just sit there, not saying a word. There aren't any words for a night like that. We wouldn't even look at each other. We'd see the lights of the town far off and know that other people had climbed other hills before us and that there was nothing better in the world. Nothing could be made better; all of the houses and ceremonies and guarantees in the world are nothing compared to a night like this. The cities and the people in the rooms in the houses in those cities at night are one thing; the hills and the open air and the stars and holding hands are something else.

"And then, finally, without speaking, the two of you will turn your heads in the moonlight and look at each other.

"And so you're on the hill all night long. Is there anything really wrong with this, can you honestly say there is anything wrong?"

"No," said a voice, "the only thing wrong on a night like that is that there is a world and you must come back to it."

That was his friend, Joseph, speaking, fifteen years ago. Dear Joseph, with whom he had talked so many days through; their adolescent philosophizings, their problems of great import. Now Joseph was married and swallowed by the black streets of Chicago, and himself taken West by time, and all of their philosophy for nothing.

He remembered the month after he had married Helen. They had driven across country, the first and last time she had consented to the "brutal," as she called it, journey by automobile. In the moonlit evenings they had gone through the wheat country and the corn country of the Middle West and once, at twilight, looking straight ahead, Thomas had said, "What do you say, would you like to spend the night out?"

"Out?" Helen said.

"Here," he said, with a great appearance of casualness. He motioned his hand to the side of the road. "Look at all that land, the hills. It's a warm night. It'd be nice to sleep out."

"My God!" Helen had cried. "You're not serious?"

"I just thought."

"The damn country's running with snakes and bugs. What a way to spend the night, getting burrs in my stockings, tramping around some farmer's property."

"No one would ever know."

"But *I'd* know, my dear," said Helen.

"It was just a suggestion."

"Dear Tom, you *were* only joking, weren't you?"

"Forget I ever said anything," he said.

They had driven on in the moonlight to a boiling little night motel where moths fluttered about the raw electric lights. There had been an iron bed in a paint-smelling tiny room where you could hear the beer tunes from the roadhouse all night and hear the continental vans pounding by late, late toward dawn. . . .

He walked through the green forest and listened to the various silences there. Not one silence, but several; the silence that the moss made underfoot, the silence the shadows made depending from the trees, the silence of small streams exploring tiny countries on all sides as he came into a clearing.

He found some wild strawberries and ate them. To hell with the car, he thought. I don't care if someone takes it apart wheel by wheel, and carries it off. I don't care if the sun melts it into slag on the spot.

He lay down and cradled his head on his arms and went to sleep.

The first thing he saw when he wakened was his wrist-watch. Six forty-five. He had slept most of the day away. Cool shadows had crept up all about him. He shivered and moved to sit up and then did not move again, but lay there with his face upon his arm, looking ahead.

The girl who sat a few yards away from him, with her hands in her lap, smiled.

"I didn't hear you come up," he said.

She had been very quiet.

For no reason at all in the world, except a secret reason, Thomas felt his heart pounding silently and swiftly.

She remained silent. He rolled over on his back and closed his eyes.

"Do you live near here?"

She lived not far away.

"Born and raised here?"

She had never been anywhere else.

"It's a beautiful country," he said.

A bird flew into a tree.

"Aren't you afraid?"

He waited but there was no answer.

"You don't know me," he said.

But on the other hand, neither did *he* know *her*.

"That's different," he said.

Why was it different?

"Oh, you know, it just *is*."

After what seemed half an hour of waiting, he opened his eyes and looked at her for a long while. "You are real, aren't you? I'm not dreaming this?"

She wanted to know where he was going.

"Somewhere I don't want to go."

Yes, that was what so many people said. So many passed through on their way to somewhere they didn't like.

"That's me," he said. He raised himself slowly. "Do you know, I've just realized, I haven't eaten since early today."

She offered him the bread and cheese and cookies she was carrying from town. They didn't speak while he ate, and he ate very slowly, afraid that some motion, some gesture, some word, might make her run away. The sun was down the sky and the air was even fresher now, and he examined everything very carefully.

He looked at her and she was beautiful, twenty-one, fair, healthy, pink cheeked, and self-contained.

The sun was gone. The sky lingered its colors for a time, while they sat in the clearing.

At last he heard a whispering. She was getting up. She put out her hand to take his. He stood beside her and they looked at the woods around them and the distant hills.

They began to walk away from the path and the car, away from the highway and the town. A spring moon rose over the land while they were walking.

The breath of nightfall was rising up out of the separate

blades of grass, a warm sighing of air, quiet and endless. They reached the top of the hill and without a word sat there watching the sky. He thought to himself that this was impossible, that such things did not happen; he wondered who she was, and what she was doing here.

Ten miles away, a train whistled in the spring night and went on its way over the dark evening earth, flashing a brief fire.

And then, again, he remembered the old story, the old dream, the thing he and his friend had discussed so many years ago. There must be one night in your life that you will remember forever. There must be one night for everyone. And if you know that the night is coming on and that this night will be that particular night, then take it and don't question it and don't talk about it to anyone ever after that. For if you let it pass it might not come again. Many have let it pass, many have seen it go by and have never seen another like it, when all the circumstances of weather, light, moon and time, of night hill and warm grass and train and town and distance were balanced upon the trembling of a finger.

He thought of Helen and he thought of Joseph. Joseph. Did it ever work out for you, Joseph; were you ever at the right place at the right time, and did all go well with you? There was no way of knowing; the brick city had taken Joseph and lost him in the tile subways and black elevateds and noise.

As for Helen, not only had she never known a night like this, but she had never *dreamed* of such a thing, there was no place in her mind for this.

So here I am, he thought quietly, thousands of miles from everything and everyone.

Across the soft black country now came the sound of a courthouse clock ringing the hour. One. Two. Three. One of those great stone courthouses that stood in the green square of every small American town at the turn of the century, cool stone in the summertime, high in the night sky, with round dial faces glowing in four directions. Five, six. He counted the bronze announcements of the hour, stopping at nine. Nine o'clock on a late spring night on a breathing, warm, moonlit hill in the interior of a great continent, his hand touching another hand, thinking, this year I'll be thirty-three. But it didn't come too late and I didn't let it pass, and this is the night.

Slowly now, carefully, like a statue coming to life, turning and turning still more, he saw her head move about so her eyes could look upon him. He felt his own head turning, also, as it had done so many times in his imagination. They gazed at each other for a long time.

———

He woke during the night. She was awake, near him.

"Who are you?" he whispered.

She said nothing.

"I could stay another night," he said.

But he knew that one can never stay another night. One night is the night and only one. After that, the gods turn their backs.

"I could come back in a year or so."

Her eyes were closed but she was awake.

"But I don't know who you are," he said.

"You could come with me," he said, "to New York."

But he knew she could never be there or anywhere but here, on this night.

"And I can't stay here," he said, knowing that this was the truest and most empty part of all.

He waited for a time and then said again, "Are you real? Are you really real?"

They slept. The moon went down the sky toward morning.

———

He walked out of the hills and the forest at dawn, to find the car covered with dew. He unlocked it and climbed in behind the wheel, and sat for a moment, looking back at the path he had made in the wet grass. He moved over, preparatory to getting out of the car again. He put his hand on the inside of the door and gazed steadily out.

The forest was empty and still, the path was deserted, the highway was motionless and serene. There was no movement anywhere in a thousand miles.

He started the car motor and let it idle.

The car was pointed east where the orange sun was now rising slowly.

"All right," he said, quietly. "Everyone, here I come. What a shame you're all still alive. What a shame the world isn't just hills and hills and nothing else to drive over but hills and never coming to a town."

He drove away east without looking back.

WEST OF OCTOBER

The four cousins, Tom, William, Philip, and John, had come to visit the Family at the end of summer. There was no room in the big old house, so they were stashed out on little cots in the barn, which shortly thereafter burned.

Now the Family was no ordinary family. Each member of it was more extraordinary than the last.

To say that most of them slept days and worked at odd jobs nights, would fall short of commencement.

To remark that some of them could read minds, and some fly with lightnings to land with leaves, would be an understatement.

To add that some could not be seen in mirrors while others could be found in multitudinous shapes, sizes, and textures in the same glass, would merely repeat gossip that veered into truth.

There were uncles, aunts, cousins, and grandparents by the toadstool score and the mushroom dozen.

They were just about every color you could mix in one restless night.

Some were young and others had been around since the Sphinx first sank its stone paws deep in tidal sands.

In all, in numbers, background, inclination, and talent, a most incredible and miraculous mob. And the most incredible of them all was:

Cecy.

Cecy. She was the reason, the real reason, the central reason for any of the Family to come visit, and not only to visit but to circle her and stay. For she was as multitudinous as a pomegranate. Her talent was single but kaleidoscopic. She was all the senses of all the creatures in the world. She was all the motion picture houses and stage play theaters and all the art galleries of time. You could ask almost anything of her and she would gift you with it.

Ask her to yank your soul like an aching tooth and drift it in clouds to cool your spirit, and yanked you were, drawn high to drift in such clouds as sowed rain to grow grass and seed-sprout flowers.

Ask her to seize that same soul and bind it in the flesh of a tree, and you awoke next morning with apples popping out of your branches and birds singing in your green-leafed head.

Ask to live in a frog, and you spent days afloat and nights croaking strange songs.

Ask to be pure rain and you fell on everything. Ask to be the moon and suddenly you looked down and saw your pale illumination bleaching lost towns to the color of tombstones and tuberoses and spectral ghosts.

Cecy. Who extracted your soul and pulled forth your impacted wisdom, and could transfer it to animal, vegetable, or mineral; name your poison.

No wonder the Family came. No wonder they stayed long past lunch, way beyond dinner, far into midnights the week after next!

And here were the four cousins, come to visit.

And along about sunset of the first day, each of them said, in effect: "Well?"

They were lined up by Cecy's bed in the great house, where she lay for long hours, both night and noon, because her talents were in such demand by both family and friends.

"Well," said Cecy, her eyes shut, a smile playing about her lovely mouth. "What would your pleasure be?"

"I—" said Tom.

"Maybe—" said William and Philip.

"Could you—" said John.

"Take you on a visit to the local insane asylum," guessed Cecy, "to peek in people's very strange heads?"

"Yes!"

"Said and done!" said Cecy. "Go lie on your cots in the barn." They ran. They lay. "That's it. Over, up, and—out!" she cried.

Like corks, their souls popped. Like birds, they flew. Like bright unseen needles they shot into various and assorted ears in the asylum just down the hill and across the valley.

"Ah!" they cried in delight at what they found and saw.

While they were gone, the barn burned down.

In all the shouting and confusion, the running for water, the general ramshackle hysteria, everyone forgot what was in the barn or where the high-flying cousins might be going, or what Cecy, asleep, was up to. So deep in her rushing sleep was this favorite daughter, that she heard not the flames, nor the dread moment when the walls fell in and four human-shaped torches self-destroyed. The cousins themselves did not feel the repercussions of their own bodies being snuffed for some few moments. Then a clap of silent thunder banged across country, shook the skies, knocked the wind-blown essences of lost cousin through mill-fans to lodge in trees, while Cecy, with a gasp, sat straight up in bed.

Running to the window, she looked out and gave one shriek

that shot the cousins home. All four, at the moment of concussion, had been in various parts of the county asylum, opening trapdoors in wild people's heads and peeking in at maelstroms of confetti and wondering at the colors of madness, and the dark rainbow hues of nightmare.

All the Family stood by the collapsed barn, stunned. Hearing Cecy's cry, they turned.

"What happened?" cried John from her mouth.

"Yes, what!" said Philip, moving her lips.

"My God," gasped William, staring from her eyes.

"The barn burned," said Tom. "We're *dead!*"

The Family, soot-faced in the smoking yard, turned like a traveling minstrel's funeral and stared up at Cecy in shock.

"Cecy?" asked Mother, wildly. "Is there someone, I mean, *with* you?"

"Yes, me, Tom!" shouted Tom from her lips.

"And me, John."

"Philip!"

"William!"

The souls counted off from the young woman's mouth.

The Family waited.

Then, as one, the four young men's voices asked the final, most dreadful question:

"Didn't you save just *one* body?"

The Family sank an inch into the earth, burdened with a reply they could not give.

"But—" Cecy held on to her own elbows, touched her own chin, her mouth, her brow, inside which four live ghosts knocked elbows for room. "But—what'll I *do* with them?" Her eyes searched over all those faces below in the yard. "My boy cousins can't stay here. They simply can't stand around in my *head!*"

What she cried after that, or what the cousins babbled, crammed like pebbles under her tongue, or what the Family said, running like burned chickens in the yard, was lost.

Like Judgment Day thunders, the rest of the barn fell.

———

With a hollow roar the fire went up the kitchen chimney. An October wind leaned this way and that on the roof, listening to all the Family talk in the dining room below.

"It seems to me," said Father.

"Not seems, but *is*!" said Cecy, her eyes now blue, now yellow, now hazel, now brown.

"We must farm the young cousins out. Find temporary hospices for them, until such time as we can cull new bodies—"

"The quicker the better," said a voice from Cecy's mouth now high, now low, now two gradations between.

"Joseph might be loaned out to Bion, Tom given to Leonard, William to Sam, Philip to—"

All the uncles, so named, snapped their hackles and stirred their boots.

Leonard summed up for all. "Busy. Overworked. Bion with his shop, Sam with his arm."

"Gah—." Misery sprang from Cecy's mouth in four-part harmony.

Father sat down in darkness. "Good grief, there must be *some* one of us with plenty of time to waste, a small room to let in the backside of their subconscious or the topside of their trapdoor Id! Volunteers! *Stand!*"

The Family sucked an icy breath, for suddenly Grandma was on her feet, but pointing her witch-broom cane.

"That man right there's got all the time in the world. I hereby solicit, name, and nominate *him*!"

As if their heads were on a single string, everyone turned to blink at Grandpa.

Grandpa leaped up as if shot. "No!"

"Hush." Grandma shut her eyes on the question, folded her arms, purring, over her bosom. "You got all the time in the world."

"No, by Joshua and Jesus!"

"This," Grandma pointed around by intuition, eyes closed, "is the Family. No one in the world like us. We're particular strange-fine. We sleep days, walk nights, fly the winds and airs, wander storms, read minds, hate wine, like blood, do magic, live forever or a thousand years, whichever comes first. In sum, we're the Family. That being true and particular there's no one to lean on, turn to, when trouble comes—"

"I won't—"

"Hush." One eye as large as the Star of India opened, burned, dimmed down, shut. "You spit mornings, whittle afternoons, and catbox the nights. The four nice cousins can't stay in Cecy's upper floor. It's not proper, four wild young men in a slim girl's head." Grandma's mouth sweetened itself. "Besides, there's a lot *you* can teach the cousins. You been around long before Napoleon walked in and then ran *out* of Russia, or Ben Franklin got the pox. Good if the boys were tucked in your ear for a spell. What's inside, God knows, but it might, I say might, improve their posture. Would you deny them *that*?"

"Jumping Jerusalem!" Grandpa leaped to his feet. "I won't have them all wrestling two falls out of three between my left ear and my right! Kick the sides out of my head. Knock my eyes like basketballs around inside my skull! My brain's no boardinghouse. One at a time! Tom can pull my eyelids up in the morning. William can help me shove the food in, noons. John can snooze in my cold pork-marrow half-into dusk. Philip can dance in my dusty attic nights. Time to myself is what I ask. And clean up when they *leave!*"

"Done!" Grandma circled like an orchestra leader, waving at the ghosted air. "One at a time, did you *hear*, boys?"

"We heard!" cried an anvil chorus from Cecy's mouth.

"Move 'em in!" said Grandpa.

"Gangway!" said four voices.

And since no one had bothered to say which cousin went first, there was a surge of phantoms on the air, a huge tide-drift of storm and unseen wind.

Four different expressions lit Grandpa's face. Four different earthquakes shook his brittle frame. Four different smiles ran scales along his piano teeth. Before Grandpa could protest, at four different gaits and speeds, he was run out of the house, across the lawn, and down the abandoned railroad tracks toward town, yelling against and laughing for the wild hours ahead.

The Family stood lined up on the porch, staring after the rushing parade of one.

"Cecy! *Do* something!"

But Cecy, exhausted, was fast asleep in her chair.

———

That *did* it.

At noon the next day the big, dull blue, iron engine panted into the railroad station to find the Family lined up on the platform, Grandpa leaned and supported in their midst. They not so much walked but carried him to the day coach, which smelled of fresh varnish and hot plush. Along the way, Grandpa, eyes shut, spoke in a variety of voices that everyone pretended not to hear.

They propped him like an ancient doll in his seat, fastened his straw hat on his head like putting a new roof on an old building, and talked into his face.

"Grandpa, sit up. Grandpa, mind your hat. Grandpa, along the way don't drink. Grandpa, you *in* there? Get out of the way, cousins, let the old man speak."

"I'm here." Grandpa's mouth and eyes gave some birdlike twitches. "And suffering for their sins. *Their* whiskey makes *my* misery. Damn!"

"No such thing!" "Lies!" "We did nothing!" cried a number of voices from one side, then the other of his mouth. "No!"

"Hush!" Grandma grabbed the old man's chin and focused his bones with a shake. "West of October is Cranamockett, not a long trip. We got all kinds of folks there, uncles, aunts, cousins, some with and some without children. Your job is to board the cousins out and—"

"Take a load off my mind," muttered Grandpa, a tear trickling down from one trembling eyelid.

"But if you can't unload the damn fools," advised Grandma, "bring 'em back alive!"

"If I live through it."

"Goodbye!" said four voices from under his tongue.

"Goodbye!" Everyone waved from the platform. "So long, Grandpa, Tom, William, Philip, John!"

"*I'm* here now, *too!*" said a young woman's voice.

Grandpa's mouth had popped wide.

"Cecy!" cried everyone. "Farewell!"

"Good night, nurse!" said Grandpa.

The train chanted away into the hills, west of October.

———

The train rounded a long curve. Grandpa leaned and creaked his body.

"Well," whispered Tom, "here we are."

"Yes." A long pause. William went on: "Here we are."

A long silence. The train whistled.

"I'm tired," said John.

"*You're* tired!" Grandpa snorted.

"Bit stuffy in here," said Philip.

"Got to expect that. Grandpa's ten thousand years old, aren't you, Grandpa?"

"Four hundred; shut *up!*" Grandpa gave his own skull a thump with his fingers. A panic of birds knocked about in his head. "Cease!"

"There," whispered Cecy, quieting the panic. "I've slept well and I'll come for *part* of the trip, Grandpa, to teach you how to hold, stay, and keep the resident crows and vultures in your cage."

"Crows! Vultures!" the cousins protested.

"Silence," said Cecy, tamping the cousins like tobacco in an ancient uncleaned pipe. Far away, her body lay in her bedroom as always, but her mind wove around them softly; touched, pushed, enchanted, kept. "Enjoy. Look around."

The cousins looked.

And indeed, wandering in the upper keeps of Grandfather's head was like surviving in a mellow attic in which memories, transparent wings folded, lay piled all about in ribboned bundles, in files, packets, shrouded figures, strewn shadows. Here and there, a special bright memory, like a single ray of amber light, struck in upon and shaped here a golden hour, there a summer day. There was a smell of worn leather and burnt horsehair and the faintest scent of uric acid from the jaundiced beams that ached about them as they jostled invisible elbows.

"Look," murmured the cousins. "I'll be darned. *Sure!*"

For now, quietly indeed, they were peering through the dusty panes of the old man's eyes, viewing the great hellfire train that bore them and the green–turning–to–brown autumn world swinging by, all of it passing as traffic does before an old house with cobwebbed windows. When they worked Grandpa's mouth it was like ringing a dulled clapper in a rusty churchbell. The sounds of the world wandered in through his hairy ears like static on a badly tuned radio.

"Still," Tom admitted, "it's better than having no body at all."

"I'm dizzy," said John. "Not used to bifocals. Can you take your glasses off, Grandpa?"

"Nope."

The train banged across a bridge in thunders.

"Think I'll take a look around," said Tom.

Grandpa felt his limbs stir.

"Stick right where you are, young man!"

Grandpa shut his eyes tight.

"Put up the shades, Grandpa! Let's see the sights!"

His eyeballs swiveled under the lids.

"Here comes a pretty girl, built one brick atop another! Quick!"

Grandpa tightened his lids.

"Most beautiful girl in the *world*!"

Grandpa couldn't help but open one eye.

"Ah!" said everyone. "*Right*, Grandpa?"

"Nope!"

The young woman curved this way and that, leaning as the train pushed or pulled her; as pretty as something you might win at a carnival by knocking the milk bottles down.

"Bosh!" Grandpa slammed his windows shut.

"Open, Sesame!"

Instantly, within, he felt his eyeballs redirected.

"Let go!" shouted Grandpa. "Grandma'll *kill* me!"

"She'll never *know*!"

The young woman turned as if called. She lurched back as if she might fall on *all* of them.

"Stop!" cried Grandpa. "Cecy's with us! She's innocent and—"

"Innocent!" The great attic rocked with laughter.

"Grandfather," said Cecy, very softly. "With all the night excursions I have made, all the traveling I have done, I am not—"

"Innocent," said the four cousins.

"Look here!" protested Grandpa.

"No, *you* look," whispered Cecy. "I have sewn my way through bedroom windows on a thousand summer nights. I have lain in cool snowbeds of white pillows and sheets, and I have swum unclothed in rivers on August noons and lain on riverbanks for birds to see—"

"I—" Grandpa screwed his fists into his ears—"will not listen!"

"Yes." Cecy's voice wandered in cool meadows remembering. "I have been in a girl's warm summer face and looked out at a young man, and I have been in that same young man, the same instant, breathing out fiery breaths, gazing at that forever summer girl. I have lived in mating mice or circling lovebirds or bleeding-heart doves. I have hidden in two butterflies fused on a blossom of clover—"

"Damn!" Grandpa winced.

"I've been in sleighs on December midnights when snow fell and smoke plumed out the horses' pink nostrils and there were fur blankets piled high with six young people hidden warm and delving and wishing and finding and—"

"Stop! I'm sunk!" said Grandpa.

"Bravo!" said the cousins. "More!"

"—and I have been inside a grand castle of bone and flesh—the most beautiful woman in the world . . . !"

Grandpa was amazed and held still.

For now it was as if snow fell upon and quieted him. He felt a stir of flowers about his brow, and a blowing of July morning wind about his ears, and all through his limbs a burgeoning of warmth, a growth of bosom about his ancient flat chest, a fire struck to bloom in the pit of his stomach. Now, as she talked, his lips softened and colored and knew poetry and might have let it pour forth in incredible rains, and his worn and iron-rusty fingers tumbled in his lap and changed to cream and milk and melting apple-snow. He looked down at them, stunned, clenched his fists to stop this womanish thing!

"No! Give me back my hands! Wash my mouth out with soap!"

"Enough talk," said an inner voice, Philip.

"We're wasting time," said Tom.

"Let's go say hello to that young lady across the aisle," said John. "All those in favor?"

"Aye!" said the Salt Lake Tabernacle choir from one single throat. Grandpa was yanked to his feet by unseen wires.

"Any dissenters?"

"Me!" thundered Grandpa.

Grandpa squeezed his eyes, squeezed his head, squeezed his ribs. His entire body was that incredibly strange bed that sank to smother its terrified victims. "Gotcha!"

The cousins ricocheted about in the dark.

"Help! Cecy! Light! Give us light! Cecy!"

"I'm here!" said Cecy.

The old man felt himself touched, twitched, tickled, now behind the ears, now the spine. Now his knees knocked, now his ankles cracked. Now his lungs filled with feathers, his nose sneezed soot.

"Will, his left leg, move! Tom, the right leg, *hup!* Philip, right arm, John, the left! Fling! Me for his flimsy turkey-bone body! Ready? Set!"

"Heave!"

"Double-time. Run!"

Grandpa ran.

But he didn't run across the aisle, he ran down it, gasping, eyes bright.

"Wait!" cried the Greek chorus. "The lady's back there! Someone trip him! Who's got his legs? Will? Tom!"

Grandpa flung the vestibule door wide, leaped out on the windy platform and was about to hurl himself out into a meadow of swiftly flashing sunflowers when:

"Freeze! Statues!" said the chorus stuffed in his mouth.

And statue he became on the backside of the swiftly vanishing train.

A moment later, spun about, Grandpa found himself back inside. As the train rocketed around a curve, he sat on the young lady's hands.

"Excuse," Grandpa leaped up, "me—"

"Excused." The lady rearranged her sat-on hands.

"No trouble, please, no, no!" Grandpa collapsed on the seat across from her, eyes clammed shut. "Damn! Hell! Statues, everyone! Bats, back in the belfry! Damn!"

The cousins grinned and melted the wax in his ears.

"Remember," hissed Grandpa behind his teeth, "you're young in there, I'm a mummy out here!"

"But—" sighed the chamber quartet fiddling behind his lids—"we'll act to *make* you young!"

He felt them light a fuse in his stomach, a bomb in his chest.

"No!"

Grandpa yanked a cord in the dark. A trapdoor popped wide. The cousins fell down into a rich and endless maze of color and remembrance. Three-dimensional shapes as rich and almost as warm as the girl across the aisle. The cousins fell, shouting.

"Watch it!"

"I'm lost!"

"Tom?"

"I'm somewhere in Wisconsin! How'd I get *here*?"

"*I'm* on a Hudson River boat. William?"

Far off, William called: "London. My God! Newspapers say the date's August twenty-second, nineteen hundred!"

"Can't be! Cecy?!"

"Not Cecy! Me!" said Grandpa, everywhere at once. "You're still between my ears, dammit, and using my other times and places as guest towels. Mind your head, the ceilings are low!"

"Ah ha," said William. "And is this the Grand Canyon I gaze upon, or a wrinkle in your nut?"

"Grand Canyon," said Grandpa. "Nineteen twenty-one."

"A woman!" cried Tom, "stands before me!"

And indeed the woman was beautiful in the spring, two hundred years ago. Grandpa recalled no name. She had only been someone passing as he hunted wild strawberries on a summer noon.

Tom reached out toward the beautiful memory.

"Get away!" shouted Grandpa.

And the girl's face, in the light summer air, flew apart. She drifted away, away, vanishing down the road, and at last gone.

"Damn and blast!" cried Tom.

The other cousins were in a rampage, opening doors, running paths, raising windows.

"Look! Oh, my gosh! Look!" they all shouted.

The memories lay side by side, neat as sardines a million deep, a million wide. Put by in seconds, minutes, hours. Here a dark girl brushing her hair. Here the same girl walking, running, or asleep. All her actions kept in honey-combs the color of her summer cheeks. The bright flash of her smile. You could pick her up, turn her round, send her away, call her back. All you had to say was Italy, 1797, and she danced through a warm pavilion, or swam in moonlit waters.

"Grandfather! Does Grandma know about her?"

"There *must* be other women!"

"Thousands!" cried Grandpa.

Grandpa flung back a lid. "Here!"

A thousand women wandered through a department store.

"Well done, Grandpa!"

From ear to ear, Grandpa felt the rummaging and racing over mountains, scoured deserts, down alleys, through cities.

Until John seized one lone and lovely lady by the arm.

He caught a woman by the hand.

"Stop!" Grandpa rose up with a roar. The people on the train stared at him.

"Got you!" said John.

The beautiful woman turned.

"Fool!" snarled Grandpa.

The lovely woman's flesh burned away. The upraised chin grew gaunt, the cheeks hollow, the eyes sank in wrinkles.

John drew back. "Grandmother, it's *you*!"

"Cecy!" Grandpa was trembling violently. "Stash John in a bird, a stone, a well! Anywhere, but not in my damn fool head! Now!"

"Out you go, John!" said Cecy.

And John vanished.

Into a robin singing on a pole that flashed by the train window.

Grandmother stood withered in darkness. Grandpa's gentle inward gaze touched her again, to reclothe her younger flesh. New color poured into her eyes, cheeks, and hair. He hid her safely away in a nameless and far-off orchard.

Grandpa opened his eyes.

Sunlight sprang in on the last three cousins.

The young woman still sat across the aisle.

Grandfather shut his eyes again but it was too late. The cousins rose up behind his gaze.

"We're fools!" said Tom. "Why bother with old times! New is right *there*! That girl! Yes?"

"Yes!" whispered Cecy. "Listen! I'll put Grandpa's mind over in *her* body. Then bring her mind over to hide in Grandpa's head! Grandpa's body will sit here straight as a ramrod, and inside it we'll all be acrobats, gymnasts! fiends! The conductor will pass, never guessing! Grandpa will sit here. His head full of wild laughter, unclothed mobs while his real mind will be trapped over there in that fine girl's head! What fun in the middle of a train coach on a hot afternoon, with nobody knowing."

"Yes!" said everyone at once.

"No," said Grandpa, and pulled forth two white tablets from his pocket and swallowed them.

"Stop him!" shouted William.

"Drat!" said Cecy. "It was such a fine, lovely, wicked plan."

"Good night, everybody," said Grandpa. The medicine was working. "And you—" he said, looking with gentle sleepiness at the young lady across the aisle. "You have just been rescued from a fate, young lady, worse than ten thousand deaths."

"Beg pardon?" The young lady blinked.

"Innocence, continue in thy innocence," said Grandpa, and fell asleep.

The train pulled into Cranamockett at six o'clock. Only then was John allowed back from his exile in the head of that robin on a fence miles behind.

There were absolutely no relatives in Cranamockett willing to take in the cousins.

At the end of three days, Grandfather rode the train back to Illinois, the cousins still in him, like peach stones.

And there they stayed, each in a different territory of Grandpa's sun-or-moonlit attic keep.

Tom took residence in a remembrance of 1840 in Vienna with a crazed actress, William lived in Lake County with a flaxen-haired Swede of some indefinite years, while John shuttled from fleshpot to fleshpot, 'Frisco, Berlin, Paris, appearing, on occasion, as a wicked glitter in Grandpa's eyes. Philip, on the other hand, locked himself deep in a potato-bin cellar, where he read all the books Grandpa ever read.

But on some nights Grandpa edges over under the covers toward Grandma.

"You!" she cries. "At your age! Git!" she screams.

And she beats and beats and beats him until, laughing in five voices, Grandpa gives up, falls back, and pretends to sleep, alert with five kinds of alertness, for another try.

THE LAST CIRCUS

Red Tongue Jurgis (we called him that because he ate candy red-hots all the time) stood under my window one cold October morning and yelled at the metal weathercock on top of our house. I put my head out the window and blew steam. "Hi, Red Tongue!"

"Jiggers!" he said. "Come on! The circus!"

Three minutes later I ran out of the house polishing two apples on my knee. Red Tongue was dancing to keep warm. We agreed that the last one to reach the train yard was a damnfool old man.

Eating apples, we ran through the silent town.

We stood by the rails in the dark train yard and listened to them humming. Far away in the cold dark morning country, we knew, the circus was coming. The sound of it was in the rails, trembling. I put my ear down to hear it traveling. "Gosh," I said.

And then, there was the locomotive charging on us with fire and light and a sound like a black storm, clouds following it. Out of boxcars red and green lanterns swung and in the boxcars were snorts and screams and yells. Elephants stepped down and cages rolled and everything mixed around until, in the first light, the animals and men were marching, Red Tongue and I with them, through the town, out to the meadowlands where every grass blade was a white crystal and every bush rained if you touched it.

"Just think, RT," I said. "One minute there's nothing there but land. And *now* look at it."

We looked. The big tent bloomed out like one of those Japanese flowers in cold water. Lights flashed on. In half an hour there were pancakes frying somewhere and people laughing.

We stood looking at everything. I put my hand on my chest and felt my heart thumping my fingers like those trick shop palpitators you buy for two bits. All I wanted to do was look and smell.

"Home for breakfast!" cried RT and knocked me down so he got a head start running.

"Tuck your tongue in and wash your face," said Mom, looking up from her kitchen stove.

"Pancakes!" I said, amazed at her intuition.

"How was the circus?" Father lowered his newspaper and looked over it at me.

"Swell," I said. "Boy!"

I washed my face in cold tap water and scraped my chair out just as Mom set the pancakes down. She handed me the syrup jug. "Float them," she said.

While I was chewing, Father adjusted the paper in his hands and sighed. "I don't know what it's coming to."

"You shouldn't read the paper in the morning," Mom said. "It ruins your digestion."

"Look at this," cried Father, flicking the paper with his finger. "Germ warfare, atom bomb, hydrogen bomb. That's *all* you read!"

"Personally," said Mother, "I've a big washing this week."

Father frowned. "That's what's wrong with the world; people on a powder keg doing their wash." He sat up and leaned forward. "Why it says here this morning, they've got a new atom bomb that would wipe Chicago clean off the map. And as for our town—nothing left but a smudge. The thing I keep thinking is it's a darn shame."

"What?" I asked.

"Here we've taken a million years to get where we are. We build towns and build cities out of nothing. Why, a hundred years ago, this town wasn't nowhere to be seen. Took a lot of time and sweat and trouble, and now we've got it all one brick on another and what happens? BANG!"

"It won't happen to us, I bet," I said.

"No?" Father snorted. "Why not?"

"It just *couldn't*," I said.

"You two leave off," Mom nodded at me. "You're too young to understand." She nodded at Pop. "You're old enough to know better."

We ate in silence. Then I said to Pop, "What was it like before this town was here?"

"Nothing at all. Just the lake and the hills is all."

"Indians?"

"Not many around here. Just empty woods and hills is all."

"Pass the syrup," said Mom.

———

"Whambo!" cried RT, "I'm an atom bomb! Boom!"

We were waiting in line at the Elite theater. It was the biggest day of the year. We had lugged pop all morning at the circus to earn show tickets. Now, in the afternoon, we were seeing cowboys and Indians on the movie screen, and, this evening, the circus itself! We felt rich and we laughed all the time. RT kept squinting through his atomic ring, yelling, "Whoom! You're disintegrated!"

Cowboys chased Indians across the screen. Half an hour later the Indians chased the cowboys back the other way. After everybody was tired of stomping, the cartoon came on, and then a newsreel.

"Look, the atom bomb!" RT settled down for the first time.

The big gray cloud lifted on the screen, blew apart, battleships and cruisers burst open and rain fell.

RT held my arm tight, staring up at the burning whiteness. "Ain't that something, Doug, ain't it?" He jabbed my ribs.

"It's a whooperdoo, all right," I said, jabbing him back, giggling. "Wish I had an atom bomb! Blooie, there goes the school!"

"Bam! Goodbye Clara Holmquist!"

"Bang! There goes Officer O'Rourke!"

———

For supper there were Swedish meatballs, hot buns, Boston beans and green salad. Father looked very serious and strange and tried to bring up some important scientific facts he had read in a magazine, but Mom shook her head.

I watched Pop. "You feeling okay, Pop?"

"I'm going to cancel our paper subscription," said Mom. "You're worrying yourself right into ulcers. You hear me, Dad?"

"Boy," I said, "did I see a *film*! The atom bomb blew up a whole battleship down at the Elite."

Father dropped his fork and stared at me. "Sometimes, Douglas, you have the uncanny ability to say just the wrong thing at the wrong time."

I saw Mother squinting at me to catch my eye. "It's late," she said. "You'd better run on to the circus."

As I was getting my hat and coat I heard Father say in a low and thoughtful voice, "How would it be to sell the business?

You know, we've always wanted to travel; go to Mexico maybe. A small town. Settle down."

"You're talking like a child," whispered Mother. "I won't hear you carry on this way."

"I know it's foolish. Don't mind me. But you're right; better cancel the paper."

———

A wind was blowing the trees half over and the stars were all out and the circus lay in the country hills, in the meadow, like a big toadstool. Red Tongue and I had popcorn in one hand, taffy in the other, and cotton candy on our chins. "Lookit my beard!" Red Tongue shouted. Everybody was talking and pushing under the bright light bulbs and a man smacked a canvas with a bamboo cane and shouted about The Skeleton, The Blubber Lady, The Illustrated Man, The Seal Boy, while RT and I jostled through to the lady who tore our tickets in half.

We balanced our way up to sit on the slat seats just when the bass drums exploded and the jeweled elephants lumbered out, and from then on there were hot searchlights, men shooting from fiery howitzers, ladies hung by their white teeth imitating butterflies high up in the clouds of cigarette smoke while trapeze men rode back and forth among the ropes and poles, and lions trotted softly around the sawdust-floored cage while the trainer in white pants shot smoke and flame at them from a silver pistol. "Look!" RT and I cried, blinking here, gaping there, chuckling, ohing, ahing, amazed, incredulous, surprised, and entertained, out of breath, eyes wide, mouths open. Chariots roared around the track, clowns jumped from burning hotels, grew hair, changed from giants to midgets in a steam box. The band crashed and tooted and hooted and everywhere was color and warmth and sequins shining and the crowd thundering.

But along about the end of the show I looked up. And there, behind me, was a little hole in the canvas. And through that hole I could see the old meadowland, the wind blowing over it and the stars shining alone out there. The cold wind tugged at the tent very gently. And all of a sudden, turning back to the warm riot all around me, I was cold too. I heard Red Tongue laughing beside me and I half-saw some men riding a silver bike on a high, far-away, thin thread, the snare drum going tatatatatatatatata, everyone quiet. And when that was over, there were two hundred clowns whacking each other's heads with bats and Red Tongue almost fell from his seat, screaming with it. I sat there and didn't move and at last Red Tongue turned and looked at me and said, "Hey, what's wrong, Doug?"

"Nothing," I said. I shook myself. I looked up at the red circus poles and the rope lines and the flaring lights. I looked at the zinc-oxide clowns and made myself laugh. "Lookit there, RT, that fat one over there!"

The band played "The Old Gray Mare She Ain't What She Used to Be."

"It's all over," said Red Tongue, breathlessly.

We sat while the thousands of stunned people walked away mumbling and laughing and pressing at each other. The tent was thick with cigar smoke and the musical instruments lay curled up and abandoned for a moment on the wooden dock where the band had shocked us with wave after wave of brass.

We didn't move because neither of us wanted it to be over.

"Guess we better go," said RT, not stirring.

"Let's wait," I said, tonelessly, not looking at anything. I felt the wood slat aching under my bottom after the long strange hours of music and color. Men were moving and slapping the collapsing chairs down into themselves to be toted away. The canvas strippings were being unhooked. Everywhere was the jingle and the snap and clatter of the circus falling apart.

The tent was empty.

We stood on the midway, the wind blowing dust in our eyes, leaves whipping off the trees. And the wind carried away all the dead leaves and all the restless people. The sideshow bulbs blinked off. We walked to the top of a nearby hill and stood there in the windy dark, our teeth chattering, watching the blue lights drift in the blackness, the white shapes of elephants floating, the sounds of men cursing and stakes being pried up. And then, like an immense sighing bellows, the main tent settling to earth.

An hour later the gravel road was amove with cars and trucks and golden cages. The pale meadow lay empty. The moon was rising and rime formed over every wet thing. RT and I walked slowly down across the meadow, smelling the sawdust. "That's all that's left," said Red Tongue. "Sawdust."

"Here's a stake hole," I said. I pointed. "There's another."

"You'd never know they were ever here," said RT. "It's like making it up in your mind." The wind blew across the empty meadow and we stood watching the black trees shake. There was not a light or a sound; even all of the circus smell had finally blown away.

"Welp," said RT, scuffing his shoes. "We'll get the tar beat out of us if we ain't home *an hour ago!*" He smiled.

We walked back together down the lonely country road, the wind at our backs, our hands deep in our pockets, our heads down. We walked past the deep silent ravine and then we walked through the little streets of the town, past sleeping houses, where here and there a radio quietly played, and there was the sound of a last cricket, and our heels thumping on the rough bricks in the middle of the long street, under the swaying, dim arc lamps at each corner.

I looked at all the houses and all the picket fences and all the slanting roofs and lighted windows and I looked at every tree and at all the bricks under my feet. I looked at my shoes and I looked over at RT trudging beside me, his teeth chattering. And I saw the courthouse clock a mile away, lifting up its moist white face in the moonlight, all the municipal buildings black and big. "G'night, Doug." I didn't answer as RT walked slowly on down the street between the houses at midnight and turned a far corner.

I crept upstairs and was in bed in a minute, looking out through my window at the town.

My brother Skip must have heard me crying for a long time before he put his hand over to feel my arm. "What's wrong, Doug?" he asked.

"Nothing," I sobbed quietly, eyes closed. "Just the circus."

Skip waited. The wind blew around the house. "What about it?" he asked.

"Nothing—except it won't come again."

"Sure it will," he said.

"No, it's gone. And it won't come back again. It's all gone where it was, nothing of it left."

"Try to get some sleep." Skip turned over.

I stopped crying. Somewhere, across town, a few windows were still glowing. Down at the rail station, an engine hooted and started and went rushing off between the hills.

I waited in the dark room, holding my breath, while one by silent one, the small, far-away windows of the little houses went dark.

THE LAUREL AND HARDY
LOVE AFFAIR

He called her Stanley, she called him Ollie.

That was the beginning, that was the end, of what we will call the Laurel and Hardy love affair.

She was twenty-five, he was thirty-two when they met at one of those dumb cocktail parties where everyone wonders what they are doing there. But no one goes home, so everyone drinks too much and lies about how grand a late afternoon it all was.

They did not, as often happens, see each other across a crowded room, and if there was romantic music to background their collision, it couldn't be heard. For everyone was talking at one person and staring at someone else.

They were, in fact, ricocheting through a forest of people, but finding no shade trees. He was on his way for a needed drink, she was eluding a love-sick stranger, when they locked paths in the exact center of the fruitless mob. They dodged left and right a few times, then laughed and he, on impulse, seized his tie and twiddled it at her, wiggling his fingers. Instantly, smiling, she lifted her hand to pull the top of her hair into a frouzy tassel, blinking and looking as if she had been struck on the head.

"Stan!" he cried, in recognition.

"Ollie!" she exclaimed. "Where have you *been?*"

"Why don't you do something to *help* me!" he exclaimed, making wide fat gestures.

They grabbed each other's arms, laughing again.

"I—" she said, and her face brightened even more. "I—I know the exact place, not two miles from here, where Laurel and Hardy, in nineteen thirty, carried that piano crate up and down one hundred and fifty steps!"

"Well," he cried, "let's get *out* of here!"

His car door slammed, his car engine roared.

Los Angeles raced by in late afternoon sunlight.

He braked the car where she told him to park. "Here!"

"I can't believe it," he murmured, not moving. He peered around at the sunset sky. Lights were coming on all across Los Angeles, down the hill. He nodded. "Are *those* the steps?"

"All one hundred and fifty of them." She climbed out of the open-topped car. "Come on, Ollie."

"Very well," he said, "Stan."

They walked over to the bottom of yet another hill and gazed up along the steep incline of concrete steps toward the sky. The faintest touch of wetness rimmed his eyes. She was quick to pretend not to notice, but she took his elbow. Her voice was wonderfully quiet:

"Go on up," she said, "Go on. Go."

She gave him a tender push.

He started up the steps, counting, and with each half-whispered count, his voice took on an extra decibel of joy. By the time he reached fifty-seven he was a boy playing a wondrous old-new game, and he was lost in time, and whether he was carrying the piano up the hill or whether it was chasing him down, he could not say.

"Hold it!" he heard her call, far away, "right there!"

He held still, swaying on step fifty-eight, smiling wildly, as if accompanied by proper ghosts, and turned.

"Okay," she called, "now come back down."

He started down, color in his cheeks and a peculiar suffering of happiness in his chest. He could hear the piano following now.

"Hold it right *there!*"

She had a camera in her hands. Seeing it, his right hand flew instinctively to his tie to flutter it on the evening air.

"Now, *me!*" she shouted, and raced up to hand him the camera. And he marched down and looked up and there she was, doing the thin shrug and the puzzled and hopeless face of Stan baffled by life but loving it all. He clicked the shutter, wanting to stay here forever.

She came slowly down the steps and peered into his face.

"Why," she said, "you're *crying.*"

She placed her thumbs under his eyes to press the tears away. She tasted the result. "Yep," she said. "*Real* tears."

He looked at her eyes, which were almost as wet as his.

"Another fine mess you've got us in," he said.

"Oh, Ollie," she said.

"Oh, Stan," he said.

He kissed her, gently.

And then he said:

"Are we going to know each other forever?"

"Forever," she said.

———

And that was how the long love affair began.

They had real names, of course, but those don't matter, for

Laurel and Hardy always seemed the best thing to call themselves.

For the simple fact was that she was fifteen pounds underweight and he was always trying to get her to add a few pounds. And he was twenty pounds overweight and she was always trying to get him to take off more than his shoes. But it never worked and was finally a joke, the best kind, which wound up being:

"You're Stan, no two ways about it, and I'm Ollie, let's face it. And, oh God, dear young woman, let's enjoy the mess, the wonderful mess, all the while we're in!"

It was, then, while it lasted, and it lasted some while, a French parfait, an American perfection, a wildness from which they would never recover to the end of their lives.

From that twilight hour on the piano stairs on their days were long, heedless, and full of that amazing laughter that paces the beginning and the run-along rush of any great love affair. They only stopped laughing long enough to kiss and only stopped kissing long enough to laugh at how odd and miraculous it was to find themselves with no clothes to wear in the middle of a bed as vast as life and as beautiful as morning.

And sitting there in the middle of warm whiteness, he shut his eyes and shook his head and declared, pompously:

"I have *nothing* to say!"

"Yes, you do!" she cried. "*Say* it!"

And he said it and they fell off the edge of the earth.

———

Their first year was pure myth and fable, which would grow outsize when remembered thirty years on. They went to see new films and old films, but mainly Stan and Ollie. They memorized all the best scenes and shouted them back and forth as they drove around midnight Los Angeles. He spoiled her by treating her childhood growing up in Hollywood as very special, and she spoiled him by pretending that his yesterday on roller skates out front of the studios was not in the past but right now.

She proved it one night. On a whim she asked him where he had roller-skated as a boy and collided with W. C. Fields. Where had he asked Fields for his autograph, and where was it that Fields signed the book, handed it back, and cried, "There you are, you little son-of-a-bitch!"

"Drive me there," she said.

And at ten o'clock that night they got out of the car in front of Paramount Studio and he pointed to the pavement near the gate and said, "He stood there," and she gathered him in her arms and kissed him and said, gently, "Now where was it you had your picture taken with Marlene Dietrich?"

He walked her fifty feet across the street from the studio. "In the late afternoon sun," he said, "Marlene stood here." And she kissed him again, longer this time, and the moon rising like an obvious magic trick, filling the street in front of the empty studio. She let her soul flow over into him like a tipped fountain, and he received it and gave it back and was glad.

"Now," she said, quietly, "where was it you saw Fred Astaire in nineteen thirty-five and Ronald Colman in nineteen thirty-seven and Jean Harlow in nineteen thirty-six?"

And he drove her to those three different places all around Hollywood until midnight and they stood and she kissed him as if it would never end.

And that was the first year. And during that year they went up and down those long piano steps at least once a month and had champagne picnics halfway up, and discovered an incredible thing:

"I think it's our mouths," he said. "Until I met you, I never knew I had a mouth. Yours is the most amazing in the world, and it makes me feel as if mine were amazing, too. Were you ever really kissed before I kissed you?"

"Never!"

"Nor was I. To have lived this long and not known mouths."

"Dear mouth," she said, "shut up and kiss."

But then at the end of the first year they discovered an even more incredible thing. He worked at an advertising agency and was nailed in one place. She worked at a travel agency and would soon be flying everywhere. Both were astonished they had never noticed before. But now that Vesuvius had erupted and the fiery dust was beginning to settle, they sat and looked at each other one night and she said, faintly:

"Goodbye. . . ."

"What?" he asked.

"I can see goodbye coming," she said.

He looked at her face and it was not sad like Stan in the films, but just sad like herself.

"I feel like the ending of that Hemingway novel where two people ride along in the late day and say how it would be if they could go on forever but they know now they won't," she said.

"Stan," he said, "this is no Hemingway novel and this can't be the end of the world. You'll never leave me."

But it was a question, not a declaration and suddenly she moved and he blinked at her and said,

"What are you doing down there?"

"Nut," she said, "I'm kneeling on the floor and I'm asking for your hand. Marry me, Ollie. Come away with me to France. I've got a new job in Paris. No, don't say anything. Shut up. No one has to know I've got the money this year and will support you while you write the great American novel—"

"But—" he said.

"You've got your portable typewriter, a ream of paper, and

me. Say it, Stan, will you come? Hell, don't marry me, we'll live in sin, but fly with me, yes?"

"And watch us go to hell in a year and bury us forever?"

"Are you that afraid, Ollie? Don't you believe in me or you or anything? God, why are men such cowards, and why the hell do you have such thin skins and are afraid of a woman like a ladder to lean on. Listen, I've got things to do and you're coming with me. I can't leave you here, you'll fall down those damn stairs. But if I have to, I will. I want everything now, not tomorrow. That means you, Paris, and my job. Your novel will take time, but you'll do it. Now, do you do it here and feel sorry for yourself, or do we live in a coldwater walk-up flat in the Latin Quarter a long way off from here. This is my one and only offer, Stan. I've never proposed before, I won't ever propose again, it's hard on my knees. Well?"

"Have we had this conversation before?" he said.

"A dozen times in the last year, but you never listened, you were hopeless."

"No, in love and helpless."

"You've got one minute to make up your mind. Sixty seconds." She was staring at her wristwatch.

"Get up off the floor," he said, embarrassed.

"If I do, it's out the door and gone," she said. "Forty-nine seconds to go, Ollie."

"Stan," he groaned.

"Thirty," she read her watch. "Twenty. I've got one knee off the floor. Ten. I'm beginning to get the other knee up. Five. One."

And she was standing on her feet.

"What brought this on?" he asked.

"Now," she said, "I am heading for the door. I don't know. Maybe I've thought about it more than I dared even notice. We are very special wondrous people, Ollie, and I don't think our like will ever come again in the world, at least not to us, or I'm lying to myself and I probably am. But I must go and you are free to come along, but can't face it or don't know it. And now—" she reached out. "My hand is on the door and—"

"And?" he said, quietly.

"I'm crying," she said.

He started to get up but she shook her head.

"No, don't. If you touch me I'll cave in, and to hell with that. I'm going. But once a year will be forbearance day, or forgiveness day or whatever in hell you want to call it. Once a year I'll show up at our flight of steps, no piano, same hour, same time as that night when we first went there and if you're there to meet me I'll kidnap you or you me, but don't bring along and show me your damn bank balance or give me any of your lip."

"Stan," he said.

"My God," she mourned.

"What?"

"This door is heavy. I can't move it." She wept. "There. It's moving. There." She wept more. "I'm gone."

The door shut.

"Stan!" He ran to the door and grabbed the knob. It was wet. He raised his fingers to his mouth and tasted the salt, then opened the door.

The hall was already empty. The air where she had passed was just coming back together. Thunder threatened when the two halves met. There was a promise of rain.

———

He went back to the steps on October 4 every year for three years, but she wasn't there. And then he forgot for two years but in the autumn of the sixth year, he remembered and went back in the late sunlight and walked up the stairs because he saw something halfway up and it was a bottle of good champagne with a ribbon and a note on it, delivered by someone, and the note read:

"Ollie, dear Ollie. Date remembered. But in Paris. Mouth's not the same, but happily married. Love. Stan."

And after that, every October he simply did not go to visit the stairs. The sound of that piano rushing down that hillside, he knew, would catch him and take him along to where he did not know.

And that was the end, or almost the end, of the Laurel and Hardy love affair.

There was, by amiable accident, a final meeting.

Traveling through France fifteen years later, he was walking on the Champs-Élysées at twilight one afternoon with his wife and two daughters, when he saw this handsome woman coming the other way, escorted by a very sober-looking older man and a very handsome dark-haired boy of twelve, obviously her son.

As they passed, the same smile lit both their faces in the same instant.

He twiddled his necktie at her.

She tousled her hair at him.

They did not stop. They kept going. But he heard her call back along the Champs-Élysées, the last words he would ever hear her say:

"Another fine mess you've got us in!" And then she added the old, the familiar name by which he had gone in the years of their love.

And she was gone and his daughters and wife looked at him and one daughter said, "Did that lady call you Ollie?"

"What lady?" he said.

"Dad," said the other daughter, leaning in to peer at his face. "You're crying."

"No."

"Yes, you are. *Isn't* he, Mom?"

"Your papa," said his wife, "as you well know, cries at telephone books."

"No," he said, "just one hundred fifty steps and a piano. Remind me to show you girls, someday."

They walked on and he turned and looked back a final time. The woman with her husband and son turned at that very moment. Maybe he saw her mouth pantomime the words, So long, Ollie. Maybe he didn't. He felt his own mouth move, in silence: So long, Stan.

And they walked in opposite directions along the Champs-Élysées in the late light of an October sun.

I SUPPOSE YOU ARE WONDERING WHY WE ARE HERE?

The restaurant was empty when he arrived. It was six o'clock, early, the big crowds if they came would come later, which was perfect, for he had a dozen busy things to do. He watched his hands lay out the napkins in front of three places, then arrange and rearrange the wineglasses, then place and replace the knives, forks, and spoons as if he himself were the maître d' or some sort of latter-day sorcerer. He heard himself muttering under his breath, and part of the time it was a sort of mindless chant and the rest an incantation, for he really didn't know how to do all this, but it had to be done.

He himself opened the wine, while the owners of the restaurant stood in the back, whispering with the chef and nodding at him as if he were the maniac-in-charge.

In charge of what, he was not quite sure. His own life? Not quite. Not by half. Sometimes not at all. But tonight, one way or another, it would have to change. Tonight might at least give him a few answers or a little peace.

He poured some wine in a glass, sniffed it, sipped it, eyes shut, waiting for the taste. All right. Not great, but all right.

He rearranged the cutlery for the third time, thinking, I have two problems. My daughters who might as well be Martians living on Mars, and my mother and father, the greatest problem of all.

Because they had been dead for twenty years.

No matter. If he prayed, if he silently begged, if he summoned them with immense will, controlling his heartbeat and restless mind, focusing his thoughts on the near grass meadow, it would happen. His mother and father would somehow recycle their dusts, arise, walk, stroll along the night avenues for three blocks, and step into this restaurant as matter-of-factly, just as if—

God, I haven't even had a full glass of wine yet, he thought, and turned abruptly to step outside.

Out in the summer night, with the restaurant screen door half-open, he stared down the dusking street toward the graveyard gates. Yes. Almost ready. *He* was, that is. But . . . were *they*? Was the time right? For him, of course, but . . . Would the napkins placed, the cutlery arranged in symbols of need, the good wine waiting, would all of it truly *do* the job?

Cut it out, he thought, and turned his gaze from the far graveyard entrance to the nearby phone booth. He let the screen door shut, walked to the booth, dropped in his dime, and dialed a number.

His daughter's voice, on the answering machine, sounded. He shut his eyes and hung up, shaking his head, not saying anything. He tried a second number. The second daughter simply didn't answer. He hung up, took a final look at that graveyard off away there in the growing dark, and hurried back inside the restaurant.

There he did the whole thing over again, the glasses, the napkins, the cutlery, touching, retouching, placing and replacing, to energize it all, to make all the objects, as well as himself, believe. Then he nodded and sat down, stared hard at the cutlery, the plates, the wineglasses, took three deep breaths, shut his eyes, concentrated, and prayed very hard, waiting.

He knew that if he sat here long enough and wished hard enough—

They would arrive, sit down, greet him as always; his mother would kiss him on the cheek, his father would grab his hand and tighten on it, hard, the loud greetings would at last quiet down and the last supper at this small-town restaurant would finally begin.

Two minutes passed. He heard his watch ticking on his wrist. Nothing.

Another minute passed. He concentrated. He prayed. His heart sounded quietly. Nothing.

Another minute. He listened to his own breathing. Now, he thought. Now, dammit. Come *on!*

His heart jumped.

The front door to the restaurant had opened.

He did not look up, he trapped his breath, and kept his eyes shut.

Someone was walking toward his table. Someone arrived. Someone was looking down at him.

"I thought you'd never invite us to dinner again," said his mother.

He opened his eyes just as she leaned down to kiss him on the brow.

"Long time no see!" His father reached out, seized his hand, and gripped it tight. "How goes it, son?"

The son leaped up, almost spilling the wine.

"Fine, Dad. Hi, Mom! Sit down, my God, oh my God, sit down!"

But they did not sit down. They stood looking at each other in a kind of stunned bewilderment until: "Don't make such a fuss, it's only us," said his mother. "It's been so long since you called. We—"

"It has been a long time, son." His father was still holding his hand in an iron grip. Now, he winked to show it was okay. "But, we understand. You're busy. You okay, boy?"

"Okay," said the son. "I mean—I've *missed* you!" And here he grabbed both of them, impulsively, and hugged them, his eyes watering. "How have you been—" He stopped and blushed. "I mean—"

"Don't be embarrassed, son," said his father. "We're great. For a while there it was tough. I mean, it was all so new. How in hell do you describe it. You can't, so I won't—"

"George, for goodness' sake, cut the cackle and get us a table," said his mother.

"This *is* our table," said the son, pointing at the empty places. He suddenly realized he had forgotten to light the candle, and did so, with trembling hands. "Sit down. Have some wine!"

"Your father shouldn't drink wine," his mother started to say.

"For God's sake," his father said, "it doesn't make any difference *now*."

"I forgot." His mother felt herself in a strange, tentative way, as if she had just tried on a new dress and the seams were awry. "I keep forgetting."

"It's the same as forgetting you're alive." His father barked a laugh. "People live seventy years and after a while don't *notice*. Forget to say, hell, I'm alive! When that happens, you might as well be—"

"George," said his mother.

"Look at it this way," said his father, sitting down and leaving his wife and son standing. "Before you're born's one condition, living's a second condition, and after you're through is a third. In each state you forget to notice, say: Hey, I'm on first base, I'm on second! Well, hell, here we are on third, and like your mom says, she sometimes forgets. I can have as much damned wine as I want!"

He poured wine all around, and drank his, much too quickly. "Not bad!"

"How can you *tell*?" said the son, then bit his tongue.

But his father had not heard, and patted the seat beside him. "Come on, Ma!"

"Don't call me Ma. I'm Alice!"

"Ma-Alice, come *on*!"

His mother slid in on one side, and the son slid in on the other side of his father.

For the first time, as they got settled, the son had a chance to really look at what his parents were wearing.

His father wore a tweed jacket and knickers for golfing and high, brightly patterned, Argyle socks. His shoes were a light sunburnt orange, highly polished, his tie was black with tangerine stripes, and on his head he wore a cap with a broad brim, made of some brown tweed stuff, very fresh looking and new.

"You look great, Dad. Mom—"

She was wearing her good Lodge go-to-meeting coat, a gray woolen affair, under which she wore a blue and white silk dress with a light blue scarf at her neck. On her head was a kind of mushroom cloche, the sort of cap aging flappers wore, with ruby stickpins thrust through to hold it tight to their marcelled curls.

"Where have I seen your outfits before?" asked the son.

But before they could answer, he remembered: a snapshot of himself and his brother on the front lawn some Memorial Day or July 4 long years ago. There they were, secretly pinching one another, dressed in their knickers and coats and caps, their folks behind them, squinting out at a noon that would last forever.

His father read his thoughts and said, "Right after Baptist

service, Easter noon, nineteen twenty-seven. Wore my golf clothes. Ma had a fit."

"What are you both yammering about?" His mother fussed in her purse, drew forth a mirror, and checked her Tangee mouth, etching it with her little finger.

"Nothing, Alice-Ma." His father refilled his glass but this time, seeing his son watching, drank the wine slower. "Not bad, once you get used to it. It's not the hard stuff, though. Whiskey is more like it. Where's the menu? Hell, here it is. Let's have a look."

His father took a long time angling the menu and peering at the print.

"What's this French stuff on the list?" he cried. "Why can't they use *English*? Who do they think they *are*?"

"It *is* in English, dad. See. *There*." The son underlined several items on the menu with his fingernail.

"Hell," snorted his father, staring at the lines, "why didn't they *say* so?"

"Pa," said his mother, "just read the English and *choose*."

"Always had trouble choosing. What's everyone else eating? What's that man over *there* eating?" His father leaned and craned his neck, staring at the table across the way. "Looks good. Think I'll have *that*!"

"Your father," said his mother, "has always ordered this way. If that man was having carpet tacks and pork bellies, he'd order *that*."

"I remember," said the son, quietly, and drank his wine. He held his breath and at last let it out. "What'll *you* have, Mom?"

"What are *you* having, son?"

"Hamburger steak—"

"That's what *I'll* have," said his mother, "to save trouble."

"Mom," said the son. "It's no trouble. There are three dozen items on the menu."

"No," she said, and put the menu down and covered it with her napkin as if it were a small cold body. "That's it. My son's taste is *my* taste."

He reached for the wine bottle and suddenly realized it was empty. "Good grief," he said, "did we drink it *all*?"

"*Someone* did. Get some more, son. Here, while you're waiting, take some of mine." The father poured half of his wine into his son's glass. "I could drink a soup bowl of that stuff."

More wine was brought, opened, poured.

"Watch your liver!" said his mother.

"Is that a threat, or a toast?" said his father.

As they drank, the son realized that somehow the evening had got out of hand; they were not talking about the things he most dearly wanted to talk about.

"Here's to your health, son!"

"And yours, Dad. Mom!"

Again he had to stop, flushing, for he suddenly remembered that meadow down the street from which they had come, that quiet place of marble huts with great names cut on the Grecian roofs, and too many crosses and not half enough angels.

"Your health," said the son, quietly.

His mother at last raised her glass and nibbled at the wine like a field mouse.

"Oh." She wrinkled her nose. "Sour."

"No, it's not, ma," said the son, "that's just the cellar taste. It's not a bad wine, really—"

"If it's so good," said his mother, "why are you gulping it so fast?"

"Mother," said his father. "Well!"

And here his father exploded a laugh, brisked his palms together, and leaned on the table with false earnestness.

"I suppose you are wondering," he said, "why we are *here*?"

"*You* didn't call, father. *He* did. Your son."

"Just a joke, Ma. Well, son, why *did* you?"

They were both staring at him, waiting.

"Why did I *what*?"

"Call us *here*!"

"Oh, that—"

The son refilled his glass. He was beginning to perspire. He wiped his lips and brow with his napkin.

"Wait a minute," he said. "It'll come to me—"

"Don't push, Father, let the boy breathe."

"Sure, sure," said his father. "But we took a lot of trouble to dress up and find time and come here. On top of which—"

"Father."

"No, Alice, let me finish. Son of mine, good boy, that *place* you got us into is not of the *best*."

"It's all right," said his mother.

"No, it's not, and you know it." The father picked up a fork and drew a picture of the place on the tablecloth. "It's too damn small, too far from everywhere. No view. And, the heating, my God, the heating!"

"Well, it *does* get cold in the winter," admitted his mother.

"Cold, hell. So cold it runs cracks up one side and down the other of all the places out there. Oh, and another thing. I don't like some of our neighbors."

"You *never* liked neighbors anytime, anywhere, anyhow," said his mother. "People next door moved out: Thank *God*, you said. New people moved in: *Oh*, God, you said."

"Well, these are the worst, they take the cake. Son, can you *do* anything about it?"

"Do?" said the son, and thought: my God, they don't know where they've come from, they don't know where they've been for twenty years, they can't guess why it's cold—

"Too hot in summer," added his father. "Melts you in your shoes. Don't *look* at me that way, Mother. Son wants to hear.

He'll do something about it, won't you, son? Find us a *new* place—"

"Yes, Dad."

"You got a headache, son?"

"No." The son opened his eyes, and reached for the bottle. "I'll look into it. I promise."

I wonder, he thought, has anyone ever moved anyone out of a place like that to another place, all for a view, all for better neighbors? Would the law allow? Where could he take them? Where might they go? North Chicago, maybe? There was a place there on a hill—

The waiter arrived just then to take their orders.

"Whatever *he's* having." His mother pointed at the son.

"Whatever that man over *there* is eating," said the father.

"Hamburger steak," said the son.

The waiter went away and came back and they ate quickly.

"Is this a speed contest?"

"Slow down, boy. Whoa."

And suddenly it was all over. Exactly one hour had passed as the son put down his knife and fork and finished his fourth glass of wine. Suddenly his face burst into a smile.

"I *remember!*" he cried. "I mean, it's come back to me. Why I called, why I *brought* you here!"

"Well?" said his mother.

"Spit it out, son," said his father.

"I," said the son.

"Yes?"

"I—"

"Yes, yes?"

"I," said the son, "love you."

His words pushed his parents back in their seats. Their shoulders sagged and they glanced at each other out of the corners of their eyes, quietly, with their heads lowered.

"Hell, son," said his father. "We know that."

"We love you, too," said his mother.

"Yes," said his father, quietly. "Yes."

"But we try not to think about it," said his mother. "It makes us too unhappy when you don't call."

"Mother!" cried the son, and stopped himself from saying: you've forgotten *again*!

Instead, he said: "I'll call more often."

"No need," said his father.

"I will, believe me, I will!"

"Don't make promises you can't live up to, is what I say. But now," said the father, drinking more wine, "son, what else did you want to see us about?"

"What else?" The son was shocked. Wasn't it enough he protested his great and enduring love—"Well. . . ." The son slowed. His gaze wandered through the restaurant window to the silent phone booth where he had placed those calls.

"My children—" he said.

"Children!" The old man exploded. "By God, I'd forgot myself. What *were* they now—?"

"Daughters, of course," said the wife, punching her husband's arm. "What's wrong with you?"

"If you don't know what's been wrong with me for twenty years, you'll never know." The father turned to the son. "Daughters, of course. Must be full-grown now. Little tads, last time we saw—"

"Let son tell us about them," said the mother.

"There's nothing to tell." The son paused awkwardly. "Hell. Lots. But it doesn't make sense."

"Try us," said the father.

"Sometimes—"

"Yes?"

"Sometimes," the son continued, slowly, eyes down, "I have

this feeling my daughters, mind you, my *daughters* have passed away and you, *you're* alive! Does that make any sense?"

"About as much sense as most families make," said the father, taking out, cutting, and sucking at a fresh cigar. "You always *did* talk funny, son."

"Pa," said the mother.

"Well, he *did* and he *does*, dammit. Talk funny, that is. But go ahead, talk on, and while you're at it give me some more wine. Go on."

The son poured wine and said, "I can't figure them out. So I've got two problems. That's why I summoned you. Number one, I missed you. Number two, I miss *them*. *There's* a joke for you. How can that *be*?"

"On the face of it—" the father began.

"That's life," said the mother, nodding, very wise.

"That's all the advice you can *give*?" cried the son.

"Sorry, we know you went to a lot of trouble, and the dinner was fine and the wine jim-dandy, but we're out of practice, boy. We can't even remember what *you* were like! So how can we help? We can't!" The father lit a match and watched it flame around the cigar as he drew fire. "No, son. On top of which, we got another problem here. Hate to mention it. Don't know how to say it—"

"What your father means is—"

"No, let me say it, Alice. I hope you'll take this in the kindly spirit with which I offer it, boy—"

"Whatever it is, Dad, I will," said the son.

"God, this is hard." The father slammed down his cigar and finished another glass of wine. "Damn and hell, the fact *is*, son, the reason why we didn't see you more often over the years is—" He held his breath, then exploded it: "You were a *bore*!"

A bomb had been tossed on the table to explode. Stunned, all three stared at one another.

"What?" asked the son.

"I said—"

"No, no, I heard you," said the son. "I heard. I bore you." He tasted the words. They had a strange flavor. "*I* bore *you? My God!* I *bore* you!"

His face reddened, tears burst from his eyes and he began to roar with laughter, beating the table with his right fist and holding to his aching chest with his left, and then wiping his eyes with a napkin. "*I* bore *you!"*

His mother and father waited for a decent interval before they, in turn, began to snort, whiffle, stop up their breaths, and then let it out in a great proclamation of relief and hilarity.

"Sorry, son!" cried the father, tears running down about his laughing mouth.

"He didn't really mean—" gasped the mother, rocking back and forth, giggles escaping with each breath.

"Oh, he did, he did!" shouted the son. "He did!"

And now everyone in the restaurant was looking up at the merry trio.

"More wine!" said the father.

"More wine."

And by the time the last bottle of wine was uncorked and poured, the three had settled into a smiling, gasping, beautiful silence. The son lifted his glass in a toast.

"Here's to boredom!"

Which set them all off again, firing guffaws, sucking air, pounding the table, eyes gummed shut with happy tears, knocking each other's ribs with their elbows.

"Well, son," said the father, at last, quieting. "It's late. We really *must* be going."

"Where?" laughed the son, and grew still. "Oh, yes. I forgot."

"Oh, don't look so down in the mouth," said his mother. "That place isn't half as bad as Father makes out."

"But," said the son, quietly, "isn't *it* a bit—boring—also?"

"Not once you get the hang of it. Finish the wine. Here goes."

They drank the last of the wine, laughed a bit, shook their heads, then walked to the restaurant door and out into a warm summer night. It was only eight o'clock and a fine wind blew up from the lake, and there was a smell of flowers in the air that made you want to just walk on forever.

"Let me go part way with you," offered the son.

"Oh, that's not necessary."

"We can make it alone, son," said the father. "It's better that way."

They stood looking at each other.

"Well," said the son, "it's been nice."

"No, not really. Loving, yes, loving, because we're family and we love you, son, and you love us. But nice? I don't know if that fits. Boring, yes, boring, and loving, loving and boring. Good night, son."

And they milled around each other and hugged and kissed and wept and then gave one last great hoot of laughter, and there went his parents, along the street under the darkening trees, heading for the meadow place.

The son stood for a long moment, watching his parents getting smaller and smaller with distance and then he turned, almost without thinking, and stepped into the phone booth, dialed, and got the answering machine.

"Hello, Helen," he said, and paused because it was hard to find words, difficult to say. "This is Dad. About that dinner next Thursday? Could we cancel? No special reason. Overwork. I'll call next week, set a new date. Oh, and could you call Debby and tell *her*? Love you. 'Bye."

He hung up and looked down the long dark street. Way off there, his parents were just turning in at the iron graveyard gates. They saw him watching, gave him a wave, and were gone.

Mom. Dad, he thought. Helen. Debby. And again: Helen, Debby, Mom, Dad. I *bore* them. *I* bore *them!* I will be *damned!*

And then, laughing until the tears rolled out of his eyes, he turned and strolled back into the restaurant. His laughter made a few people look up from their tables.

He didn't mind, because the wine, as he finished it, wasn't all that bad.

LAFAYETTE, FAREWELL

There was a tap on the door, the bell was not rung, so I knew who it was. The tapping used to happen once a week, but in the past few weeks it came every other day. I shut my eyes, said a prayer, and opened the door.

Bill Westerleigh was there, looking at me, tears streaming down his cheeks.

"Is this *my* house or *yours*?" he said.

It was an old joke now. Several times a year he wandered off, an eighty-nine-year-old man, to get lost within a few blocks. He had quit driving years ago because he had wound up thirty miles out of Los Angeles instead of at the center where we were. His best journey nowadays was from next door, where he lived with his wondrously warm and understanding wife, to here, where he tapped, entered, and wept. "Is this *your* house or *mine*?" he said, reversing the order.

"Mi casa es su casa." I quoted the old Spanish saying.

"And thank God for that!"

I led the way to the sherry bottle and glasses in the parlor and poured two glasses while Bill settled in an easy chair across from me. He wiped his eyes and blew his nose on a handkerchief which he then folded neatly and put back in his breast pocket.

"Here's to you, buster." He waved his sherry glass. "The sky is full of 'em. I hope you come back. If not, we'll drop a black wreath where we think your crate fell."

I drank and was warmed by the drink and then looked a long while at Bill.

"The Escadrille been buzzing you again?" I asked.

"Every night, right after midnight. Every morning now. And, the last week, noons. I try not to come over. I tried for three days."

"I know. I missed you."

"Kind of you to say, son. You have a good heart. But I know I'm a pest, when I have my clear moments. Right now I'm clear and I drink your hospitable health."

He emptied his glass and I refilled it.

"You want to talk about it?"

"You sound just like a psychiatrist friend of mine. Not that I ever went to one, he was just a friend. Great thing about coming over here is it's free, and sherry to boot." He eyed his drink pensively. "It's a terrible thing to be haunted by ghosts."

"We all have them. That's where Shakespeare was so bright. He taught himself, taught us, taught psychiatrists. Don't do bad, he said, or your ghosts will get you. The old remembrance, the conscience which doth make cowards and scare midnight men, will rise up and cry, Hamlet, remember me, Macbeth, you're marked, Lady Macbeth, you, too! Richard the Third, beware, we walk the dawn camp at your shoulder and our shrouds are stiff with blood."

"God, you talk purty." Bill shook his head. "Nice living next door to a writer. When I need a dose of poetry, here you are."

"I tend to lecture. It bores my friends."

"Not me, dear buster, not me. But you're right. I mean, what we were talking about. Ghosts."

He put his sherry down and then held to the arms of his easy chair, as if it were the edges of a cockpit.

"I fly all the time now. It's nineteen eighteen more than it's nineteen eighty-seven. It's France more than it's the U.S. of A. I'm up there with the old Lafayette. I'm on the ground near Paris with Rickenbacker. And there, just as the sun goes down, is the Red Baron. I've had quite a life, haven't I, Sam?"

It was his affectionate mode to call me by six or seven assorted names. I loved them all. I nodded.

"I'm going to do your story someday," I said. "It's not every writer whose neighbor was part of the Escadrille and flew and fought against von Richthofen."

"You couldn't write it, dear Ralph, you wouldn't know what to say."

"I might surprise you."

"You might, by God, you might. Did I ever show you the picture of myself and the whole Lafayette Escadrille team lined up by our junky biplane the summer of 'eighteen?"

"No," I lied, "let me see."

He pulled a small photo from his wallet and tossed it across to me. I had seen it a hundred times but it was a wonder and a delight.

"That's me, in the middle left, the short guy with the dumb smile next to Rickenbacker." Bill reached to point.

I looked at all the dead men, for most were long dead now, and there was Bill, twenty years old and lark-happy, and all the other young, young, oh, dear God, young men lined up, arms around each other, or one arm down holding helmets and goggles, and behind them a French 7-1 biplane, and beyond, the flat airfield somewhere near the Western front. Sounds of flying came out of the damned picture. They always did, when I held it. And sounds of wind and birds. It was like a miniature TV screen. At any moment I expected the Lafayette Escadrille to burst into action, spin, run, and take off into that absolutely clear and endless sky. At that very moment in time, in the photo, the Red Baron still lived in the clouds; he would be there forever now and never land, which was right and good, for we wanted him to stay there always, that's how boys and men feel.

"God, I love showing you things." Bill broke the spell. "You're so damned appreciative. I wish I had had you around when I was making films at MGM."

That was the other part of William (Bill) Westerleigh. From fighting and photographing the Western front half a mile up, he had moved on, when he got back to the States. From the Eastman labs in New York, he had drifted to some flimsy film studios in Chicago, where Gloria Swanson had once starred, to Hollywood and MGM. From MGM he had shipped to Africa to camera-shoot lions and the Watusi for *King Solomon's Mines.* Around the world's studios, there was no one he didn't know or who didn't know him. He had been principal cameraman on some two hundred films, and there were two bright gold Academy Oscars on his mantel next door.

"I'm sorry I grew up so long after you," I said. "Where's that photo of you and Rickenbacker alone? And the one signed by von Richthofen."

"You don't want to see *them*, buster."

"Like hell I don't!"

He unfolded his wallet and gently held out the picture of the two of them, himself and Captain Eddie, and the single snap of von Richthofen in full uniform, and signed in ink below.

"All gone," said Bill. "Most of 'em. Just one or two, and me left. And it won't be long"—he paused—"before there's not even me."

And suddenly again, the tears began to come out of his eyes and roll down and off his nose.

I refilled his glass.

He drank it and said:

"The thing is, I'm not afraid of *dying*. I'm just afraid of dying and going to *hell*!"

"You're not going there, Bill," I said.

"Yes, I am!" he cried out, almost indignantly, eyes blazing, tears streaming around his gulping mouth. "For what I did, what I can *never* be forgiven for!"

I waited a moment. "What was that, Bill?" I asked quietly.

"All those young boys I killed, all those young men I destroyed, all those beautiful people I murdered."

"You never did that, Bill," I said.

"Yes! I did! In the sky, dammit, in the air over France, over Germany, so long ago, but Jesus, there they are every night now, alive again, flying, waving, yelling, laughing like boys, until I fire my guns between the propellers and their wings catch fire and spin down. Sometimes they wave to me, *okay*! as they fall. Sometimes they curse. But, Jesus, every night, every morning now, the last month, they never leave. Oh, those beautiful boys, those lovely young men, those fine faces, the great shining and loving eyes, and down they go. And *I* did it. And I'll burn in hell for it!"

"You will not, I repeat *not*, burn in hell," I said.

"Give me another drink and shut up," said Bill. "What do *you* know about who burns and who doesn't? Are you Catholic? No. Are you Baptist? Baptists burn more slowly. There. Thanks."

I had filled his glass. He gave it a sip, the drink for his mouth meeting the stuff from his eyes.

"William," I sat back and filled my own glass. "No one burns in hell for war. War's that way."

"We'll *all* burn," said Bill.

"Bill, at this very moment, in Germany, there's a man your age, bothered with the same dreams, crying in his beer, remembering too much."

"As well they should! They'll burn, he'll burn too,

remembering my friends, the lovely boys who got themselves screwed into the ground when their propellers chewed the way. Don't you see? They didn't know. I didn't know. No one told them, no one told us!"

"What?"

"What war *was*. Christ, we didn't know it would come after us, find us, so late in time. We thought it was all over; that we had a way to forget, put it off, bury it. Our officers didn't say. Maybe they just didn't know. None of us did. No one guessed that one day, in old age, the graves would bust wide, and all those lovely faces come up, and the whole war with 'em! How could we guess that? How could we know? But now the time's here, and the skies are full, and the ships just won't come down, unless they burn. And the young men won't stop waving at me at three in the morning, unless I kill them all over again. Jesus Christ. It's so terrible. It's so sad. How do I save them? What do I do to go back and say, Christ, I'm sorry, it should never have happened, someone should have warned us when we were happy: war's not just dying, it's remembering and remembering *late* as well as soon, I wish them well. How do I say *that,* what's the next *move?*"

"There is no move," I said quietly. "Just sit here with a friend and have another drink. I can't think of anything to do. I wish I could. . . ."

Bill fiddled with his glass, turning it round and round.

"Let me tell you, then," he whispered. "Tonight, maybe tomorrow night's the last time you'll ever see me. Hear me out."

He leaned forward, gazing up at the high ceiling and then out the window where storm clouds were being gathered by wind.

"They've been landing in our backyards, the last few nights. You wouldn't have heard. Parachutes make sounds like kites, soft kind of whispers. The parachutes come down on our back lawns.

Other nights, the bodies, without parachutes. The good nights are the quiet ones when you just hear the silk and the threads on the clouds. The bad ones are when you hear a hundred and eighty pounds of aviator hit the grass. Then you can't sleep. Last night, a dozen things hit the bushes near my bedroom window. I looked up in the clouds tonight and they were full of planes and smoke. Can you make them stop? Do you *believe* me?"

"That's the one thing; I *do* believe."

He sighed, a deep sigh that released his soul.

"Thank *God!* But what do I do *next?*"

"Have you," I asked, "tried talking to them? I mean," I said, "have you asked for their *forgiveness?*"

"Would they *listen?* Would they forgive? My God," he said. "Of course! Why not? Will you come *with* me? Your back-yard. No trees for them to get strung up in. Christ, or on your porch. . . ."

"The porch, I think."

I opened the living-room French doors and stepped out. It was a calm evening with only touches of wind motioning the trees and changing the clouds.

Bill was behind me, a bit unsteady on his feet, a hopeful grin, part panic, on his face.

I looked at the sky and the rising moon.

"Nothing out here," I said.

"Oh, Christ, yes, there is. Look," he said. "No, wait. Listen."

I stood turning white cold, wondering why I waited, and listened.

"Do we stand out in the middle of your garden, where they can see us? You don't have to if you don't want."

"Hell," I lied. "I'm not afraid." I lifted my glass. "To the La-fayette Escadrille?" I said.

"No, no!" cried Bill, alarmed. "Not tonight. They mustn't hear *that.* To *them*, Doug. *Them.*" He motioned his glass at the sky where the clouds flew over in squadrons and the moon was a round, white, tombstone world.

"To von Richthofen, and the beautiful sad young men."

I repeated his words in a whisper.

And then we drank, lifting our empty glasses so the clouds and the moon and the silent sky could see.

"I'm ready," said Bill, "if they want to come get me now. Better to die out here than go in and hear them landing every night and every night in their parachutes and no sleep until dawn when the last silk folds in on itself and the bottle's empty. Stand right over there, son. That's it. Just half in the shadow. Now."

I moved back and we waited.

"What'll I say to them?" he asked.

"God, Bill," I said, "I don't know. They're not my friends."

"They weren't mine, either. More's the pity. I *thought* they were the enemy. Christ, isn't that a dumb stupid halfass word. The enemy! As if such a thing ever really happened in the world. Sure, maybe the bully that chased and beat you up in the schoolyard, or the guy who took your girl and laughed at you. But them, those beauties, up in the clouds on summer days or autumn afternoons? No, no!"

He moved further out on the porch.

"All right," he whispered. "Here I am."

And he leaned way out, and opened his arms as if to embrace the night air.

"Come on! What you waiting for!"

He shut his eyes.

"Your turn," he cried. "My God, you *got* to hear, you got to come. You beautiful bastards, *here*!"

And he tilted his head back as if to welcome a dark rain.

"Are they coming?" he whispered aside, eyes clenched.

"No."

Bill lifted his old face into the air and stared upward, willing the clouds to shift and change and become something more than clouds.

"Damn it!" he cried, at last. "I killed you all. Forgive me or come kill me!" And a final angry burst. "Forgive me. I'm sorry!"

The force of his voice was enough to push me completely back into shadows. Maybe that did it. Maybe Bill, standing like a small statue in the middle of my garden, made the clouds shift and the wind blow south instead of north. We both heard, a long way off, an immense whisper.

"Yes!" cried Bill, and to me, aside, eyes shut, teeth clenched, "You *hear*!"

We heard another sound, closer now, like great flowers or blossoms lifted off spring trees and run along the sky.

"There," whispered Bill.

The clouds seemed to form a lid and make a vast silken shape which dropped in serene silence upon the land. It made a shadow that crossed the town and hid the houses and at last reached our garden and shadowed the grass and put out the light of the moon and then hid Bill from my sight.

"Yes! They're coming," cried Bill. "Feel them? One, two, a dozen! Oh, God, yes."

And all around, in the dark, I thought I heard apples and plums and peaches falling from unseen trees, the sound of boots hitting my lawn, and the sound of pillows striking the grass like bodies, and the swarming of tapestries of white silk or smoke flung across the disturbed air.

"Bill!"

"No!" he yelled. "I'm okay! They're all around. Get back! *Yes!*"

There was a tumult in the garden. The hedges shivered with propeller wind. The grass lay down its nape. A tin watering can blew across the yard. Birds were flung from trees. Dogs all around the block yelped. A siren, from another war, sounded ten miles away. A storm had arrived, and was that thunder or field artillery?

And one last time, I heard Bill say, almost quietly, "I didn't know, oh, God, I didn't know what I was doing." And a final fading sound of "Please."

And the rain fell briefly to mix with the tears on his face.

And the rain stopped and the wind was still.

"Well." He wiped his eyes, and blew his nose on his big hankie, and looked at the hankie as if it were the map of France. "It's time to go. Do you think I'll get lost again?"

"If you do, come here."

"Sure." He moved across the lawn, his eyes clear. "How much do I owe you, Sigmund?"

"Only *this*," I said.

I gave him a hug. He walked out to the street. I followed to watch.

When he got to the corner, he seemed to be confused. He turned to his right, then his left. I waited and then called gently:

"To your *left*, Bill!"

"God bless you, buster!" he said, and waved.

He turned and went into his house.

———

They found him a month later, wandering two miles from home. A month after that he was in the hospital, in France all the time now, and Rickenbacker in the bed to his right and von Richthofen in the cot to his left.

The day after his funeral the Oscar arrived, carried by his wife, to place on my mantel, with a single red rose beside it, and the picture of von Richthofen, and the other picture of the gang lined up in the summer of '18 and the wind blowing out of the picture and the buzz of planes. And the sound of young men laughing as if they might go on forever.

Sometimes I come down at three in the morning when I can't sleep and I stand looking at Bill and his friends. And sentimental sap that I am, I wave a glass of sherry at them.

"Farewell, Lafayette," I say. "Lafayette, farewell."

And they all laugh as if it were the grandest joke that they ever heard.

BANSHEE

It was one of those nights, crossing Ireland, motoring through the sleeping towns from Dublin, where you came upon mist and encountered fog that blew away in rain to become a blowing silence. All the country was still and cold and waiting. It was a night for strange encounters at empty crossroads with great filaments of ghost spider web and no spider in a hundred miles. Gates creaked far across meadows, where windows rattled with brittle moonlight.

It was, as they said, banshee weather. I sensed, I knew this as my taxi hummed through a final gate and I arrived at Courtown House, so far from Dublin that if that city died in the night, no one would know.

I paid my driver and watched the taxi turn to go back to the living city, leaving me alone with twenty pages of final screenplay in my pocket, and my film director employer waiting inside. I stood in the midnight silence, breathing in Ireland and breathing out the damp coal mines in my soul.

Then, I knocked.

The door flew wide almost instantly. John Hampton was there, shoving a glass of sherry into my hand and hauling me in.

"Good God, kid, you got me curious. Get that coat off. Give me the script. Finished it, eh? So *you* say. You got me curious. Glad you called from Dublin. The house is empty. Clara's in Paris with the kids. We'll have a good read, knock the hell out of your scenes, drink a bottle, be in bed by two and—what's that?"

The door still stood open. John took a step, tilted his head, closed his eyes, listened.

The wind rustled beyond in the meadows. It made a sound in the clouds like someone turning back the covers of a vast bed.

I listened.

There was the softest moan and sob from somewhere off in the dark fields.

Eyes still shut, John whispered, "You know what that is, kid?"

"What?"

"Tell you later. Jump."

With the door slammed, he turned about and, the grand lord of the empty manor, strode ahead of me in his hacking coat, drill slacks, polished half-boots, his hair, as always, wind-blown from swimming upstream or down with strange women in unfamiliar beds.

Planting himself on the library hearth, he gave me one of those beacon flashes of laugh, the teeth that beckoned like a lighthouse beam swift and gone, as he traded me a second sherry for the screenplay, which he had to seize from my hand.

"Let's see what my genius, my left ventricle, my right arm, has birthed. Sit. Drink. Watch."

He stood astride the hearthstones, warming his backside, leafing my manuscript pages, conscious of me drinking my sherry much too fast, shutting my eyes each time he let a page drop and flutter to the carpet. When he finished he let the last page sail, lit a small cigarillo and puffed it, staring at the ceiling, making me wait.

"You son of a bitch," he said at last, exhaling. "It's good. Damn you to hell, kid. It's good!"

My entire skeleton collapsed within me. I had not expected such a midriff blow of praise.

"It needs a little cutting, of course!"

My skeleton reassembled itself.

"Of course," I said.

He bent to gather the pages like a great loping chimpanzee and turned. I felt he wanted to hurl them into the fire. He watched the flames and gripped the pages.

"Someday, kid," he said quietly, "you must teach me to write."

He was relaxing now, accepting the inevitable, full of true admiration.

"Someday," I said, laughing, "you must teach me to direct."

"*The Beast* will be *our* film, son. Quite a team."

He arose and came to clink glasses with me.

"Quite a team we are!" He changed gears. "How are the wife and kids?"

"They're waiting for me in Sicily where it's warm."

"We'll get you to them, and sun, straight off! I—"

He froze dramatically, cocked his head, and listened.

"Hey, what goes on—" he whispered.

I turned and waited.

This time, outside the great old house, there was the merest thread of sound, like someone running a fingernail over the paint, or someone sliding down out of the dry reach of a tree. Then there was the softest exhalation of a moan, followed by something like a sob.

John leaned in a starkly dramatic pose, like a statue in a stage pantomime, his mouth wide, as if to allow sounds entry to the inner ear. His eyes now unlocked to become as huge as hen's eggs with pretended alarm.

"Shall I tell you what that sound is, kid? A banshee!"

"A what?" I cried.

"Banshee!" he intoned. "The ghosts of old women who haunt the roads an hour before someone dies. *That's* what that sound was!" He stepped to the window, raised the shade, and peered out. "Sh! Maybe it means—*us!*"

"Cut it out, John!" I laughed, quietly.

"No, kid, no." He fixed his gaze far into the darkness, savoring his melodrama. "I lived here ten years. Death's out there. The banshee always *knows!* Where were we?"

He broke the spell as simply as that, strode back to the hearth and blinked at my script as if it were a brand-new puzzle.

"You ever figure, Doug, how much *The Beast* is like me? The hero plowing the seas, plowing women left and right, off round the world and no stops? Maybe that's why I'm doing it. You ever wonder how many women I've had? Hundreds! I—"

He stopped, for my lines on the page had shut him again. His face took fire as my words sank in.

"Brilliant!"

I waited, uncertainly.

"No, not that!" He threw my script aside to seize a copy of the London *Times* off the mantel. "*This!* A brilliant review of your new book of stories!"

"What?" I jumped.

"Easy, kid. I'll *read* this grand review to you! You'll love it. Terrific!"

My heart took water and sank. I could see another joke coming on or, worse, the truth disguised as a joke.

"Listen!"

John lifted the *Times* and read, like Ahab, from the holy text.

"'Douglas Rogers's stories may well be the huge success of American literature—'" John stopped and gave me an innocent blink. "How you like it so far, kid?"

"Continue, John," I mourned. I slugged my sherry back. It was a toss of doom that slid down to meet a collapse of will.

" '—but here in London,' " John intoned, " 'we ask more from our tellers of tales. Attempting to emulate the ideas of Kipling, the style of Maugham, the wit of Waugh, Rogers drowns somewhere in the mid-Atlantic. This is ramshackle stuff, mostly bad shades of superior scribes. Douglas Rogers, go home!' "

I leaped up and ran, but John with a lazy flip of his underhand, tossed the *Times* into the fire where it flapped like a dying bird and swiftly died in flame and roaring sparks.

Imbalanced, staring down, I was wild to grab that damned paper out, but finally glad the thing was lost.

John studied my face, happily. My face boiled, my teeth ground shut. My hand, struck to the mantel, was a cold rock fist.

Tears burst from my eyes, since words could not burst from my aching mouth.

"What's wrong, kid?" John peered at me with true curiosity, like a monkey edging up to another sick beast in its cage. "You feeling poorly?"

"John, for Christ's sake!" I burst out. "Did you have to do *that*!"

I kicked at the fire, making the logs tumble and a great firefly wheel of sparks gush up the flue.

"Why, Doug, I didn't think—"

"Like hell you didn't!" I blazed, turning to glare at him with tear-splintered eyes. "What's *wrong* with you?"

"Hell, nothing, Doug. It was a fine review, great! I just added a few lines, to get your goat!"

"I'll never know now!" I cried. "Look!"

I gave the ashes a final, scattering kick.

"You can buy a copy in Dublin tomorrow, Doug. You'll see. They love you. God, I just didn't want you to get a big head, right. The joke's over. Isn't it enough, dear son, that you have just written the finest scenes you ever wrote in your life for your truly great screenplay?" John put his arm around my shoulder.

That was John: kick you in the tripes, then pour on the wild sweet honey by the larder ton.

"Know what your problem is, Doug?" He shoved yet another sherry in my trembling fingers. "Eh?"

"What?" I gasped, like a sniveling kid, revived and wanting to laugh again. "What?"

"The thing is, Doug—" John made his face radiant. His eyes fastened to mine like Svengali's. "You don't love me half as much as I love you!"

"Come on, John—"

"No, kid, I *mean* it. God, son, I'd kill for you. You're the greatest living writer in the world, and I love you, heart and soul. Because of that, I thought you could take a little leg-pull. I see that I was wrong—"

"No, John," I protested, hating myself, for now he was making *me* apologize. "It's all right."

"I'm sorry, kid, truly sorry—"

"Shut up!" I gasped a laugh. "I still love you. I—"

"That's a boy! Now—" John spun about, brisked his palms together, and shuffled and reshuffled the script pages like a cardsharp. "Let's spend an hour cutting this brilliant, superb scene of yours and—"

For the third time that night, the tone and color of his mood changed.

"Hist!" he cried. Eyes squinted, he swayed in the middle of the room, like a dead man underwater. "Doug, you hear?"

The wind trembled the house. A long fingernail scraped an attic pane. A mourning whisper of cloud washed the moon.

"Banshees." John nodded, head bent, waiting. He glanced up, abruptly. "Doug? Run out and *see*."

"Like hell I will."

"No, go on out," John urged. "This has been a night of mis-
conceptions, kid. You doubt *me*, you doubt *it*. Get my overcoat,
in the hall. Jump!"

He jerked the hall closet door wide and yanked out his
great tweed overcoat which smelled of tobacco and fine whiskey. Clutching it in his two monkey hands, he beckoned it like
a bullfighter's cape. "Huh, *toro!* Hah!"

"John," I sighed, wearily.

"Or are you a coward, Doug, are you yellow? You—"

For this, the fourth, time, we both heard a moan, a cry, a
fading murmur beyond the wintry front door.

"It's waiting, kid!" said John, triumphantly. "Get out there.
Run for the *team!*"

I was in the coat, anointed by tobacco scent and booze as
John buttoned me up with royal dignity, grabbed my ears, kissed
my brow.

"I'll be in the stands, kid, cheering you on. I'd go with
you, but banshees are shy. Bless you, son, and if you don't come
back—I loved you like a son!"

"Jesus," I exhaled, and flung the door wide.

But suddenly John leaped between me and the cold blowing moonlight.

"Don't go out there, kid. I've changed my mind! If you got
killed—"

"John," I shook his hands away. "You *want* me out there.
You've probably got Kelly, your stable girl, out there now, making noises for your big laugh—"

"Doug!" he cried in that mock-insult serious way he had,
eyes wide, as he grasped my shoulders. "I swear to God!"

"John," I said, half-angry, half-amused, "so long."

I ran out the door to immediate regrets. He slammed and
locked the portal. Was he laughing? Seconds later, I saw his silhouette at the library window, sherry glass in hand, peering out

at this night theater of which he was both director and hilarious audience.

I spun with a quiet curse, hunched my shoulders in Caesar's cloak, ignored two dozen stab wounds given me by the wind, and stomped down along the gravel drive.

I'll give it a fast ten minutes, I thought, worry John, turn his joke inside out, stagger back in, shirt torn and bloody, with some fake tale of my own. Yes, by God, *that* was the trick—

I stopped.

For in a small grove of trees below, I thought I saw something like a large paper kite blossom and blow away among the hedges.

Clouds sailed over an almost full moon, and ran islands of dark to cover me.

Then there it was again, further on, as if a whole cluster of flowers were suddenly torn free to snow away along the colorless path. At the same moment, there was the merest catch of a sob, the merest door-hinge of a moan.

I flinched, pulled back, then glanced up at the house.

There was John's face, of course, grinning like a pumpkin in the window, sipping sherry, toast-warm and at ease.

"Ohh," a voice wailed somewhere. ". . . God. . . ."

It was then that I saw the woman.

She stood leaning against a tree, dressed in a long, moon-colored dress over which she wore a hip-length heavy woolen shawl that had a life of its own, rippling and winging out and hovering with the weather.

She seemed not to see me or if she did, did not care; I could not frighten her, nothing in the world would ever frighten her again. Everything poured out of her steady and unflinching gaze toward the house, that window, the library, and the silhouette of the man in the window.

She had a face of snow, cut from that white cool marble

that makes the finest Irish women; a long swan neck, a generous if quivering mouth, and eyes a soft and luminous green. So beautiful were those eyes, and her profile against the blown tree branches, that something in me turned, agonized, and died. I felt that killing wrench men feel when beauty passes and will not pass again. You want to cry out: Stay. I love you. But you do not speak. And the summer walks away in her flesh, never to return.

But now the beautiful woman, staring only at that window in the far house, spoke.

"Is he in there?" she said.

"What?" I heard myself say.

"Is that him?" she wondered. "The beast," she said, with quiet fury. "The monster. Himself."

"I don't—"

"The great animal," she went on, "that walks on two legs. He stays. All others go. He wipes his hands on flesh; girls are his napkins, women his midnight lunch. He keeps them stashed in cellar vintages and knows their years but not their names. Sweet Jesus, and is that *him*?"

I looked where she looked, at the shadow in the window, far off across the croquet lawn.

And I thought of my director in Paris, in Rome, in New York, in Hollywood, and the millraces of women I had seen John tread, feet printing their skins, a dark Christ on a warm sea. A picnic of women, dancing on tables, eager for applause and John, on his way out, saying, "Dear, lend me a fiver. That beggar by the door kills my heart—"

I watched this young woman, her dark hair stirred by the night wind, and asked:

"Who *should* he be?"

"Him," she said. "Him that lives there and loved me and now does not." She shut her eyes to let the tears fall.

"He doesn't live there anymore," I said.

"He does!" She whirled, as if she might strike or spit. "Why do you lie?"

"Listen." I looked at the new but somehow old snow in her face. "That was another time."

"No, there's only *now*!" She made as if to rush for the house. "And I love him still, so much I'd kill for it, and myself lost at the end!"

"What's his name?" I stood in her way. "His *name*?"

"Why, Will, of course. Willie. William."

She moved. I raised my arms and shook my head.

"There's only a Johnny there now. A John."

"You lie! I feel him there. His name's changed, but it's *him*. Look! Feel!"

She put her hands up to touch on the wind toward the house, and I turned and sensed with her and it was another year, it was a time between. The wind said so, as did the night and the glow in that great window where the shadow stayed.

"That's him!"

"A friend of mine," I said, gently.

"No friend of anyone, ever!"

I tried to look through her eyes and thought: my God, has it always been this way, forever some man in that house, forty, eighty, a hundred years ago! Not the same man, no, but all dark twins, and this lost girl on the road, with snow in her arms for love, and frost in her heart for comfort, and nothing to do but whisper and croon and mourn and sob until the sound of her weeping stilled at sunrise but to start again with the rising of the moon.

"That's my friend in there," I said, again.

"If that be true," she whispered fiercely, "then you are my enemy!"

I looked down the road where the wind blew dust through the graveyard gates.

"Go back where you came from," I said.

She looked at the same road and the same dust, and her voice faded. "Is there to be no peace, then," she mourned. "Must I walk here, year on year, and no come-uppance?"

"If the man in there," I said, "was really your Will, your William, what would you have me do?"

"Send him out to me," she said, quietly.

"What would you do with him?"

"Lie down with him," she murmured, "and ne'er get up again. He would be kept like a stone in a cold river."

"Ah," I said, and nodded.

"Will you ask him, then, to be sent?"

"No. For he's not yours. Much like. Near similar. And breakfasts on girls and wipes his mouth on their silks, one century called this, another that."

"And no love in him, ever?"

"He says the word like fishermen toss their nets in the sea," I said.

"Ah, Christ, and I'm caught!" And here she gave such a cry that the shadow came to the window in the great house across the lawn. "I'll stay here the rest of the night," she said. "Surely he will feel me here, his heart will melt, no matter what his name or how deviled his soul. What year is this? How long have I been waiting?"

"I won't tell you," I said. "The news would crack your heart."

She turned and truly looked at me. "Are you one of the good ones, then, the gentle men who never lie and never hurt and never have to hide? Sweet God, I wish I'd known you first!"

The wind rose, the sound of it rose in her throat. A clock struck somewhere far across the country in the sleeping town.

"I must go in," I said. I took a breath. "Is there no way for me to give you rest?"

"No," she said, "for it was not you that cut the nerve."

"I see," I said.

"You don't. But you try. Much thanks for that. Get in. You'll catch your death."

"And you—?"

"Ha!" she cried. "I've long since caught mine. It will not catch again. Get!"

I gladly went. For I was full of the cold night and the white moon, old time, and her. The wind blew me up the grassy knoll. At the door, I turned. She was still there on the milky road, her shawl straight out on the weather, one hand upraised.

"Hurry," I thought I heard her whisper, "tell him he's needed!"

I rammed the door, slammed into the house, fell across the hall, my heart a bombardment, my image in the great hall mirror a shock of colorless lightning.

John was in the library drinking yet another sherry, and poured me some. "Someday," he said, "you'll learn to take anything I say with more than a grain of salt. Jesus, look at you! Ice cold. Drink that down. Here's another to go after it!"

I drank, he poured, I drank. "Was it all a joke, then?"

"What *else*?" John laughed, then stopped.

The croon was outside the house again, the merest fingernail of mourn, as the moon scraped down the roof.

"There's your banshee," I said, looking at my drink, unable to move.

"Sure, kid, sure, unh-huh," said John. "Drink your drink, Doug, and I'll read you that great review of your book from the London *Times* again."

"You burned it, John."

"Sure, kid, but I recall it all as if it were this morn. Drink up."

"John," I said, staring into the fire, looking at the hearth where the ashes of the burned paper blew in a great breath. "Does . . . did . . . that review really exist?"

"My God, of course, sure, yes. Actually. . . ." Here he paused and gave it great imaginative concern. "The *Times* knew my love for you, Doug, and asked me to review your book." John reached his long arm over to refill my glass. "I did it. Under an assumed name, of course, now ain't that swell of me? But I had to be fair, Doug, had to be fair. So I wrote what I truly felt were the good things, the not-so-good things in your book. Criticized it just the way I would when you hand in a lousy screenplay scene and I make you do it over. Now ain't that A-one double absolutely square of me? Eh?"

He leaned at me. He put his hand on my chin and lifted it and gazed long and sweetly into my eyes.

"You're not upset?"

"No," I said, but my voice broke.

"By God, now, if you aren't. Sorry. A joke, kid, only a joke." And here he gave me a friendly punch on the arm.

Slight as it was, it was a sledgehammer striking home.

"I wish you hadn't made it up, the joke, I wish the article was real," I said.

"So do I, kid. You look bad. I—"

The wind moved around the house. The windows stirred and whispered.

Quite suddenly I said, for no reason that I knew:

"The banshee. It's out there."

"That was a joke, Doug. You got to watch out for me."

"No," I said, looking at the window. "It's there."

John laughed. "You saw it, did you?"

"It's a young and lovely woman with a shawl on a cold night. A young woman with long black hair and great green eyes and a complexion like snow and a proud Phoenician prow of a nose. Sound like anyone you ever in your life knew, John?"

"Thousands." John laughed more quietly now, looking to see the weight of my joke. "Hell—"

"She's waiting for you," I said. "Down at the bottom of the drive."

John glanced, uncertainly, at the window.

"That was the sound we heard," I said. "She described you or someone like you. Called you Willie, Will, William. But I *knew* it was you."

John mused. "Young, you say, and beautiful, and out there right this moment . . . ?"

"The most beautiful woman I've ever seen."

"Not carrying a knife—?"

"Unarmed."

John exhaled. "Well, then, I think I should just go out there and have a chat with her, eh, don't you think?"

"She's waiting."

He moved toward the front door.

"Put on your coat, it's a cold night," I said.

He was putting on his coat when we heard the sound from outside, very clear, this time. The wail and then the sob and then the wail.

"God," said John, his hand on the doorknob, not wanting to show the white feather in front of me. "She's *really* there."

He forced himself to turn the knob and open the door. The wind sighed in, bringing another faint wail with it.

John stood in the cold weather, peering down that long walk into the dark.

"Wait!" I cried, at the last moment.

John waited.

"There's one thing I haven't told you," I said. "She's out there, all right. And she's walking. But . . . she's dead."

"I'm not afraid," said John.

"No," I said, "but I am. You'll never come back. Much as I hate you right now, I can't let you go. Shut the door, John."

The sob again, and then the wail.

"Shut the door."

I reached over to knock his hand off the brass doorknob, but he held tight, cocked his head, looked at me and sighed.

"You're really good, kid. Almost as good as me. I'm putting you in my next film. You'll be a star."

Then he turned, stepped out into the cold night, and shut the door, quietly.

I waited until I heard his steps on the gravel path, then locked the door, and hurried through the house, putting out the lights. As I passed through the library, the wind mourned down the chimney and scattered the dark ashes of the London *Times* across the hearth.

I stood blinking at the ashes for a long moment, then shook myself, ran upstairs two at a time, banged open my tower room door, slammed it, undressed, and was in bed with the covers over my head when a town clock, far away, sounded one in the deep morning.

And my room was so high, so lost in the house and the sky, that no matter who or what tapped or knocked or banged at the door below, whispering and then begging and then screaming—

Who could possibly hear?

PROMISES, PROMISES

When she opened the door to her apartment, she could see that he had been crying. The tears had just finished rolling down his cheeks and he had not bothered to brush them away.

"Tom, for God's sake, what's happened? Come in!"

She pulled at him. He seemed not to feel her pulling, but at last looked down, saw that it might be a good idea, and stepped in. He looked around at her apartment as if she had changed the furniture and done over all the walls.

"I'm sorry to bother you," he said.

"Bother, hell." She steered him across the room. "Sit down. You look awful. Let me get you a drink."

"That would be nice, sitting down before I fall down," he said, vaguely. "Having a drink. I don't remember if I've had any food today. Maybe."

She brought him some brandy, poured it, glanced at his face, poured some more.

"Take it easy. Make it last." She watched him gulp it down. "What happened?"

"It's Beth," he gasped, eyes shut, the tears running. ". . . and you."

"To hell with me, what about Beth?"

"She fell and hit her head. She's been in the hospital for two days, unconscious."

"Oh, my God. . . ." She moved swiftly to kneel and put her arms around him as if he might fall. "Why didn't you *call* me?"

"I did, but I was at the hospital with Clara, and every time I called you, no answer. The rest of the time, Clara was so near, if she heard me talking to you—God—it's bad enough having a daughter you feel might . . . at any moment . . . anyway I tried, and here I am."

"Lord, no wonder you look so bad. Beth, now. She isn't . . . ? She didn't . . . ?"

"No, she didn't die. Thank God, oh, thank God!"

And he wept openly now, holding the empty brandy glass and letting his tears drop and melt into his coatfront.

She sank back on her knees and wept, too, holding tight to his hand.

"Jesus," she said softly, "Jesus."

"If you knew how often I've said that name on this weekend. I've never been religious, but all of a sudden, anything, I thought, anything I can say, do, pray, anything. I've never cried so much in my life. I've never prayed so hard."

He had to stop talking, as a fresh burst of grief shook his shoulders. When he quieted down, he managed to find and speak the rest in a whisper:

"She's all right, okay, she came out of it just two hours ago. She'll recover, the doctor is sure. The doctor says. If he gave me a bill for a million dollars right now, I'd spend the rest of my life paying it, she's worth all that."

"I know she is. Daughters always are, or most are, for their fathers."

He sank back in the chair, and she remained crouched by his knees, waiting for him to get his breath. At last, she said:

"How did it happen?"

"One of those stupid things. She put up a flimsy stepladder in the closet to reach some Christmas ornaments. The damn thing broke, she fell and hit her head, hard. We didn't know. We were in another part of the house. We've always respected her privacy. But after an hour, when her door stayed shut and we heard nothing, my wife, for some reason, just went in. All of a sudden, she was yelling. I ran, and there was Beth on the floor, lots of blood, she had struck her head on the edge of a bookcase. I almost fell, getting to her. I tried to pick her up, but suddenly I was so weak I couldn't even move myself, my God, she felt dead, loose, the way dead people are. I couldn't feel her pulse, my own was so loud. I somehow found the phone but couldn't make my fingers work the dial. Clara took the phone away from me and dialed the paramedics. When she got them, I grabbed the phone back, but couldn't speak, Clara had to tell them—Jesus, I almost cost Beth her life! I was paralyzed. What if I'd been alone? Would I have been able to talk? Would she have died? Without Clara, well, the paramedics were there in five minutes, God bless them, five instead of half an hour. They got Beth to the hospital. I rode along like an extra dead man in the ambulance. Clara followed with the car. At the hospital, they wouldn't let us see Beth for an hour, they were fighting to save her. When the doctor came out, he said it was touch and go, fifty-fifty for the next day, two days. Think of it . . . waiting for two whole days, not knowing. We stayed at the hospital until two in the morning, when they made us go home, said they'd call if there was any change. We went home and cried all night. I don't think we stopped for more than ten minutes at a time. Have you ever cried constantly for a full night, have you ever wanted to kill yourself you were so full of grief? God, we're spoiled. This was the first *real* nightmare in all our lives. We've always been well, no sickness, no accidents, no deaths. Listen to me! I can't stop talking. God, I'm tired, but I just had to come see you, Laura."

"She's all right, *really* all right?" said Laura.

"She ought to be out and around in about three days, the doctor said."

"Let me fill that." She refilled his glass and watched him drink it convulsively, as new tears gathered in her eyes. "I've seen your daughter only once, but she was, she is, a sweet girl. No wonder you—"

"No wonder." He shut his eyes, then opened them at last to look at his mistress. "Do you know what really saved her?"

"The paramedics—"

"No."

"Your doctor—"

"Those all count. But we prayed. We *prayed*, Laura. And God answered. *Something* answered. But it happened. I've never believed in prayer. I do now."

He was staring at her intently. She had to look away at last, almost flinching. She twisted her fingers together and looked at them. Her face grew suddenly pale as if she had guessed at something, then put it aside behind her eyes. At last she took a deep breath, glanced quickly at him, and asked:

"What?"

"Eh?" he said.

"*What* did you pray?" she asked.

"It," he said, "was not so much a prayer . . . as . . . a promise."

Laura grew paler, waited, took a deep breath and asked:

"What did you promise?"

He was not able to answer. Suddenly it was like not being able to dial the phone, then not being able to speak.

"Well?" said Laura.

"I promised God—"

"Yes?"

"That if he saved Beth—"

"Yes?"

"That I'd give you up and go away and never see you again!"

It came out in a terrible sighing rush.

"What!?" She sat straight up on the floor, pushed herself back, and stared at him as if he were mad.

"You heard what I said," he replied, quietly.

She leaned forward almost convulsively and shouted at him:

"How could you *possibly* have promised God *that*?"

"I had to, I did, it was the only thing I could think of." He slid down off the chair, and reaching the floor began to edge toward her, reaching out. "I was frantic, don't you see? Frantic!"

She pushed herself back from him, to increase the space between as he advanced. She looked at the window, the door, as if seeking escape and then said, almost as loud as before:

"You know that I'm now a Catholic—"

"I know, I know."

"A new one. Do you see the position you've *put* me in?"

"I didn't put you in a position, life did, my daughter's accident did. I had to make the promise to save her! What's *wrong* with you?"

"I'm in love with you, *that's* what's wrong!"

She jumped up, wheeled about, then spun back to seize her own elbows and lean down at him.

"Don't you see, you just can't go around promising God things like that! You fool, you can't take it back now!"

"I don't want to take it back," he replied, looking up at her, stunned. "You—you can't *make* me!"

"Tom, Tom," she explained, "I am deeply religious. Do you think for a moment I would demand such a thing of you? Christ, what a mess! A promise is a promise, you must keep it, but that puts me out in the cold. And if you broke that promise, I wouldn't much like you anymore for being a liar, a liar to my new God and my new faith. Good grief, you couldn't have done a better, lousier job if you had planned it!"

Seated on the floor, he now had to push himself back, then wipe his cheeks with the back of one hand.

"You *don't* think—?"

"No, no. After all, it was an accident, and she is your daughter. But you could have thought, taken time, considered, been more careful, what you said!"

"How can you be careful when you're falling out of a twenty-story building and need a net?"

She stood over him, and her shoulders slumped as if he had shot her through the chest. She felt herself fall all the way down, even as he described it. If there was a net anywhere, he couldn't share it. When she hit bottom and found herself still alive, she forced a few trembling words out:

"Oh, Tom, Tom, you—"

"I'm crying over two things," he gasped. "My daughter, who almost died. And you, who might as well be dead. I *tried* to choose. For a wild moment I thought, there *is* a choice. But I knew God would see through any damned lie I tried to make up. You can't just promise and pray and then forget it as soon as your daughter opens her eyes and smiles. I am so grateful now I could explode. I'm so sad about us, you and me, I'll cry all week and my wife will think it's just relief that Beth's coming home."

"Shut up," Laura said, quietly.

"Why?"

"Because. The more you talk, the less I can find to answer you with. Stop driving me into a corner. Stop killing me in her place. Stop."

He could only sit, growing heavy and immovable, as she turned and went in blind search of a glass and something to put in it. It took her a long while to pour and then a longer while to remember to drink whatever it was. Faced away from him, she looked only at the wall and asked:

"What did you say in your prayer?"

"I can't remember."

"Yes, you can. My God in heaven, Tom, what did you say that was so damned irreversible!"

He flushed and turned his face this way and that, not able to look at her.

"Do you mean the exact words—"

"The exact ones. I want to hear. I demand to hear. I deserve to hear. Say it."

"God," he said, his breath uneven, "this reminds me of my mother making me say prayers when I was five. I hated it. I was embarrassed, I couldn't see God anywhere, I didn't know who I was supposed to be talking to. It was so terrible, my mother gave up. Years later, I learned to pray, on my own, inside. All right, all right, don't stare at me that way. Here's what I said—"

He got up suddenly, walked to the window and looked out across the city, toward a building, any building that looked like the hospital, and focused his attention there. His voice was almost inaudible. He knew this and stopped, and started over, so she could hear:

"I said: Please, God, save her, save my daughter, let her live. If you do, I promise, I swear to give up the dearest thing in my existence. I promise to give up Laura, and never see her again. I promise, God. Please."

There was a long pause until he repeated the last word, quietly: *"Please."*

Without moving, she lifted the glass to her lips and drank the brandy straight down and, eyes shut, shook her head.

"Now, you've really done it," she said.

He turned from the window and started toward her, but stopped. "You believe me, don't you?"

"I wish I didn't, but I do. Damn!"

She hurled the glass away and watched it roll unbroken along the rug.

"You could have promised something *else*! Couldn't you, couldn't you, *couldn't* you?"

"Promise, what, what?" Not knowing where to go, he prowled the room, not able to look back at her. "What can you promise God that means anything! Money? My house? My car? Give up my Paris trip? Give up my work? God knows I love *that*! But I don't think God takes things like that. There's only one value, isn't there? For *him*? Not things, people, but . . . love. I thought and thought and I knew I had only one special last rich thing in my life that was of any priceless value that might mean something in an exchange."

"And that thing was *me*?" she said.

"Yes, dammit. Name me something else. I can't think of anything. You. My love for you has been so big, so all-consuming, so vital to my whole life, I knew it had to be the right gift, the right promise. If I said I'd give you up, God would *have* to know what a devastation it would be, what a total loss. Then he'd just *have* to give my daughter back! How could he not?"

He had stopped in the middle of the living room now. She picked up the fallen glass, looked at it, and circled him, slowly.

"I've heard and seen everything now," she said.

"Heard and seen *what*?"

"Men, one way or another, getting out of their affairs."

"Is *that* what this looks like to you?"

"How else can it look? You've been wanting out for a long time. Now you have your excuse."

He made a mourning sound, then a groan, then a sigh of exasperation.

"An excuse? No. A commitment. What else would you have wanted me to do?"

"Well, certainly not promise God to give me up!" she cried. "Why *me*?"

"Don't you know? Haven't you been listening? You're all I

had as collateral. I loved you, I love you, I will always love you. And now, though I know I'll bleed for years, I have to hand you over. Who is hurt worse here, me or you? Does it hurt more for you to be left or for me to leave? Can you really, I mean really, figure that and tell me?"

"No," she said, and her shoulders slumped again. "I'll be all right. Forgive me. It'll just take time. It's only been ten minutes since you came in that door. Christ."

She turned and walked slowly out to the kitchen. He heard her rummaging in the refrigerator. He went and sat down and held on to the armchair as if it might suddenly hurl him across the room.

She came back in with a bottle of champagne and two glasses, walking across the floor as if it were land-mined.

"What's that?" he asked, as she sat down on the floor again.

"What's it look like?" She worked the cork expertly and when it popped and hit the ceiling, she added, "We began with this, why not end with it?"

"You're angry at me—"

"Angry, hell, I'm mad clean through, and so sad I'd like to go to bed for a month and not get up again, but I will, tomorrow, dammit. Maybe this godawful champagne will help. Take your glass."

She poured and they drank and were silent for a long while.

"So this is the last time we'll ever see each other," she said.

"You don't have to put it so bluntly."

"Why not? You already have. Let's not kid around. This is the last five minutes of our lives. When you finish that, I want you out the door. I can't stand having you here. I don't want you to go. I wish I had a prayer, a promise, as strong as yours, that I believed in. I'd cry out to God with it. But I don't have that strength, and no one's dying for me, except you, and you're not really dead, just going. So, don't ever call, don't write, don't come back, don't drop in. I know, I know, that's what you intend, to go, to stay. But you might be tempted. And if you called, I'd have to die all over again. Do I sound mean, do I sound hard? I'm not. I can't handle it any other way. So—"

She lifted her glass and finished the champagne, then got up and walked to open the door to her apartment and stand by it, waiting.

"So soon?" he said, bleakly.

"Hard to believe it's been five years. But—so *soon*."

He got up and looked around as if he had left something, and then realized it was really her and came to stand before her, his hands at his sides. He didn't seem to know what to do with his arms or his body.

"Do you forgive me?"

"No, not now. But soon, yes, I must. Either that, or stop going to church. Give me time to really think about your daughter and her dying almost, and yes, I will. It's a terrible week for all of us. Part of me knows that you are being cut right down the middle. Goodbye." Her mouth whispered, *darling*, but she couldn't say it out loud.

She kissed him once, for a long moment, and when she felt the slight pull of her gravity moving him closer, broke off and stepped away.

He went out the door and halfway down the stairs turned and looked at her and said:

"Goodbye."

He turned and went the rest of the way down.

Tears exploded from her eyes. She flung herself forward to seize the top stair rail and stare blindly down.

"How dare you!" she shrieked, and stopped.

She stared at the empty stairwell, stifling her breath. The next words fell out of their own accord:

"—love your daughter—"

And then the rest, which only she could hear:

"—more than *me?*"

She backed up, groped round, found herself inside, and slammed the door, *hard*.

Downstairs, he heard.

And it was like the sound of the shutting of a tomb.

THE LOVE AFFAIR

All morning long the scent was in the clear air, of cut grain or green grass or flowers, Sio didn't know which, he couldn't tell. He would walk down the hill from his secret cave and turn about and raise his fine head and strain his eyes to see, and the breeze blew steadily, raising the tide of sweet odor about him. It was like a spring in autumn. He looked for the dark flowers that clustered under the hard rocks, probing up, but found none. He searched for a sign of grass, that swift tide that rolled over Mars for a brief week each spring, but the land was bone and pebble and the color of blood.

Sio returned to his cave, frowning. He watched the sky and saw the rockets of the Earthmen blaze down, far away, near the newly building towns. Sometimes, at night, he crept in a quiet, swimming silence down the canals by boat, lodged the boat in a hidden place, and then swam, with quiet hands and limbs, to the edge of the fresh towns, and there peered out at the hammering, nailing, painting men, at the men shouting late into the night at their labor of constructing a strange thing upon this planet. He would listen to their odd language and try to understand, and watch the rockets gather up great plumes of beautiful fire and go booming into the stars; an incredible people. And then, alive and undiseased, alone, Sio would return to his cave. Sometimes he walked many miles through the mountains to find others of his own hiding race, a few men, fewer women, to talk to, but now he had a habit of solitude, and lived alone, thinking on the destiny that had finally killed his people. He did not blame the Earthmen; it had been an accidental thing, the disease that had burned his father and mother in their sleep, and burned the fathers and mothers of great multitudes of sons.

He sniffed the air again. That strange aroma. That sweet, drifting scent of compounded flowers and green moss.

"What is it?" He narrowed his golden eyes in four directions.

He was tall and a boy still, though eighteen summers had lengthened the muscles in his arms and his legs were long from seasons of swimming in the canals and daring to run, take cover, run again, take swift cover, over the blazing dead sea bottoms or going on the long patrols with silver cages to bring back assassin-flowers and fire-lizards to feed them. It seemed that his life had been full of swimming and marching, the things young men do to take their energies and passions, until they are married and a woman soon does what mountains and rivers once did. He had carried the passion for distance and walking later into young manhood than most, and while many another man had been drifting off down the dying canals in a slim boat with a woman like a bas-relief across his body, Sio had continued leaping and sporting, much of the time by himself, often speaking alone to himself. The worry of his parents, he had been, and the despair of women who had watched his shadow lengthening handsomely from the hour of his fourteenth birthday, and nodded to each other, watching the calendar for another year and just *another* year to pass. . . .

But since the invasion and the disease, he had slowed to

stillness. His universe was sunken away by death. The sawed and hammered and freshly painted towns were carriers of disease. The weight of so much dying rested heavily on his dreams. Often he woke weeping and put his hands out on the night air. But his parents were gone and it was time, past time, for one special friend, one touching, one love.

The wind was circling and spreading the bright odor. Sio took a deeper breath and felt his flesh warm.

And then there was a sound. It was like a small orchestra playing. The music came up through the narrow stone valley to his cave.

A puff of smoke idled into the sky about a half mile away. Below, by the ancient canal, stood a small house that the men of Earth had built for an archaeological crew, a year ago. It had been abandoned and Sio had crept down to peer into the empty rooms several times, not entering, for he was afraid of the black disease that might touch him.

The music was coming from that house.

"An entire orchestra in that small house?" he wondered, and ran silently down the valley in the early afternoon light.

The house looked empty, despite the music which poured out the open windows. Sio scrambled from rock to rock, taking half an hour to lie within thirty yards of the frightful, dinning house. He lay on his stomach, keeping close to the canal. If anything happened, he could leap into the water and let the current rush him swiftly back into the hills.

The music rose, crashed over the rocks, hummed in the hot air, quivered in his bones. Dust shook from the quaking roof of the house. Paint fell in a soft snowstorm from the peeling wood.

Sio leapt up and dropped back. He could see no orchestra within. Only flowery curtains. The front door stood wide.

The music stopped and started again. The same tune was repeated ten times. And the odor that had lured him down from his stone retreat was thick here, like a clear water moving about his perspiring face.

At last, in a burst of running, he reached the window, looked in.

Upon a low table, a brown machine glistened. In the machine, a silver needle pressed a spinning black disc. The orchestra thundered! Sio stared at the strange device.

The music paused. In that interval of hissing quiet, he heard footsteps. Running, he plunged into the canal.

Falling down under the cool water, he lay at the bottom, holding his breath, waiting. Had it been a trap? Had they lured him down to capture and kill him?

A minute ticked by, bubbles escaped his nostrils. He stirred and rose slowly toward the glassy wet world above.

He was swimming and looking up through the cool green current when he saw her.

Her face was like a white stone above him.

He did not move, nor stir for a moment, but he saw her. He held his breath. He let the current slide him slowly, slowly away, and she was very beautiful, she was from Earth, she had come in a rocket that scorched the land and baked the air, and she was as white as a stone.

The canal water carried him among the hills. He climbed out, dripping.

She was beautiful, he thought. He sat on the canal rim, gasping. His chest was constricted. The blood burned in his face. He looked at his hands. Was the black disease in him? Had looking at her contaminated him?

I should have gone up, he thought, as she bent down, and clasped my hands to her neck. She killed us, she killed us. He saw her white throat, her white shoulders. What a peculiar color, he thought. But, no, he thought, she did not kill us. It was the disease. In so much whiteness, can darkness stay?

"Did she see me?" He stood up, drying in the sun. He put his hand to his chest, his brown, slender hand. He felt his heart beating rapidly. "Oh," he said. "I saw *her!*"

He walked back to the cave, not slowly, not swiftly. The music still crashed from the house below, like a festival all to itself.

Without speaking, he began, certainly and accurately, to pack his belongings. He threw pieces of phosphorous chalk, food, and several books into a cloth, and tied them up firmly. He saw that his hands shook. He turned his fingers over, his eyes wide. He stood up hurriedly, the small packet under one arm, and walked out of the cave and started up the canyon, away from the music and the strong perfume.

He did not look back.

The sun was going down the sky now. He felt his shadow move away behind to stay where he should have stayed. It was not good, leaving the cave where he had often lived as a child. In that cave he had found for himself a dozen hobbies, developed a hundred tastes. He had hollowed a kiln in the rock and baked himself fresh cakes each day, of a marvelous texture and variety. He had raised grain for food in a little mountain field. He had made himself clear, sparkling wines. He had created musical instruments, flutes of silver and thorn-metal, and small harps. He had written songs. He had built small chairs and woven the fabric of his clothing. And he had painted pictures on the cave walls in crimson and cobalt phosphorous, pictures that glowed through the long nights, pictures of great intricacy and beauty. And he had often read a book of poems that he had written when he was fifteen and which, proudly, but calmly, his parents had read aloud to a select few. It had been a good existence, the cave, his small arts.

As the sun was setting, he reached the top of the mountain pass. The music was gone. The scent was gone. He sighed and sat to rest a moment before going on over the mountains. He shut his eyes.

A white face came down through green water.

He put his fingers to his shut eyes, feeling.

White arms gestured through currents of rushing tide.

He started up, seized his packet of keepsakes, and was about to hurry off, when the wind shifted.

Faintly, faintly, there was the music. The insane, metallic blaring, music, miles away.

Faintly, the last fragrance of perfume found its way among the rocks.

As the moons were rising, Sio turned and found his way back to the cave.

The cave was cold and alien. He built a fire and ate a small dinner of bread and wild berries from the mossrocks. So soon, after he had left it, the cave had grown cold and hard. His own breathing sounded strangely off the walls.

He extinguished the fire and lay down to sleep. But now there was a dim shaft of light touching the cave wall. He knew that this light had traveled half a mile up from the windows of the house by the canal. He shut his eyes but the light was there. It was either the light or the music or the smell of flowers. He found himself looking or listening or breathing for any one of the incredible three.

At midnight he stood outside his cave.

Like a bright toy, the house lights were yellow in the valley. In one of the windows, it seemed he saw a figure dancing.

"I must go down and kill her," he said. "*That* is why I came back to the cave. To kill, to bury her."

When he was half-asleep, he heard a lost voice say, "You are a great liar." He did not open his eyes.

She lived alone. On the second day, he saw her walking in the foothills. On the third day, she was swimming, swimming for hours, in the canal. On the fourth day and the fifth day, Sio came down nearer and nearer to the house, until, at sunset at the sixth day, with dark closing in, he stood outside the window of the house and watched the woman living there.

She sat at a table upon which stood twenty tiny brass tubes of red color. She slapped a white, cool-looking cream on her face, making a mask. She wiped it on tissues which she threw in a basket. She tested one tube of color, pressing in on her wide lips, clamping her lips together, wiping it, adding another color, wiping *it* off, testing a third, a fifth, a ninth color, touching her cheeks with red, also, tweezing her brows with a silver pincers. Rolling her hair up in incomprehensible devices, she buffed her fingernails while she sang a sweet strange alien song, a song in her own language, a song that must have been very beautiful. She hummed it, tapping her high heels on the hardwood floor. She sang it walking about the room, clothed only in her white body, or lying on the bed in her white flesh, her head down, the yellow hair flaming back to the floor, while she held a fire cylinder to her red, red lips, sucking, eyes closed, to let long slow chutes of smoke slip out her pinched nostrils and lazy mouth into great ghost forms on the air. Sio trembled. The ghosts. The strange ghosts from her mouth. So casually. So easily. Without looking at them, she created them.

Her feet, when she arose, exploded on the hardwood floor. Again she sang. She whirled about. She sang to the ceiling. She snapped her fingers. She put her hands out, like birds, flying, and danced alone, her heels cracking the floor, around, around.

The alien song. He wished he could understand. He wished that he had the ability that some of his own people often had, to project the mind, to read, to know, to interpret, instantly; foreign tongues, foreign thoughts. He tried. But there was nothing. She went on singing the beautiful, unknown song, none of which he could understand:

"Ain't misbehavin', I'm savin' my love for you . . ."

He grew faint, watching her Earth body, her Earth beauty, so totally different, something from so many millions of miles away. His hands were moist, his eyelids jerked unpleasantly.

A bell rang.

There she was, picking up a strange black instrument, the function of which was not unlike a similar device of Sio's people.

"Hello, Janice? God, it's good to hear from you!"

Sio smiled. She was talking to a distant town. Her voice was thrilling to hear. But what were the words?

"God, Janice, what a hell-out-of-the-way place you sent me to. I know, honey, a vacation. But, it's sixty miles from nowhere. All I do is play cards and swim in the damned canal."

The black machine buzzed in reply.

"I can't stand it here, Janice. I know, I know. The churches. It's a damn shame they ever came up here. Everything was going so nice. What *I* want to know is when do we open up again?"

Lovely, thought Sio. Gracious. Incredible. He stood in the night beyond her open window, looking at her amazing face and body. And what were they talking about? Art, literature, music, yes, music, for she sang, she sang all of the time. An odd music, but one could not expect to understand the music of another world. Or the customs or the language or the literature. One must judge by instinct alone. The old ideas must be set aside. It was to be admitted that her beauty was not like Martian beauty, the soft slim brown beauty of the dying race. His mother had had golden eyes and slender hips. But here, this one, singing alone in the desert, she was of larger stuffs, large breasts, large hips, and the legs, yes, of white fire, and the peculiar custom of walking about without clothes, with only those strange knocking slippers on the feet. But all women of Earth did that, yes? He nodded. You must understand. The women of that far world, naked, yellow-haired, large-bodied, loud-heeled, he could see them. And the magic with the mouth and nostrils. The ghosts, the souls issuing from the lips in smoky patterns. Certainly a magical creature of fire and imagination. She shaped bodies in the air, with her brilliant mind. What else but a mind of clarity and clear genius could drink the gray, cherry red fire, and plume out architectural perfections of intricate and fine beauty from her nostrils. The genius! An artist! A creator! How was it done, how many years might one study to do this? How did one apply one's time? His head whirled with her presence. He felt he must cry out to her, "Teach me!" But he was afraid. He felt like a child. He saw the forms, the lines, the smoke swirl into infinity. She was here, in the wilderness, to be alone, to create her fantasies in absolute security, unwatched. One did not bother creators, writers, painters. One stood back and kept one's thoughts silent.

What a people! he thought. Are all of the women of that fiery green world like this? Are they fiery ghosts and music? Do they walk blazingly naked in their loud houses?

"I must watch this," he said, half-aloud. "I must study." He felt his hands curl. He wanted to touch. He wanted her to sing for him, to construct the artistic fragments in the air for him, to teach him, to tell him about that far gone world and its books and its fine music. . . .

"God, Janice, but how soon? What about the other girls? What about the other towns?"

The telephone burred like an insect.

"All of them closed down? On the whole damn planet? There must be *one* place! If you don't find a place for me soon, I'll . . . !"

Everything was strange about it. It was like seeing a woman for the first time. The way she held her head back, the way she moved her red-fingernailed hands, all new and different. She crossed her white legs, leaning forward, her elbow on a bare knee, summoning and exhaling spirits, talking, squinting at the window where he, yes, he stood in shadow, she looked right through him, oh, if she knew, what would she do?

"Who, me, afraid of living out here alone?"

She laughed, Sio laughed in cadence, in the moonlit darkness. Oh the beauty of her alien laughter, her head thrown back, the mystic clouds jetting and shaping from her nostrils.

He had to turn away from the window, gasping.

"Yeah! Sure!"

What fine rare words of living, music, poetry was she speaking now?

"Well, Janice, who's afraid of any Martian? How many are left, a dozen, two dozen. Line 'em up, bring 'em on, right? Right!"

Her laughter followed as he stumbled blindly around the corner of her house, his feet thrashing a litter of bottles. Eyes shut, he saw the print of her phosphorous skin, the phantoms leaping from her mouth in sorceries and evocations of cloud, rain and wind. Oh, to translate! Oh, gods, to *know*. Listen! What's that word, and that, and yes then, that!? Did she call out after him. No. Was that his name?

At the cave he ate but was not hungry.

He sat in the mouth of the cave for an hour, as the moons rose and hurtled across the cold sky and he saw his breath on the air, like the spirits, the fiery silences that breathed about her face, and she was talking, talking, he heard or did not hear her voice moving up the hill, among the rocks, and he could smell her breath, that breath of smoking promise, of warm words heated in her mouth.

And at last he thought, I will go down and speak to her very quietly, and speak to her every night until she understands what I say and I know her words and she then comes with me back into the hills where we will be content. I will tell her of my people and my being alone and how I have watched her and listened to her for so many nights. . . .

But . . . she is Death.

He shivered. The thought, the words would not go away.

How could he have forgotten?

He need only touch her hand, her cheek, and he would wither in a few hours, a week at the latest. He would change color and fall in folds of ink and turn to ash, black fragments of leaf that would break and fly away in the wind.

One touch and . . . Death.

But a further thought came. She lives alone, away from the others of her race. She must like her own thoughts, to be so much apart. Are we not the same, then? And, because she is separate from the towns, perhaps the Death is not in her . . . ? Yes! Perhaps!

How fine to be with her for a day, a week, a month, to swim with her in the canals, to walk in the hills and have her sing that strange song and he, in turn, would touch the old harp books and let them sing back to her! Wouldn't that be worth anything, everything? A man died when he was alone, did he not? So, consider the yellow lights in the house below. A month of real understanding and being and living with beauty and a maker of ghosts, the souls that came from the mouth, wouldn't it be a chance worth taking? And if death came . . . how fine and original it would be!

He stood up. He moved. He lit a candle in a niche of the cave where the images of his parents trembled in the light. Outside, the dark flowers waited for the dawn when they would quiver and open and she would be here to see them and tend them and walk with him in the hills. The moons were gone now. He had to fix his special sight to see the way.

He listened. Below in the night, the music played. Below in the dark, her voice spoke wonders across time. Below in the shadows, her white flesh burned, and the ghosts danced about her head.

He moved swiftly now.

At precisely nine forty-five that night, she heard the soft tapping at her front door.

ONE FOR HIS LORDSHIP, AND ONE FOR THE ROAD!

Someone's born, and it may take the best part of a day for the news to ferment, percolate, or otherwise circumnavigate across the Irish meadows to the nearest town, and the dearest pub, which is Heeber Finn's.

But let someone die, and a whole symphonic band lifts in the fields and hills. The grand ta-ta slams across country to ricochet off the pub slates and shake the drinkers to calamitous cries for: more!

So it was this hot summer day. The pub was no sooner opened, aired, and mobbed than Finn, at the door, saw a dust flurry up the road.

"That's Doone," muttered Finn.

Doone was the local anthem sprinter, fast at getting out of cinemas ahead of the damned national tune, and swift at bringing news.

"And the news is bad," murmured Finn. "It's *that* fast he's running!"

"Ha!" cried Doone, as he leaped across the sill. "It's done, and he's dead!"

The mob at the bar turned.

Doone enjoyed his moment of triumph, making them wait.

"Ah, God, here's a drink. Maybe that'll make you talk!"

Finn shoved a glass in Doone's waiting paw. Doone wet his whistle and arranged the facts.

"Himself," he gasped, at last. "Lord Kilgotten. Dead. And not an hour past!"

"Ah, God," said one and all, quietly. "Bless the old man. A sweet nature. A dear chap."

For Lord Kilgotten had wandered their fields, pastures, barns, and this bar all the years of their lives. His departure was like the Normans rowing back to France or the damned Brits pulling out of Bombay.

"A fine man," said Finn, drinking to the memory, "even though he *did* spend two weeks a year in London."

"How old was he?" asked Brannigan. "Eighty-five? Eighty-eight? We thought we might have buried him long since."

"Men like that," said Doone, "God has to hit with an axe to scare them off the place. Paris, now, we thought that might have slain him, years past, but no. Drink, that should have drowned him, but he swam for the shore, no, no. It was that teeny bolt of lightning in the field's midst, an hour ago, and him under the tree picking strawberries with his nineteen-year-old secretary lady."

"Jesus," said Finn. "There's no strawberries this time of year. It was *her* hit him with a bolt of fever. Burned to a crisp!"

That fired off a twenty-one-gun salute of laughs that hushed itself down when they considered the subject and more towns-folk arrived to breathe the air and bless himself.

"I wonder," mused Heeber Finn, at last, in a voice that would make the Valhalla gods sit still at table, and not scratch, "I wonder. What's to become of all that wine? The wine, that is, which Lord Kilgotten has stashed in barrels and bins, by the quarts and the tons, by the scores and precious thousands in his cellars and attics, and, who knows, under his bed?"

"Aye," said everyone, stunned, suddenly remembering. "Aye. Sure. *What?*"

"It has been left, no doubt, to some damn Yank drift-about cousin or nephew, corrupted by Rome, driven mad by Paris, who'll jet in tomorrow, who'll seize and drink, grab and run, and Kilcock and us left beggared and buggered on the road behind!" said Doone, all in one breath.

"Aye." Their voices, like muffled dark velvet drums, marched toward the night. "Aye."

"There *are* no relatives!" said Finn. "No dumb Yank nephews or dimwit nieces falling out of gondolas in Venice, but swimming this way. I have made it my business to know."

Finn waited. It was his moment now. All stared. All leaned to hear his mighty proclamation.

"Why not, I been thinking, if Kilgotten, by God, left all ten thousand bottles of Burgundy and Bordeaux to the citizens of the loveliest town in Eire? To *us!*"

There was an antic uproar of comment on this, cut across when the front doorflaps burst wide and Finn's wife, who rarely visited the sty, stepped in, glared around and snapped:

"Funeral's in an hour!"

"An hour?" cried Finn. "Why, he's only just cold—"

"Noon's the time," said the wife, growing taller the more she looked at this dreadful tribe. "The doc and the priest have just come from the Place. Quick funerals was his lordship's will. 'Uncivilized,' said Father Kelly, 'and no hole dug.' 'But there *is!*' said the Doc. 'Hanrahan was supposed to die yesterday but took on a fit of mean and survived the night. I treated and treated him, but the man persists! Meanwhile, there's his hole, unfilled. Kilgotten can have it, dirt and headstone.' All's invited. Move your bums!"

The double-wing doors whiffled shut. The mystic woman was gone.

"A funeral!" cried Doone, prepared to sprint.

"No!" Finn beamed. "Get out. Pub's closed. A *wake!*"

———

"Even Christ," gasped Doone, mopping the sweat from his brow, "wouldn't climb down off the cross to walk on a day like this."

"The heat," said Mulligan, "*is* intolerable."

Coats off, they trudged up the hill, past the Kilgotten gate-house, to encounter the town priest, Father Padraic Kelly, doing the same. He had all but his collar off, and was beet-faced in the bargain.

"It's hell's own day," he agreed, "*none* of us will keep!"

"Why all the rush?" said Finn, matching fiery stride for stride with the holy man. "I smell a rat. What's up?"

"Aye," said the priest. "There *was* a secret codicil in the will—"

"I *knew* it!" said Finn.

"What?" asked the crowd, fermenting close behind in the sun.

"It would have caused a riot if it got out," was all Father Kelly would say, his eyes on the graveyard gates. "You'll find out at the penultimate moment."

"Is that the moment before or the moment after the end, Father?" asked Doone, innocently.

"Ah, you're so dumb you're pitiful," sighed the priest. "Get your ass through that gate. Don't fall in the hole!"

Doone did just that. The others followed, their faces assuming a darker tone as they passed through. The sun, as if to observe this, moved behind a cloud, and a sweet breeze came up for some moment of relief.

"There's the hole." The priest nodded. "Line up on both sides of the path, for God's sake, and fix your ties, if you have some, and check your flies, above all. Let's run a nice show for Kilgotten, and here he *comes!*"

And here, indeed, came Lord Kilgotten, in a box carried on the planks of one of his farm wagons, a simple good soul to be sure, and behind that wagon, a procession of other vehicles, cars, trucks that stretched half down the hill in the now once more piercing light.

"What a procession!" cried Finn.

"I never seen the like!" cried Doone.

"Shut up," said the priest, politely.

"My God," said Finn. "Do you see the *coffin?*"

"We see, Finn, we *see!*" gasped all.

For the coffin, trundling by, was beautifully wrought, finely nailed together with silver and gold nails, but the special strange wood of it?

Plankings from wine-crates, staves from boxes that had sailed from France only to collide and sink in Lord Kilgotten's cellars!

A storm of exhalations swept the men from Finn's pub. They toppled on their heels. They seized each other's elbows.

"*You* know the words, Finn," whispered Doone. "Tell us the *names!*"

Finn eyed the coffin made of vintage shipping crates, and at last exhaled:

"Pull out my tongue and jump on it. Look! There's Château Lafite Rothschild, nineteen seventy. Châteauneuf du Pape, 'sixty-eight! Upside down, *that* label, Le Corton! Downside up: La Lagune! What style, my God, what class! I wouldn't so much mind being buried in burned-stamp-labeled wood like that myself!"

"I wonder," mused Doone, "can he *read* the labels from *inside?*"

"Put a sock in it," muttered the priest. "Here comes the *rest!*"

If the body in the box was not enough to pull clouds over the sun, this second arrival caused an even greater ripple of uneasiness to oil the sweating men.

"It was as if," Doone recalled, later, "someone had slipped, fallen in the grave, broken an ankle, and *spoiled* the whole afternoon!"

For the last part of the procession was a series of cars and trucks ramshackle-loaded with French vineyard crates, and finally a great old brewery wagon from early Guinness days, drawn by a team of proud white horses, draped in black, and sweating with the surprise they drew behind.

"I will be damned," said Finn. "Lord Kilgotten's brought his own wake *with* him!"

"Hurrah!" was the cry. "What a dear soul."

"He must've known the days would ignite a nun, or kindle a priest, and our tongues on our chests!"

"Gangway! Let it pass!"

The men stood aside as all the wagons, carrying strange labels from southern France and northern Italy, making tidal sounds of bulked liquids, lumbered into the churchyard.

"Someday," whispered Doone, "we must raise a statue to Kilgotten, a philosopher of friends!"

"Pull up your socks," said the priest. "It's too soon to tell. For here comes something *worse* than an undertaker!"

"What could be worse?"

With the last of the wine wagons drawn up about the grave, a single man strode up the road, hat on, coat buttoned, cuffs properly shot, shoes polished against all reason, mustache waxed and cool, unmelted, a prim case like a lady's purse tucked under his clenched arm, and about him an air of the ice houses, a thing fresh born from a snowy vault, tongue like an icicle, stare like a frozen pond.

"Jesus," said Finn.

"It's a *lawyer*!" said Doone.

All stood aside.

The lawyer, for that is what it was, strode past like Moses as the Red Sea obeyed, or King Louis on a stroll, or the haughtiest tart on Piccadilly: choose *one*.

"It's Kilgotten's law," hissed Muldoon. "I seen him stalking Dublin like the Apocalypse. With a lie for a name: Clement! Half-ass Irish, full-ass Briton. The *worst*!"

"What can be worse than death?" someone whispered.

"We," murmured the priest, "shall soon see."

"Gentlemen!"

A voice called. The mob turned.

Lawyer Clement, at the rim of the grave, took the prim briefcase from under his arm, opened it, and drew forth a symboled and ribboned document, the beauty of which bugged the eye and rammed and sank the heart.

"Before the obsequies," he said. "Before Father Kelly orates, I have a message, this codicil in Lord Kilgotten's will, which I shall read aloud."

"I bet it's the eleventh Commandment," murmured the priest, eyes down.

"What would the eleventh Commandment *be*?" asked Doone, scowling.

"Why not: 'THOU SHALT SHUT UP AND LISTEN,'" said the priest. "*Ssh*."

For the lawyer was reading from his ribboned document and his voice floated on the hot summer wind, like this:

"'And whereas my wines are the finest—'"

"They are *that*!" said Finn.

"'—and whereas the greatest labels from across the world fill my cellars, and whereas the people of this town, Kilcock, do not appreciate such things, but prefer the—er—hard stuff . . .'"

"Who *says*!?" cried Doone.

"Back in your ditch," warned the priest, *sotto voce.*

"'I do hereby proclaim and pronounce,'" read the lawyer, with a great smarmy smirk of satisfaction, "'that contrary to the old adage, a man can *indeed* take it with him. And I so order, write, and sign this codicil to my last will and testament in what might well be the final month of my life.' Signed, William, Lord Kilgotten. Last month, on the seventh."

The lawyer stopped, folded the paper and stood, eyes shut, waiting for the thunderclap that would follow the lightning bolt.

"Does that mean," asked Doone, wincing, "that the lord intends to—?"

Someone pulled a cork out of a bottle.

It was like a fusillade that shot all the men in their tracks.

It was only, of course, the good lawyer Clement, at the rim of the damned grave, corkscrewing and yanking open the plug from a bottle of La Vieille Ferme '73!

"Is this the *wake*, then?" Doone laughed, nervously.

"It is *not*," mourned the priest.

With a smile of summer satisfaction, Clement, the lawyer, poured the wine, glug by glug, down into the grave, over the wine-carton box in which Lord Kilgotten's thirsty bones were hid.

"Hold on! He's gone mad! Grab the bottle! No!"

There was a vast explosion, like that from the crowd's throat that has just seen its soccer champion slain midfield!

"Wait! My God!"

"Quick. Run, get the lord!"

"Dumb," muttered Finn. "His lordship's *in* that box, and his wine is *in* the grave!"

Stunned by this unbelievable calamity, the mob could only stare as the last of the first bottle cascaded down into the holy earth.

Clement handed the bottle to Doone, and uncorked a second.

"Now, wait just one moment!" cried the voice of the Day of Judgment.

And it was, of course, Father Kelly, who stepped forth, bringing his higher law with him.

"Do you mean to say," cried the priest, his cheeks blazing, his eyes smoldering with bright sun, "you are going to dispense all that stuff in Kilgotten's pit?"

"That," said the lawyer, "is my intent."

He began to pour the second bottle. But the priest stiff-armed him, to tilt the wine back.

"And do you mean for us to just stand and *watch* your blasphemy?!"

"At a wake, yes, that would be the polite thing to do." The lawyer moved to pour again.

"Just hold it, right there!" The priest stared around, up, down, at his friends from the pub, at Finn their spiritual leader, at the sky where God hid, at the earth where Kilgotten lay playing Mum's the Word, and at last at lawyer Clement and his damned, ribboned codicil. "Beware, man, you are provoking civil strife!"

"Yah!" cried everyone, atilt on the air, fists at their sides, grinding and ungrinding invisible rocks.

"What year is this wine?" Ignoring them, Clement calmly eyed the label in his hands. "Le Corton. Nineteen seventy. The best wine in the finest year. Excellent." He stepped free of the priest and let the wine spill.

"*Do* something!" shouted Doone. "Have you no curse handy?"

"Priests do not curse," said Father Kelly. "But, Finn, Doone, Hannahan, Burke. Jump! Knock heads."

The priest marched off and the men rushed after to knock their heads in a bent-down ring and a great whisper with the father. In the midst of the conference the priest stood up to see what Clement was doing. The lawyer was on his third bottle.

"Quick!" cried Doone. "He'll waste the *lot!*"

A fourth cork popped, to another outcry from Finn's team, the Thirsty Warriors, as they would later dub themselves.

"Finn!" the priest was heard to say, deep in the heads-together, "you're a genius!"

"I am!" agreed Finn, and the huddle broke and the priest hustled back to the grave.

"Would you mind, sir," he said, grabbing the bottle out of the lawyer's grip, "reading one *last* time, that damned codicil?"

"Pleasure." And it was. The lawyer's smile flashed as he fluttered the ribbons and snapped the will.

"'—that contrary to the old adage, a man can indeed take it with him—'"

He finished and folded the paper, and tried another smile, which worked to his own satisfaction, at least. He reached for the bottle confiscated by the priest.

"Hold on." Father Kelly stepped back. He gave a look to the crowd who waited on each fine word. "Let me ask you a question, Mr. Lawyer, sir. Does it anywhere say there just *how* the wine is to get into the grave?"

"Into the grave is into the grave," said the lawyer.

"As long as it finally *gets* there, *that's* the important thing, do we agree?" asked the priest, with a strange smile.

"I can pour it over my shoulder, or toss it in the air," said the lawyer, "as long as it lights to either side or atop the coffin, when it comes down, all's well."

"Good!" exclaimed the priest. "Men! One squad here. One battalion over there. Line up! Doone!"

"Sir?"

"Spread the rations. Jump!"

"Sir!" Doone jumped.

To a great uproar of men bustling and lining up.

"I," said the lawyer, "am going to find the police!"

"Which is *me*," said a man at the far side of the mob, "Officer Bannion. Your complaint?"

Stunned, lawyer Clement could only blink and at last in a squashed voice, bleat: "I'm leaving."

"You'll not make it past the gate alive," said Doone, cheerily.

"I," said the lawyer, "am staying. But—"

"But?" inquired Father Kelly, as the corks were pulled and the corkscrew flashed brightly along the line.

"You go against the letter of the law!"

"No," explained the priest, calmly, "we but shift the punctuation, cross new t's, dot new i's."

"Tenshun!" cried Finn, for all was in readiness.

On both sides of the grave, the men waited, each with a full bottle of vintage Château Lafite Rothschild or Le Corton or Chianti.

"Do we drink it *all*?" asked Doone.

"Shut your gab," observed the priest. He eyed the sky. "Oh, Lord." The men bowed their heads and grabbed off their caps. "Lord, for what we are about to receive, make us truly thankful. And thank you, Lord, for the genius of Heeber Finn, who thought of this—"

"Aye," said all, gently.

"'Twas nothin'," said Finn, blushing.

"And bless this wine, which may circumnavigate along the way, but finally wind up where it should be going. And if today and tonight won't do, and all the stuff not drunk, bless us as we return each night until the deed is done and the soul of the wine's at rest."

"Ah, you *do* speak dear," murmured Doone.

"Sh!" hissed all.

"And in the spirit of this time, Lord, should we not ask our good lawyer friend Clement, in the fullness of his heart, to join *with* us?"

Someone slipped a bottle of the best in the lawyer's hands. He seized it, lest it should break.

"And finally, Lord, bless the old Lord Kilgotten, whose years of saving-up now help us in this hour of putting-away. *Amen.*"

"Amen," said all.

"Tenshun!" cried Finn.

The men stiffened and lifted their bottles.

"One for his lordship," said the priest.

"And," added Finn, "one for the road!"

There was a dear sound of drinking and, years later, Doone remembered, a glad sound of laughter from the box in the grave.

"It's all right," said the priest, in amaze.

"Yes." The lawyer nodded, having heard. "It's all right."

AT MIDNIGHT IN THE MONTH OF JUNE

We had been waiting a long, long time in the summer night, as the darkness pressed warmer to the earth and the stars turned slowly over the sky. He sat in total darkness, his hands lying easily on the arms of the Morris chair. He heard the town clock strike nine and ten and eleven, and then at last twelve. The breeze from an open back window flowed through the midnight house in an unlit stream that touched him like a dark rock where he sat silently watching the front door—silently watching.

At midnight, in the month of June. . . .

The cool night poem by Mr. Edgar Allan Poe slid over his mind like the waters of a shadowed creek.

The lady sleeps! Oh, may her sleep,
Which is enduring, so be deep!

He moved down the black shapeless halls of the house, stepped out of the back window, feeling the town locked away in bed, in dream, in night. He saw the shining snake of garden hose coiled resiliently in the grass. He turned on the water. Standing alone, watering the flower bed, he imagined himself a conductor leading an orchestra that only night-strolling dogs might hear, passing on their way to nowhere with strange white smiles. Very carefully he planted both feet and his tall weight into the mud beneath the window, making deep, well-outlined prints. He stepped inside again and walked, leaving mud, down the absolutely unseen hall, his hands seeing for him.

Through the front porch window he made out the faint outline of a lemonade glass, one-third full, sitting on the porch rail where *she* had left it. He trembled quietly.

Now, he could feel her coming home. He could feel her moving across town, far away, in the summer night. He shut his eyes and put his mind out to find her, and felt her moving along in the dark; he knew just where she stepped down from a curb and crossed a street, and up on a curb and tack-tacking, tack-tacking along under the June elms and the last of the lilacs, with a friend. Walking the empty desert of night, he *was* she. He felt a purse in his hands. He felt long hair prickle his neck, and his mouth turn greasy with lipstick. Sitting still, he was walking, walking, walking on home after midnight.

"Good night!"

He heard but did not hear the voices, and she was coming nearer, and now she was only a mile away and now only a matter of a thousand yards, and now she was sinking, like a beautiful white lantern on an invisible wire, down into the cricket and frog and water-sounding ravine. And he knew the texture of the wooden ravine stairs as if, a boy, he was rushing down them, feeling the rough grain and the dust and the leftover heat of the day. . . .

He put his hands out on the air, open. The thumbs of his hands touched, and then the fingers, so that his hands made a circle, enclosing emptiness, there before him. Then, very slowly, he squeezed his hands tighter and tighter together, his mouth open, his eyes shut.

He stopped squeezing and put his hands, trembling, back on the arms of the chair. He kept his eyes shut.

Long ago, he had climbed, one night, to the top of the court-house tower fire escape, and looked out at the silver town, at the town of the moon, and the town of summer. And he had seen all the dark houses with two things in them, people and sleep, the two elements joined in bed and all their tiredness and terror breathed upon the still air, siphoned back quietly, and breathed out again, until that element was purified, the problems and hatreds and horrors of the previous day exorcised long before morning and done away with forever.

He had been enchanted with the hour, and the town, and he had felt very powerful, like the magic man with the marionettes who strung destinies across a stage on spider threads. On the very top of the courthouse tower he could see the least flicker of leaf turning in the moonlight five miles away; the last light, like a pink pumpkin eye, wink out. The town did not escape his eye—it could do nothing without his knowing its every tremble and gesture.

And so it was tonight. He felt himself a tower with the clock in it pounding slow and announcing hours in a great bronze tone, and gazing upon a town where a woman, hurried or slowed by fitful gusts and breezes now of terror and now of self-confidence, took the chalk-white midnight sidewalks home, fording solid avenues of tar and stone, drifting among fresh-cut lawns, and now running, running down the steps, through the ravine, up the hill, up the hill!

He heard her footsteps before he really heard them. He heard her gasping before there was a gasping. He fixed his gaze to the lemonade glass outside, on the banister. Then the real sound, the real running, the gasping, echoed wildly outside. He sat up. The footsteps raced across the street, the sidewalk, in a panic. There was a babble, a clumsy stumble up the porch steps, a key ratcheting the door, a voice yelling in a whisper, praying to itself. "Oh, God, dear God!" Whisper! Whisper! And the woman crashing in the door, slamming it, bolting it, talking, whispering, talking to herself in the dark room.

He felt, rather than saw, her hand move toward the light switch.

He cleared his throat.

———

She stood against the door in the dark. If moonlight could have struck in upon her, she would have shimmered like a small pool of water on a windy night. He felt the fine sapphire jewels come out upon her face, and her face all glittering with brine.

"Lavinia," he whispered.

Her arms were raised across the door like a crucifix. He heard her mouth open and her lungs push a warmness upon the air. She was a beautiful dim white moth; with the sharp needle point of terror he had her pinned against the wooden door. He could walk all around the specimen, if he wished, and look at her, look at her.

"Lavinia," he whispered.

He heard her heart beating. She did not move.

"It's me," he whispered.

"Who?" she said, so faint it was a small pulse-beat in her throat.

"I won't tell you," he whispered. He stood perfectly straight in the center of the room. God, but he felt *tall*! Tall and dark and very beautiful to himself, and the way his hands were out before him was as if he might play a piano at any moment, a lovely melody, a waltzing tune. The hands were wet, they felt as if he had dipped them into a bed of mint and cool menthol.

"If I told you who I am, you might not be afraid," he whispered. "I want you to be afraid. Are you afraid?"

She said nothing. She breathed out and in, out and in, a small bellows which, pumped steadily, blew upon her fear and kept it going, kept it alight.

"Why did you go to the show tonight?" he whispered. "*Why* did you go to the show?"

No answer.

He took a step forward, heard her breath take itself, like a sword hissing in its sheath.

"Why did you come back through the ravine, alone?" he whispered. "You *did* come back alone, didn't you? Did you think you'd meet me in the middle of the bridge? Why did you go to the show tonight? Why did you come back through the ravine, alone?"

"I—" she gasped.

"You," he whispered.

"No—" she cried, in a whisper.

"Lavinia," he said. He took another step.

"Please," she said.

"Open the door. Get out. And run," he whispered.

She did not move.

"Lavinia, open the door."

She began to whimper in her throat.

"Run," he said.

In moving he felt something touch his knee. He pushed, something tilted in space and fell over, a table, a basket, and a half-dozen unseen balls of yarn tumbled like cats in the dark, rolling softly. In the one moonlit space on the floor beneath the window, like a metal sign pointing, lay the sewing shears. They were winter ice in his hand. He held them out to her suddenly, through the still air.

"Here," he whispered.

He touched them to her hand. She snatched her hand back.

"Here," he urged.

"Take this," he said, after a pause.

He opened her fingers that were already dead and cold to the touch, and stiff and strange to manage, and he pressed the scissors into them. "Now," he said.

He looked out at the moonlit sky for a long moment, and when he glanced back it was some time before he could see her in the dark.

"I waited," he said. "But that's the way it's always been. I waited for the others, too. But they all came looking for me, finally. It was that easy. Five lovely ladies in the last two years. I waited for them in the ravine, in the country, by the lake, everywhere I waited, and they came out to find me, and found me. It was always nice, the next day, reading the newspapers. And you went looking tonight, I know, or you wouldn't have come back alone through the ravine. Did you scare yourself there, and run? Did you think I was down there waiting for you? You should have *heard* yourself running up the walk! Through the door! And *locking* it! You thought you were safe inside, home at last, safe, safe, safe, didn't you?"

She held the scissors in one dead hand, and she began to cry. He saw the merest gleam, like water upon the wall of a dim cave. He heard the sounds she made.

"No," he whispered. "You have the scissors. Don't cry."

She cried. She did not move at all. She stood there, shivering, her head back against the door, beginning to slide down the length of the door toward the floor.

"Don't cry," he whispered.

"I don't like to hear you cry," he said. "I can't stand to hear that."

He held his hands out and moved them through the air until one of them touched her cheek. He felt the wetness of that cheek, he felt her warm breath touch his palm like a summer moth. Then he said only one more thing:

"Lavinia," he said, gently. "Lavinia."

———

How clearly he remembered the old nights in the old times, in
the times when he was a boy and them all running, and running, and hiding and hiding, and playing hide-and-seek. In the
first spring nights and in the warm summer nights and in the
late summer evenings and in those first sharp autumn nights
when doors were shutting early and porches were empty except for blowing leaves. The game of hide-and-seek went on
as long as there was sun to see by, or the rising snow-crusted
moon. Their feet upon the green lawns were like the scattered
throwing of soft peaches and crab apples, and the counting of
the Seeker with his arms cradling his buried head, chanting to
the night: five, ten, fifteen, twenty, twenty-five, thirty, thirty-five,
forty, forty-five, fifty. . . . And the sound of thrown apples fading,
the children all safely closeted in tree or bush shade, under the
latticed porches with the clever dogs minding not to wag their
tails and give their secret away. And the counting done: eighty-
five, ninety, ninety-five, a hundred!

Ready or not, here I come!

And the Seeker running out through the town wilderness
to find the Hiders, and the Hiders keeping their secret laughter
in their mouths, like precious June strawberries, with the help of
clasped hands. And the Seeker seeking after the smallest heartbeat in the high elm tree or the glint of a dog's eye in a bush,
or a small water sound of laughter that could not help but burst
out as the Seeker ran right on by and did not see the shadow
within the shadow. . . .

He moved into the bathroom of the quiet house, thinking all this, enjoying the clear rush, the tumultuous gushing of
memories like a waterfalling of the mind over a steep precipice,
falling and falling toward the bottom of his head.

God, how secret and tall they had felt, hidden away. God,

how the shadows mothered and kept them, sheathed in their own triumph. Glowing with perspiration, how they crouched like idols and thought they might hide *forever*! While the silly Seeker went pelting by on his way to failure and inevitable frustration.

Sometimes the Seeker stopped right *at* your tree and peered up at you crouched there in your visible warm wings, in your great colorless windowpane bat wings, and said, "I *see* you there!" But you said nothing. "You're *up* there all right." But you said nothing. "Come on *down*!" But not a word, only a victorious Cheshire smile. And doubt coming over the Seeker below. "It is *you*, isn't it?" The backing off and away. "Aw, I *know* you're up there!" No answer. Only the tree sitting in the night and shaking quietly, leaf upon leaf. And the Seeker, afraid of the dark within darkness, loping away to seek easier game, something to be named and certain of. "All right for *you*!"

He washed his hands in the bathroom, and thought, Why am I washing my hands? And then the grains of time sucked back up the flue of the hour-glass again and it was another year. . . .

He remembered that sometimes when he played hide-and-seek they did not find him at all; he would not let them find him. He said not a word, he stayed so long in the apple tree that he was a white-fleshed apple; he lingered so long in the chestnut tree that he had the hardness and the brown brightness of the autumn nut. And God, how powerful to be undiscovered, how immense it made you, until your arms were branching, growing out in all directions, pulled by the stars and the tidal moon until your secretness enclosed the town and mothered it with your compassion and tolerance. You could do anything in the shadows, anything. If you chose to do it, you could do it. How powerful to sit above the sidewalk and see people pass under, never aware you were there and watching, and might put out an arm to brush their noses with the five-legged spider of your hand and brush their thinking minds with terror.

He finished washing his hands and wiped them on a towel.

But there was always an end to the game. When the Seeker had found all the other Hiders and these Hiders in turn were Seekers and they were all spreading out, calling your name, looking for you, how much more powerful and important *that* made you.

"Hey, hey! Where *are* you! Come in, the game's *over!*"

But you not moving or coming in. Even when they all collected under your tree and saw, or thought they saw you there at the very top, and called up at you. "Oh, come down! Stop fooling! Hey! We see you. We know you're there!"

Not answering even then—not until the final, the fatal thing happened. Far off, a block away, a silver whistle screaming, and the voice of your mother calling your name, and the whistle again. "Nine o'clock!" her voice wailed. "Nine o'clock! Home!"

But you waited until all the children were gone. Then, very carefully unfolding yourself and your warmth and secretness, and keeping out of the lantern light at corners, you ran home alone, alone in darkness and shadow, hardly breathing, keeping the sound of your heart quiet and in yourself, so if people heard anything at all they might think it was only the wind blowing a dry leaf by in the night. And your mother standing there, with the screen door wide. . . .

He finished wiping his hands on the towel. He stood a moment thinking of how it had been the last two years here in town. The old game going on, by himself, playing it alone, the children gone, grown into settled middle age, but now, as before, himself the final and last and only Hider, and the whole town seeking and seeing nothing and going on home to lock their doors.

But tonight, out of a time long past, and on many nights

now, he had heard that old sound, the sound of the silver whistle, blowing and blowing. It was certainly not a night bird singing, for he knew each sound so well. But the whistle kept calling and calling and a voice said, *Home* and *Nine o'clock*, even though it was now long after midnight. He listened. There was the silver whistle. Even though his mother had died many years ago, after having put his father in an early grave with her temper and her tongue. "Do this, do that, do this, do that, do this, do that, do this, do that. . . ." A phonograph record, broken, playing the same cracked turn again, again, again, her voice, her cadence, around, around, around, around, repeat, repeat, repeat.

And the clear silver whistle blowing and the game of hide-and-seek over. No more of walking in the town and standing behind trees and bushes and smiling a smile that burned through the thickest foliage. An automatic thing was happening. His feet were walking and his hands were doing and he knew everything that must be done now.

His hands did not belong to him.

He tore a button off his coat and let it drop into the deep dark well of the room. It never seemed to hit bottom. It floated down. He waited.

It seemed never to stop rolling. Finally, it stopped.

His hands did not belong to him.

He took his pipe and flung that into the depths of the room. Without waiting for it to strike emptiness, he walked quietly back through the kitchen and peered outside the open, blowing, white-curtained window at the footprints he had made there. He was the Seeker, seeking now, instead of the Hider hiding. He was the quiet searcher finding and sifting and putting away clues, and those footprints were now as alien to him as something from a prehistoric age. They had been made a million years ago by some other man on some other business; they were no part of him at all. He marveled at their precision and deepness and form in the moonlight. He put his hand down almost to touch them, like a great and beautiful archaeological discovery! Then he was gone, back through the rooms, ripping a piece of material from his pants cuff and blowing it off his open palm like a moth.

His hands were not his hands anymore, or his body his body.

He opened the front door and went out and sat for a moment on the porch rail. He picked up the lemonade glass and drank what was left, made warm by an evening's waiting, and pressed his fingers tight to the glass, tight, tight, very tight. Then he put the glass down on the railing.

The silver whistle!

Yes, he thought. Coming, coming.

The silver whistle!

Yes, he thought. Nine o'clock. Home, home. Nine o'clock. Studies and milk and graham crackers and white cool bed, home, home; nine o'clock and the silver whistle.

He was off the porch in an instant, running softly, lightly, with hardly a breath or a heartbeat, as one barefooted runs, as one all leaf and green June grass and night can run, all shadow, forever running, away from the silent house and across the street, and down into the ravine. . . .

———

He pushed the door wide and stepped into the Owl Diner, this long railroad car that, removed from its track, had been put to a solitary and unmoving destiny in the center of town. The place was empty. At the far end of the counter, the counterman glanced up as the door shut and the customer walked along the line of empty swivel seats. The counterman took the toothpick from his mouth.

"Tom Dillon, you old so-and-so! What *you* doing up this time of night, Tom?"

Tom Dillon ordered without the menu. While the food was being prepared, he dropped a nickel in the wall phone, got his number, and spoke quietly for a time. He hung up, came back, and sat, listening. Sixty seconds later, both he and the counterman heard the police siren wail by at fifty miles an hour. "Well—hell!" said the counterman. "Go get 'em boys!"

He set out a tall glass of milk and a plate of six fresh graham crackers.

Tom Dillon sat there for a long while, looking secretly down at his ripped pants cuff and muddied shoes. The light in the diner was raw and bright, and he felt as if he were on a stage. He held the tall cool glass of milk in his hand, sipping it, eyes shut, chewing the good texture of the graham crackers, feeling it all through his mouth, coating his tongue.

"Would or would you not," he asked, quietly, "call this a hearty meal?"

"I'd call that very hearty indeed," said the counterman, smiling.

Tom Dillon chewed another graham cracker with great concentration, feeling all of it in his mouth. It's just a matter of time, he thought, waiting.

"More milk?"

"Yes," said Tom.

And he watched with steady interest, with the purest and most alert concentration in all of his life, as the white carton tilted and gleamed, and the snowy milk poured out, cool and quiet, like the sound of a running spring at night, and filled the glass up all the way, to the very brim, to the very brim, and over. . . .

BLESS ME, FATHER, FOR I HAVE SINNED

It was just before midnight on Christmas Eve when Father Mellon woke, having slept for only a few minutes. He had a most peculiar urge to rise, go, and swing wide the front door of his church to let the snow in and then go sit in the confessional to wait.

Wait for what? Who would say? Who might tell? But the urge was so incredibly strong it was not to be denied.

"What's going on here?" he muttered quietly to himself, as he dressed. "I am going mad, am I not? At this hour, who could possibly want or need, and why in blazes should I—"

But dress he did and down he went and opened wide the front door of the church and stood in awe of the great artwork beyond, better than any painting in history, a tapestry of snow weaving in laces and gentling to roofs and shadowing the lamps and putting shawls on the huddled masses of cars waiting to be blessed at the curb. The snow touched the sidewalks and then his eyelids and then his heart. He found himself holding his breath with the fickle beauties and then, turning, the snow following at his back, he went to hide in the confessional.

Damn fool, he thought. Stupid old man. *Out* of here! Back to your bed!

But then he heard it; a sound at the door, and footsteps scraping on the pavestones of the church, and at last the damp rustle of some invader fresh to the other side of the confessional. Father Mellon waited.

"Bless me," a man's voice whispered, "for I have sinned!"

Stunned at the quickness of this asking, Father Mellon could only retort:

"How *could* you know the church would be open and I here?"

"I prayed, Father," was the quiet reply. "God *made* you come open up."

There seemed no answer to this, so the old priest, and what sounded like a hoarse old sinner, sat for a long cold moment as the clock itched on toward midnight, and at last the refugee from darkness repeated:

"*Bless* this sinner, father!"

But in place of the usual unguents and ointments of words, with Christmas hurrying fast through the snow, Father Mellon leaned toward the lattice window and could not help saying:

"It must be a terrible load of sin you carry to have driven you out on such a night on an impossible mission that turned possible only because God heard and pushed me out of bed."

"It *is* a terrible list, Father, as you will find!"

"Then speak, son," said the priest, "before we both freeze—"

"Well, it was this way—" whispered the wintry voice behind the thin paneling. "—Sixty years back—"

"Speak up! Sixty?!" The priest gasped. "That *long* past?"

"Sixty!" And there was a tormented silence.

"Go on," said the priest, ashamed of interrupting.

"Sixty years this week, when I was twelve," said the gray voice, "I Christmas-shopped with my grandmother in a small town back East. We walked both ways. In those days, who had a car? We walked, and coming home with the wrapped gifts, my grandma said something, I've long since forgotten what, and I got mad and ran ahead, away from her. Far off, I could hear her call and then cry, terribly, for me to come back, come back, but I wouldn't. She wailed so, I knew I had hurt her, which made me feel strong and good, so I ran even more, laughing, and beat her to the house and when she came in she was gasping and weeping as if never to stop. I felt ashamed and ran to hide. . . ."

There was a long silence.

The priest prompted. "Is that *it*?"

"The list is long," mourned the voice beyond the thin panel.

"Continue," said the priest, eyes shut.

"I did much the same to my mother, before New Year's. She angered me. I ran. I heard her cry out behind me. I smiled and ran faster. Why? Why, oh God, why?"

The priest had no answer.

"Is that it, then?" he murmured, at last, feeling strangely moved toward the old man beyond.

"One summer day," said the voice, "some bullies beat me. When they were gone, on a bush I saw two butterflies, embraced, lovely. I hated their happiness. I grabbed them in my fist and pulverized them to dust. Oh, Father, the shame!"

The wind blew in the church door at that moment and both of them glanced up to see a Christmas ghost of snow turned about in the door and falling away in drifts of whiteness to scatter on the pavings.

"There's one last terrible thing," said the old man, hidden away with his grief. And then he said:

"When I was thirteen, again in Christmas week, my dog Bo ran away and was lost three days and nights. I loved him more than life itself. He was special and loving and fine. And all of a sudden the beast was gone, and all his beauty with him. I waited.

I cried. I waited. I prayed. I shouted under my breath. I knew he would never, never come back! And then, oh, then, that Christmas Eve at two in the morning, with sleet on the sidewalks and icicles on roofs and snow falling, I heard a sound in my sleep and woke to hear him scratching the door! I bounded from bed so fast I almost killed myself! I yanked the door open and there was my miserable dog, shivering, excited, covered with dirty slush. I yelled, pulled him in, slammed the door, fell to my knees, grabbed him and wept. What a gift, what a gift! I called his name over and over, and he wept with me, all whines and agonies of joy. And then I stopped. Do you know what I did then? Can you guess the terrible thing? I beat him. Yes, beat him. With my fists, my hands, my palms, and my fists again, crying: how dare you leave, how dare you run off, how dare you do that to me, how dare you, how dare!? And I beat and beat until I was weak and sobbed and had to stop for I saw what I'd done, and he just stood and took it all as if he knew he deserved it, he had failed my love and now I was failing his, and I pulled off and tears streamed from my eyes, my breath strangled, and I grabbed him again and crushed him to me but this time cried: forgive, oh please, Bo, forgive. I didn't mean it. Oh, Bo, forgive. . . .

"But, oh, Father, he couldn't forgive me. Who was he? A beast, an animal, a dog, my love. And he looked at me with such great dark eyes that it locked my heart and it's been locked forever after with shame. *I* could not then forgive *myself.* All these years, the memory of my love and how I failed him, and every Christmas since, not the rest of the year, but every Christmas Eve, his ghost comes back, I see the dog, I hear the beating, I know my failure. Oh, God!"

The man fell silent, weeping.

And at last the old priest dared a word: "And that is why you are here?"

"Yes, Father. Isn't it awful. Isn't it terrible?"

The priest could not answer, for tears were streaming down his face, too, and he found himself unaccountably short of breath.

"Will God forgive me, Father?" asked the other.

"Yes."

"Will *you* forgive me, Father?"

"Yes. But let me tell you something now, son. When I was ten, the same things happened. My parents, of course, but then—my dog, the love of *my* life, who ran off and I hated him for leaving me, and when he came back I, too, loved and beat him, then went back to love. Until this night, I have told no one. The shame has stayed put all these years. I have confessed all to my priest-confessor. But *never* that. So—"

There was a pause.

"*So*, Father?"

"Lord, Lord, dear man, God will forgive us. At long last, we have brought it out, dared to say. And I, I will forgive you. But finally—"

The old priest could not go on, for new tears were really pouring down his face now.

The stranger on the other side guessed this and very carefully inquired, "Do you want *my* forgiveness, Father?"

The priest nodded, silently. Perhaps the other felt the shadow of the nod, for he quickly said, "Ah, well. It's *given*."

And they both sat there for a long moment in the dark and another ghost moved to stand in the door, then sank to snow and drifted away.

"Before you go," said the priest. "Come share a glass of wine."

The great clock in the square across from the church struck midnight.

"It's Christmas, Father," said the voice from behind the panel.

"The finest Christmas ever, I think."

"The finest."

The old priest rose and stepped out.

He waited a moment for some stir, some movement from the opposite side of the confessional.

There was no sound.

Frowning, the priest reached out and opened the confessional door and peered into the cubicle.

There was nothing and no one there.

His jaw dropped. Snow moved along the back of his neck.

He put his hand out to feel the darkness.

The place was empty.

Turning, he stared at the entry door, and hurried over to look out.

Snow fell in the last tones of far clocks late-sounding the hour. The streets were deserted.

Turning again, he saw the tall mirror that stood in the church entry.

There was an old man, himself, reflected in the cold glass.

Almost without thinking, he raised his hand and made the sign of blessing. The reflection in the mirror did likewise.

Then the old priest, wiping his eyes, turned a last time, and went to find the wine.

Outside, Christmas, like the snow, was everywhere.

BY THE NUMBERS!

"Company, tenshun!"

Snap.

"Company, forward—*Harch*!"

Tromp, tromp.

"Company, *halt*!"

Tromp, rattle, clump.

"Eyes right."

Whisper.

"Eyes left."

Rustle.

"About face!"

Tromp, scrape, tromp.

In the sunlight, a long time ago, the man shouted and the company obeyed. By a hotel pool under a Los Angeles sky in the summer of '52, there was the drill sergeant and there stood his team.

"Eyes front! Head up! Chin in! Chest out! Stomach sucked! Shoulders back, dammit, *back*!"

Rustle, whisper, murmur, scratch, silence.

And the drill sergeant walking forward, dressed in bathing

trunks by the edge of that pool to fix his cold bluewater gaze on his company, his squad, his team, his—

Son.

A boy of nine or ten, standing stiffly upright, staring arrow-straight ahead at military nothings, shoulders starched, as his father paced, circling him, barking commands, leaning in at him, mouth crisply enunciating the words. Both father and son were dressed in bathing togs and, a moment before, had been cleaning the pool area, arranging towels, sweeping with brooms. But now, just before noon:

"Company! By the numbers! One, two!"

"Three, four!" cried the boy.

"One, two!" shouted the father.

"Three, *four*!"

"Company halt, shoulder arms, present arms, tuck that chin, square those toes, hup!"

The memory came and went like a badly projected film in an old rerun cinema. Where had it come from, and why?

I was on a train heading north from Los Angeles to San Francisco. I was in the bar-car, alone, late at night, save for the bar man and a young-old stranger who sat directly across from me, drinking his second martini.

The old memory had come from him.

Nine feet away, his hair, his face, his startled blue and wounded eyes had suddenly cut the time stream and sent me back.

In and out of focus, I was on the train, then beside that pool, watching the hurt bright gaze of this man across the aisle, hearing his father thirty years lost, and watching the son, five thousand afternoons ago, wheeling and pivoting, turning and freezing, presenting imaginary arms, shouldering imaginary rifles.

"Tenshun!!" barked the father.

"Shun!" echoed the son.

"My God," whispered Sid, my best friend, lying beside me in the hot noon light, staring.

"My God, indeed," I muttered.

"How long has *this* been going on?"

"Years, maybe. Looks that way. Years."

"Hut, two!"

"Three, four!"

A church clock nearby struck noon; time to open the pool liquor bar.

"Company . . . *harch!*"

A parade of two, the man and boy strode across the tiles toward the half-locked gates on the open-air bar.

"Company, halt. Ready! Free locks! Hut!"

The boy snapped the locks wide.

"Hut!"

The boy flung the gate aside, jumped back, stiffened, waiting.

"Bout face, forward, harch!"

When the boy had almost reached the rim of the pool and was about to fall in, the father, with the wryest of smiles, called quietly: ". . . halt."

The son teetered on the edge of the pool.

"God damn," whispered Sid.

The father left his son standing there skeleton stiff and flag-pole erect, and went away.

Sid jumped up suddenly, staring at this.

"Sit down," I said.

"Christ, is he going to leave the kid just *waiting* there?!"

"Sit down, Sid."

"Well, for God's sake, that's inhuman!"

"He's not your son, Sid," I said, quietly. "You want to start a real fight?"

"Yeah!" said Sid. "Dammit!"

"It wouldn't do any good."

"Yes, it would. I'd like to beat hell—"

"Look at the boy's *face*, Sid."

Sid looked and began to slump.

The son, standing there in the burning glare of sun and water, was proud. The way he held his head, the way his eyes took fire, the way his naked shoulders carried the burden of goad or instruction, was all pride.

It was the logic of that pride which finally caved Sid in. Weighted with some small despair, he sank back down to his knees.

"Are we going to have to sit here all afternoon, and watch this dumb game of—" Sid's voice rose in spite of himself "— Simon Says?!"

The father heard. In the midst of stacking towels on the far side of the pool, he froze. The muscles on his back played like a pinball machine, making sums. Then he turned smartly, veered past his son who still stood balanced a half inch from the pool's rim, gave him a glance, nodded with intense, scowling approval, and came to cast his iron shadow over Sid and myself.

"I will thank you, sir," he said, quietly, "to keep your voice down, to not confuse my son—"

"I'll say any damn thing I want!" Sid started to get up.

"No, sir, you will not." The man pointed his nose at Sid; it might just as well have been a gun. "This is my pool, my turf, I have an agreement with the hotel, their territory stops out there by the gate. If I'm to run a clean, tucked-in shop, it is to be with total authority. Any dissidents—*out. Bodily.* On the gymnasium wall inside you'll find my jujitsu black belt, boxing, and rifle-marksman certificates. If you try to shake my hand, I will break your wrist. If you sneeze, I will crack your nose. One word and your dental surgeon will need two years to reshape your smile. Company, *tenshun!*"

The words all flowed together.

His son stiffened at the rim of the pool.

"Forty laps! Hut!"

"Hut!" cried the boy, and leaped.

His body striking the water and his beginning to swim furiously stopped Sid from any further outrage. Sid shut his eyes.

The father smiled at Sid, and turned to watch the boy churning the summer waters to a foam.

"There's everything I never was," he said. "Gentlemen."

He gave us a curt nod and stalked away.

Sid could only run and jump in the pool. He did twenty laps himself. Most of the time, the boy beat him. When Sid came out, the blaze was gone from his face and he threw himself down.

"Christ," he muttered, his face buried in his towel, "someday that boy *must* haul off and murder that son of a bitch!"

"As a Hemingway character once said," I replied, watching the son finish his 35th lap, "wouldn't it be nice to *think* so?"

The final time, the last day I ever saw them, the father was still marching about briskly, emptying ashtrays (no one could empty them the way *he* could), straightening tables, aligning chairs and lounges in military rows, and arranging fresh white towels on benches in crisp mathematical stacks. Even the way he swabbed the deck was geometrical. In all his marching and going, fixing and re-aligning, only on occasion did he snap his head on, flick a gaze to make sure his squad, his platoon, his company still stood frozen by the hour, a boy like a ramrod guidon, his hair blowing in the summer wind, eyes straight on the late afternoon horizon, mouth clamped, chin tucked, shoulders back.

I could not help myself. Sid was long gone. I waited on the balcony of the hotel overlooking the pool, having a final drink, not able to take my gaze off the marching father and the statue son. At dusk, the father double-timed it to the outer gate and almost as an afterthought called over his shoulder:

"Tenshun! Squad right. One, two—"

"Three, four!" cried the boy.

The boy strode through the gate, feet clubbing the cement as if he wore boots. He marched off toward the parking lot as his father snap-locked the gate with a robot's ease, took a fast scan around, raised his stare, saw me, and hesitated. His eyes burned over my face. I felt my shoulders go back, my chin drop, my shoulders flinch. To stop it, I lifted my drink, waved it carelessly at him, and drank.

What will happen, I thought, in the years ahead? Will the son grow up to kill his old man, or beat him up, or just run away to know a ruined life, always marching to some unheard shout of "Hut" or "harch!" but never "at ease!"?

Or, I thought, drinking, would the boy raise sons himself and just yell at *them* on hot noons by far pools in endless years? Would he one day stick a pistol in his mouth and kill his father the only way he knew how? Or would he marry and have *no* sons and thus bury all shouts, all drills, all sergeants? Questions, half-answers, more questions.

My glass was empty. The sun had gone, and the father and his son with it.

But now, in the flesh, straight across from me on this late-night train, heading north for unlit destinations, one of them had returned. There he was, the kid himself, the raw recruit, the child of the father who shouted at noon and told the sun to rise or set.

Merely alive? *half* alive? *all* alive?

I wasn't sure.

But there he sat, thirty years later, a young-old or old-young man, sipping on his third martini.

By now, I realized that my glances were becoming much too constant and embarrassing. I studied his bright blue, wounded eyes, for that is what they were: wounded, and at last took courage and spoke:

"Pardon me," I said. "This may seem silly, but—thirty years back, I swam weekends at the Ambassador Hotel where a military man tended the pool with his son. He—well. Are *you* that son?"

The young-old man across from me thought for a moment, looked me over with his shifting eyes and at last smiled, quietly.

"I," he said, "*am* that son. Come on over."

We shook hands. I sat and ordered a final round for us, as if we were celebrating something, or holding a wake, nobody seemed to know which. After the barman delivered the drinks, I said, "To nineteen fifty-two, a toast. A good year? Bad year? Here's to it, anyway!"

We drank and the young-old man said, almost immediately, "You're wondering what ever happened to my father."

"My God," I sighed.

"No, no," he assured me, "it's all right. A lot of people have wondered, have asked, over the years."

The boy inside the older man nursed his martini and remembered the past.

"Do you *tell* people when they ask?" I said.

"I do."

I took a deep breath. "All right, then. What *did* happen to your father?"

"He died."

There was a long pause.

"Is that *all*?"

"Not quite." The young-old man arranged his glass on the table in front of him, and placed a napkin at a precise angle to it, and fitted an olive to the very center of the napkin, reading the past there. "You remember what he was like?"

"Vividly."

"Oh, what a world of meaning you put into that 'vividly'!" The young-old man snorted faintly. "You remember his marches up, down, around the pool, left face, right, tenshun, don't move, chin-stomach in, chest out, harch two, hut?"

"I remember."

"Well, one day in nineteen fifty-three, long after the old crowd was gone from the pool, and you with them, my dad was drilling me outdoors one late afternoon. He had me standing in the hot sun for an hour or so and he yelled in my face, I can remember the saliva spray on my chin, my nose, my eyelids when he yelled: don't move a muscle! don't blink! don't twitch! don't breathe till I *tell* you! You hear, soldier? Hear? You hear! Hear?!"

"'Sir!'" I gritted between my teeth.

"As my father turned, he slipped on the tiles and fell in the water."

The young-old man paused and gave a strange small bark of a laugh.

"Did you *know*? Of course you didn't. I didn't either . . . that in all those years of working at various pools, cleaning out the showers, replacing the towels, repairing the diving boards, fixing the plumbing, he had never, my God, never learned to swim! *Never*! Jesus. It's unbelievable. Never.

"He had never *told* me. Somehow, I had never guessed! And since he had just yelled at me, instructed me, *ordered* me: eyes right! don't twitch! don't *move*! I just *stood* there staring straight ahead at the late afternoon sun. I didn't let my eyes drop to see, even once. Just straight ahead, by the numbers, as told.

"I heard him thrashing around in the water, yelling. But I couldn't understand what he said. I heard him suck and gasp and gargle and suck again, going down, shrieking, but I stood straight, chin up, stomach tight, eyes level, sweat on my brow, mouth firm, buttocks clenched, ramrod spine, and him yelling, gagging, taking water. I kept waiting for him to yell, 'At ease!' 'At ease!' he should have yelled, but he never did. So what could I do? I just stood there, like a statue, until the shrieking stopped and the water lapped the poolrim and everything got quiet. I stood there for ten minutes, maybe twenty, half an hour, until someone came out and found me there, and they looked down in the pool and saw something deep under and said Jesus Christ and finally turned and came up to me, because they knew me and my father, and at last said, At Ease.

"And then I cried."

The young-old man finished his drink.

"You see, the thing is, I couldn't be sure he wasn't faking. He'd done tricks like that before, to get me off guard, make me relax. He'd go around a corner, wait, duck back, to see if I was ramrod tall. Or he'd pretend to go in the men's room, and jump back to find me wrong. Then he'd punish me. So, standing there by the pool that day, I thought, it's a trick, to make me fall out. So I had to wait, didn't I, to be sure? . . . to be sure."

Finished, he put his empty martini glass down on the tray and sat back in his own silence, eyes gazing over my shoulder at nothing in particular. I tried to see if his eyes were wet, or if his mouth gave some special sign now that the tale was told, but I saw nothing.

"Now," I said, "I know about your father. But . . . what ever happened to *you*?"

"As you see," he said, "I'm here."

He stood up and reached over and shook my hand.

"Good night," he said.

I looked straight up in his face and saw the young boy there waiting for orders five thousand afternoons back. Then I looked at his left hand; no wedding ring there. Which meant what? No sons, no future? But I couldn't ask.

"I'm glad we met again," I heard myself say.

"Yes." He nodded, and gave my hand a final shake. "It's good to see you made it through."

Me, I thought. My God! *Me?!*

But he had turned and was walking off down the aisle, beautifully balanced, not swaying with the train's motion, this way or that. He moved in a clean, lithe, well-cared-for body, which the train's swerving could do nothing to as he went away.

As he reached the door, he hesitated, his back to me, and he seemed to be waiting for some final word, some order, some shout from someone.

Forward, I wanted to say, by the numbers! *March!*

But I said nothing.

Not knowing if it would kill him, or release him, I simply bit my tongue, and watched him open the door, slip silently through, and stride down the corridor of the next sleeping car toward a past I just might have imagined, toward a future I could not guess.

A TOUCH OF PETULANCE

On an otherwise ordinary evening in May, a week before his twenty-ninth birthday, Jonathan Hughes met his fate, commuting from another time, another year, another life.

His fate was unrecognizable at first, of course, and boarded the train at the same hour, in Pennsylvania Station, and sat with Hughes for the dinnertime journey across Long Island. It was the newspaper held by this fate disguised as an older man that caused Jonathan Hughes to stare and finally say:

"Sir, pardon me, your *New York Times* seems different from mine. The typeface on your front page seems more modern. Is that a later edition?"

"No!" The older man stopped, swallowed hard, and at last managed to say, "Yes. A very late edition."

Hughes glanced around. "Excuse me, but—all the other editions look the same. Is yours a trial copy for a future change?"

"Future?" The older man's mouth barely moved. His entire body seemed to wither in his clothes, as if he had lost weight with a single exhalation. "Indeed," he whispered. "Future change. God, what a joke."

Jonathan Hughes blinked at the newspaper's dateline:

May 2, 1999.

"Now, see here—" he protested, and then his eyes moved down to find a small story, minus picture, in the upper-left-hand corner of the front page:

WOMAN MURDERED

POLICE SEEK HUSBAND

Body of Mrs. Alice Hughes found shot to death—

The train thundered over a bridge. Outside the window, a billion trees rose up, flourished their green branches in convulsions of wind, then fell as if chopped to earth.

The train rolled into a station as if nothing at all in the world had happened.

In the silence, the young man's eyes returned to the text:

Jonathan Hughes, certified public accountant, of 112
Plandome Avenue, Plandome—

"My God!" he cried. "Get away!"

But he himself rose and ran a few steps back before the older man could move. The train jolted and threw him into an empty seat where he stared wildly out at a river of green light that rushed past the windows.

Christ, he thought, who would *do* such a thing? Who'd try to hurt us—*us*? What kind of joke? To mock a new marriage with a fine wife? Damn! And again, trembling, Damn, oh, damn!

The train rounded a curve and all but threw him to his feet. Like a man drunk with traveling, gravity, and simple rage, he swung about and lurched back to confront the old man, bent now into his newspaper, gone to earth, hiding in print. Hughes brushed the paper out of the way, and clutched the old man's shoulder. The old man, startled, glanced up, tears running from his eyes. They were both held in a long moment of thunderous traveling. Hughes felt his soul rise to leave his body.

"Who are you?"

Someone must have shouted that.

The train rocked as if it might derail.

The old man stood up as if shot in the heart, blindly crammed something in Jonathan Hughes's hand, and blundered away down the aisle and into the next car.

The younger man opened his fist and turned a card over and read a few words that moved him heavily down to sit and read the words again:

JONATHAN HUGHES, CPA
679-4990. Plandome.

"No!" someone shouted.

Me, thought the young man. Why, that old man is . . . *me*.

———

There was a conspiracy, no, several conspiracies. Someone had contrived a joke about murder and played it on him. The train roared on with five hundred commuters who all rode, swaying like a team of drunken intellectuals behind their masking books and papers, while the old man, as if pursued by demons, fled off away from car to car. By the time Jonathan Hughes had rampaged his blood and completely thrown his sanity off balance, the old man had plunged, as if falling, to the farthest end of the commuter's special.

The two men met again in the last car, which was almost empty. Jonathan Hughes came and stood over the old man, who refused to look up. He was crying so hard now that conversation would have been impossible.

Who, thought the young man, who is he crying for? Stop, please, stop.

The old man, as if commanded, sat up, wiped his eyes, blew his nose, and began to speak in a frail voice that drew Jonathan Hughes near and finally caused him to sit and listen to the whispers:

"We were born—"

"We?" cried the young man.

"We," whispered the old man, looking out at the gathering dusk that traveled like smokes and burnings past the window, "we, yes, we, the two of us, we were born in Quincy in nineteen fifty, August twenty-second—"

Yes, thought Hughes.

"—and lived at Forty-nine Washington Street and went to Central School and walked to that school all through first grade with Isabel Perry—"

Isabel, thought the young man.

"We . . ." murmured the old man. "Our" whispered the old man. "Us." And went on and on with it:

"Our woodshop teacher, Mr. Bisbee. History teacher, Miss Monks. We broke our right ankle, age ten, ice-skating. Almost drowned, age eleven; Father saved us. Fell in love, age twelve, Impi Johnson—"

Seventh grade, lovely lady, long since dead, Jesus God, thought the young man, growing old.

And that's what happened. In the next minute, two minutes, three, the old man talked and talked and gradually became younger with talking, so his cheeks glowed and his eyes brightened, while the young man, weighted with old knowledge given, sank lower in his seat and grew pale so that both almost met in mid-talking, mid-listening, and became twins in passing. There was a moment when Jonathan Hughes knew for an absolute insane certainty, that if he dared glance up he would see identical twins in the mirrored window of a night-rushing world.

He did not look up.

The old man finished, his frame erect now, his head somehow driven high by the talking out, the long-lost revelations.

"That's the past," he said.

I should hit him, thought Hughes. Accuse him. Shout at him. Why aren't I hitting, accusing, shouting?

Because. . . .

The old man sensed the question and said, "You know I'm who I say I am. I know everything there is to know about us. Now—the future?"

"Mine?"

"Ours," said the old man.

Jonathan Hughes nodded, staring at the newspaper clutched in the old man's right hand. The old man folded it and put it away.

"Your business will slowly become less than good. For what reasons, who can say? A child will be born and die. A mistress will be taken and lost. A wife will become less than good. And at last, oh believe it, yes, do, very slowly, you will come to—how shall I say it—hate her living presence. There, I see I've upset you. I'll shut up."

They rode in silence for a long while, and the old man grew old again, and the young man along with him. When he had aged just the proper amount, the young man nodded the talk to continue, not looking at the other who now said:

"Impossible, yes, you've been married only a year, a great year, the best. Hard to think that a single drop of ink could color a whole pitcher of clear fresh water. But color it could and color it did. And at last the entire world changed, not just our wife, not just the beautiful woman, the fine dream."

"You—" Jonathan Hughes started and stopped. "You— killed her?"

"We did. Both of us. But if I have my way, if I can convince you, neither of us will, she will live, and you will grow old to become a happier, finer me. I pray for that. I weep for that. There's still time. Across the years, I intend to shake you up, change your blood, shape your mind. God, if people knew what murder is. So silly, so stupid, so—ugly. But there is hope, for I have somehow got here, touched you, begun the change that will save our souls. Now, listen. You do admit, do you not, that we are one and the same, that the twins of time ride this train this hour this night?"

The train whistled ahead of them, clearing the track of an encumbrance of years.

The young man nodded the most infinitely microscopic of nods. The old man needed no more.

"I ran away. I ran to you. That's all I can say. She's been dead only a day, and I ran. Where to go? Nowhere to hide, save Time. No one to plead with, no judge, no jury, no proper witnesses save—you. Only you can wash the blood away, do you see? You *drew* me, then. Your youngness, your innocence, your good hours, your fine life still untouched, was the machine that seized me down the track. All of my sanity lies in you. If you turn away, great God, I'm lost, no, *we* are lost. We'll share a grave and never rise and be buried forever in misery. Shall I tell you what you must do?"

The young man rose.

"Plandome," a voice cried. "Plandome."

And they were out on the platform with the old man running after, the young man blundering into walls, into people, feeling as if his limbs might fly apart.

"Wait!" cried the old man. "Oh, please."

The young man kept moving.

"Don't you see, we're in this together, we must think of it together, solve it together, so you won't become me and I won't have to come impossibly in search of you, oh, it's all mad, insane, I know, I know, but listen!"

The young man stopped at the edge of the platform where cars were pulling in, with joyful cries or muted greetings, brief honkings, gunnings of motors, lights vanishing away. The old man grasped the young man's elbow.

"Good God, your wife, mine, will be here in a moment, there's so much to tell, you *can't* know what I know, there's twenty years of unfound information lost between which we must trade and understand! Are you listening? God, you *don't* believe!"

Jonathan Hughes was watching the street. A long way off a final car was approaching. He said: "What happened in the attic at my grandmother's house in the summer of nineteen fifty-eight? No one knows that but me. Well?"

The old man's shoulders slumped. He breathed more easily, and as if reciting from a promptboard said: "We hid ourselves there for two days, alone. No one ever knew where we hid. Everyone thought we had run away to drown in the lake or fall in the river. But all the time, crying, not feeling wanted, we hid up above and . . . listened to the wind and wanted to die."

The young man turned at last to stare fixedly at his older self, tears in his eyes. "*You* love me, then?"

"I had better," said the old man. "I'm all you have."

The car was pulling up at the station. A young woman smiled and waved behind the glass.

"Quick," said the old man, quietly. "Let me come home, watch, show you, teach you, find where things went wrong, correct them now, maybe hand you a fine life forever, let me—"

The car horn sounded, the car stopped, the young woman leaned out.

"Hello, lovely man!" she cried.

Jonathan Hughes exploded a laugh and burst into a manic run. "Lovely lady, hi—"

"Wait."

He stopped and turned to look at the old man with the

newspaper, trembling there on the station platform. The old man raised one hand, questioningly.

"Haven't you forgotten something?"

Silence. At last: "You," said Jonathan Hughes. "You."

———

The car rounded a turn in the night. The woman, the old man, the young, swayed with the motion.

"What did you say your name was?" the young woman said, above the rush and run of country and road.

"He didn't say," said Jonathan Hughes quickly.

"Weldon," said the old man, blinking.

"Why," said Alice Hughes. "That's *my* maiden name."

The old man gasped inaudibly, but recovered. "Well, *is* it? How curious!"

"I wonder if we're related? You—"

"He was my teacher at Central High," said Jonathan Hughes, quickly.

"And still am," said the old man. "And still am."

And they were home.

He could not stop staring. All through dinner, the old man simply sat with his hands empty half the time and stared at the lovely woman across the table from him. Jonathan Hughes fidgeted, talked much too loudly to cover the silences, and ate sparsely. The old man continued to stare as if a miracle was happening every ten seconds. He watched Alice's mouth as if it were giving forth fountains of diamonds. He watched her eyes as if all the hidden wisdoms of the world were there, and now found for the first time. By the look of his face, the old man, stunned, had forgotten why he was there.

"Have I a crumb on my chin?" cried Alice Hughes, suddenly. "Why is everyone *watching* me?"

Whereupon the old man burst into tears that shocked everyone. He could not seem to stop, until at last Alice came around
the table to touch his shoulder.

"Forgive me," he said. "It's just that you're so lovely. Please
sit down. Forgive."

They finished off the dessert and with a great display of
tossing down his fork and wiping his mouth with his napkin,
Jonathan Hughes cried, "That was fabulous. Dear wife, I love
you!" He kissed her on the cheek, thought better of it, and re-
kissed her, on the mouth. "You see?" He glanced at the old man.
"I very *much* love my wife."

The old man nodded quietly and said, "Yes, yes, I remember."

"You *remember?*" said Alice, staring.

"A toast!" said Jonathan Hughes, quickly. "To a fine wife, a
grand future!"

His wife laughed. She raised her glass.

"Mr. Weldon," said said, after a moment. "You're not
drinking? . . ."

———

It was strange seeing the old man at the door to the living
room.

"Watch this," he said, and closed his eyes. He began to move
certainly and surely about the room, eyes shut. "Over here is
the pipestand, over here the books. On the fourth shelf down
a copy of Eiseley's *The Star Thrower.* One shelf up H. G. Wells's
Time Machine, most appropriate, and over here the special chair,
and me in it."

He sat. He opened his eyes.

Watching from the door, Jonathan Hughes said, "You're not
going to cry again, are you?"

"No. No more crying."

There were sounds of washing up from the kitchen. The lovely woman out there hummed under her breath. Both men turned to look out of the room toward that humming.

"Someday," said Jonathan Hughes, "I will hate her? Someday, I will kill her?"

"It doesn't seem possible, does it? I've watched her for an hour and found nothing, no hint, no clue, not the merest period, semicolon or exclamation point of blemish, bump, or hair out of place with her. I've watched you, too, to see if *you* were at fault, *we* were at fault, in all this."

"And?" The young man poured sherry for both of them, and handed over a glass.

"You drink too much is about the sum. Watch it."

Hughes put his drink down without sipping it. "What else?"

"I suppose I should give you a list, make you keep it, look at it every day. Advice from the old crazy to the young fool."

"Whatever you say, I'll remember."

"Will you? For how long? A month, a year, then, like everything else, it'll go. You'll be busy living. You'll be slowly turning into . . . me. She will slowly be turning into someone worth putting out of the world. Tell her you love her."

"Every day."

"Promise! It's *that* important! Maybe that's where I failed myself, failed us. Every day, without fail!" The old man leaned forward, his face taking fire with his words. "Every day. Every day!"

Alice stood in the doorway, faintly alarmed.

"Anything wrong?"

"No, no." Jonathan Hughes smiled. "We were trying to decide which of us likes you best."

She laughed, shrugged, and went away.

"I think," said Jonathan Hughes, and stopped and closed his eyes, forcing himself to say it, "it's time for you to go."

"Yes, time." But the old man did not move. His voice was very tired, exhausted, sad. "I've been sitting here feeling defeated. I can't find anything wrong. I can't find the flaw. I can't advise you, my God, it's so stupid, I shouldn't have come to upset you, worry you, disturb your life, when I have nothing to offer but vague suggestions, inane cryings of doom. I sat here a moment ago and thought: I'll kill her now, get rid of her now, take the blame now, as an old man, so the young man there, you, can go on into the future and be free of her. Isn't that silly? I wonder if it would work? It's that old time-travel paradox, isn't it? Would I foul up the time flow, the world, the universe, what? Don't worry, no, no, don't look that way. No murder now. It's all been done up ahead, twenty years in your future. The old man having done nothing whatever, having been no help, will now open the door and run away to his madness."

He arose and shut his eyes again.

"Let me see if I can find my way out of my own house, in the dark."

He moved, the young man moved with him to find the closet by the front door and open it and take out the old man's overcoat and slowly shrug him into it.

"You *have* helped," said Jonathan Hughes. "You have told me to tell her I love her."

"Yes, I *did* do that, didn't I?"

They turned to the door.

"Is there hope for us?" the old man asked, suddenly, fiercely.

"Yes. I'll make sure of it," said Jonathan Hughes.

"Good, oh, good. I almost believe!"

The old man put one hand out and blindly opened the front door.

"I won't say goodbye to her. I couldn't stand looking at that lovely face. Tell her the old fool's gone. Where? Up the road to wait for you. You'll arrive someday."

"To become you? Not a chance," said the young man.

"Keep saying that. And—my God—here—" The old man fumbled in his pocket and drew forth a small object wrapped in crumpled newspaper. "You'd better keep this. I can't be trusted, even now. I might do something wild. Here. Here."

He thrust the object into the young man's hands. "Goodbye. Doesn't that mean: God be with you? Yes. Goodbye."

The old man hurried down the walk into the night. A wind shook the trees. A long way off, a train moved in darkness, arriving or departing, no one could tell.

Jonathan Hughes stood in the doorway for a long while, trying to see if there really was someone out there vanishing in the dark.

"Darling," his wife called.

He began to unwrap the small object.

She was in the parlor door behind him now, but her voice sounded as remote as the fading footsteps along the dark street.

"Don't stand there letting the draft in," she said.

He stiffened as he finished unwrapping the object. It lay in his hand, a small revolver.

Far away the train sounded a final cry, which failed in the wind.

"Shut the door," said his wife.

His face was cold. He closed his eyes.

Her voice. Wasn't there just the *tiniest* touch of petulance there?

He turned slowly, off balance. His shoulder brushed the door. It drifted. Then:

The wind, all by itself, slammed the door with a bang.

LONG DIVISION

You've had the lock *changed*!"

He sounded stunned, standing in the door looking down at the knob that he fiddled with one hand while he clenched the old door key in the other.

She took her hand off the other side of the knob and walked away.

"I didn't want any strangers coming in."

"Strangers!" he cried. Again he jiggled the knob and then with a sigh put away his key and shut the door. "Yes, I guess we are. Strangers."

She did not sit down but stood in the middle of the room looking at him.

"Let's get *to* it," she said.

"It looks like you already *have*. Jesus." He blinked at the books divided into two incredibly neat stacks on the floor. "Couldn't you have waited for me?"

"I thought it would save time," she said and nodded now to her left, now to her right. "These are mine. Those are yours."

"Let's look."

"Go ahead. But no matter how you look, these are mine, those are yours."

"Oh, no you don't!" He strode forward and began to replant the books, taking from both left and right sides of the stacks. "Let's start over."

"You'll ruin everything!" she said. "It took me hours to sort things out."

"Well," said he panting, down on one knee. "Let's take some *more* hours. *Freudian Analysis!* See? What's *that* doing on my side of the stacks. I hate Freud!"

"I thought I'd get rid of it."

"Rid of it? Call the Good Will. Don't fob the dumb books off on strangers, meaning your former husband. Let's make three stacks, one for you, one for me and one for the Salvation Army."

"You take the Salvation Army stuff *with* you and call them."

"Why can't you call from here? God, I don't want to lug the lamebrain stuff across town. Wouldn't it be simpler—"

"All right, all right, natter, natter. But stop messing with the books. Look at my stacks and then yours and see if you don't agree—"

"I see my copy of Thurber on your side, what's that doing there?"

"You gave it to me for Christmas ten years ago, don't you remember?"

"Oh," he said, and stopped. "Sure. Well—what's Willa Cather doing over there?"

"You gave me her for my birthday twelve years ago."

"It seems to me I spoiled you a lot."

"Damn right you did, a long time ago. I wish you were still spoiling me. Maybe we wouldn't be dividing up the damned books."

He flushed and turned away to kick the stacks quietly, gently with the tip of his shoe.

"Karen Horney, okay, she was a bore, too. Jung, I like Jung better, always did, but *you* can keep him."

"Thanks a billion."

"You always were one for thinking too much and not feeling."

"Anyone who carries his mattress around with him on his back shouldn't talk about thinking or feeling. Anyone who has bite marks on his neck—"

"We've been over that and it's past." He knelt down again and began to run his hand over the titles. "Here's Katherine Anne Porter's *Ship of Fools*, how in hell did you ever get through *that*? It's *yours*. John Collier's short stories! You *know* I love his work! That goes over in *my* pile!"

"Wait!" she said.

"*My* pile." He pulled the book out and tossed it along the floor.

"Don't! You'll hurt it."

"It's mine now." He gave it another shove.

"I'm glad you're not running the main library," she said.

"Here's Gogol, boring, Saul Bellow, boring, John Updike, nice style but no ideas. Boring, Frank O'Connor? Okay, but you can keep him. Henry James? Boring, Tolstoy, never could figure out the names, not boring, just confusing, keep him. Aldous Huxley? Hey, wait! You *know* I think his essays are better than his novels!"

"You can't break the set!"

"Like heck I can't. We split this baby down the middle. You get the novels, I get his ideas."

He grabbed three of the books and shoved them, skittering across the carpet.

She stepped over and began to examine the piles she had put aside for him.

"What are you doing?" he demanded.

"Just rethinking what I gave you. I think I'll take back John Cheever."

"Christ! What gives? I take *this*, you grab *that*? Put Cheever back. Here's Pushkin. Boring, Robbe-Grillet, French boring. Knut Hamsun. Scandinavian boring."

"Cut the critiques. You make me feel like I just failed my lit exam. You think you're taking all the good books and leaving me the dimwits?"

"Could be. All those Connecticut writers picking lint out of each other's navels, logrolling down Fifth Avenue, firing blanks all the way!"

"I don't suppose you find Charlie Dickens a dud?"

"Dickens!? We haven't had anyone like him in this *century!*"

"Thank God! You'll notice I gave you all the Thomas Love Peacock novels. Asimov's science fiction. Kafka? Banal."

"*Now* who's busy burning books?" He bent furiously to study first her stack, then his. "Peacock, by God, one of the great humorists of all time. Kafka? Deep. Crazy, brilliant. Asimov? A genius!"

"Ho-hum! Jesus." She sat down and put her hands in her lap and leaned forward, nodding at the hills of literature. "I think I begin to see where everything fell apart. The books you read, flotsam to me. The books I read, jetsam to you. Junk. Why didn't we realize that ten years back?"

"Lots of things you don't notice when you're——" he slowed——"in love."

The word had been spoken. She moved back in her chair, uneasily, and folded her hands and put her feet primly together. She stared at him with a peculiar brightness in her eyes.

He looked away and began to prowl the room. "Ah, hell," he said, kicking one stack, and moved across to kick the other, quietly, easily. "I don't give a damn what's in this bunch or that, I don't care, I just don't——"

"Do you have room in your car for most of these?" she said, quietly, still looking at him.

"I think so."

"Want me to help you carry them out?"

"No." There was another long moment of silence. "I can manage."

"You sure?"

"Sure."

With a great sigh he began to carry a few books over near the door.

"I've got some boxes in the car. I'll bring them up."

"Don't you want to look over the rest of the books to be sure they're ones you want?"

"Naw," he said. "You know my taste. Looks like you did it all right. It's like you just peeled two pieces of paper away from each other, and there they are, I can't believe it."

He stopped piling the books by the door and stood looking at first one fortress of volumes on one side and then the opposing castles and towers of literature, and then at his wife, seated stranded in the valley between. It seemed a long way down the valley, across the room to where she was.

At that moment, two cats, both black, one large, one small, bounded in from the kitchen, caromed off the furniture and ricocheted out of the room, with not a sound.

His hand twitched. His right foot half turned toward the door.

"Oh, no, you don't!" she said, quickly. "No cat carriers in here. Leave it outside. I'm keeping Maude and Maudlin."

"But—" he said.

"Nope," she said.

There was a long silence. At last, his shoulders slumped.

"Hell," he said, quietly. "I don't want any of the damned books. You can keep them all."

"You'll change your mind in a few days and come after them."

"I don't want them," he said. "I only want you."

"That's the terrible part of all this," she said, not moving. "I know it, and it's impossible."

"Sure. I'll be right back. I'll bring the boxes up." He opened the door and again stared at the new lock as if he couldn't believe. He took the old key from his pocket and put it on a side table near the door. "Won't need that anymore."

"No more, no," she said, so he could hardly hear her.

"I'll knock when I come back." He started out and turned. "You know all of this was just talking around the real subject we haven't even discussed yet?"

"What's that?" She looked up.

He hesitated, moved a step, and said, "Who gets the kids?"

Before she could answer, he went out and shut the door.

COME, AND BRING CONSTANCE!

His wife opened the mail at Saturday breakfast. It was the usual landslide.

"We're on every hit list in town, and beyond," he said. "I can stand the bills. But the come-ons, the premieres you don't want to attend, the benefits that benefit no one, the—"

"Who's Constance?" asked his wife.

"Who's who?" he said.

"Constance," said his wife.

And the summer morning passed quickly into November shade.

She handed over a letter from an old familiar dip up at Lake Arrowhead who was inviting him to a series of lectures on Primal Whisper, Extra Sensory Transubstantiation, EST, and Zen. The man's name, scribbled below, seemed to be "J'ujfl Kikrk." As if someone in the dark had typed the wrong letters and never gone back to correct.

The P.S. read: "If you come, bring Constance."

"Well?" said his wife, putting too much butter on her toast.

"I don't *know* any Constance," he said.

"No?"

"THERE IS NO Constance," he said.

"Really?"

"Indian scout's mother's honor."

"Indians are dirty, scouts are buggers, and your mother was an easy lady," said his wife.

"There never was, never is, and never will be," he threw the letter in the wastebasket, "a Constance."

"Then," said his wife, with a lawyer's logic, leaning against the stand, "why," she articulated, "is," she went on, "her name," she enunciated, and finished: "in the letter?"

"Where's the fan?" he said.

"What fan?"

"There's got to be one," he said, "for something awful to hit."

Meanwhile he was thinking quickly.

His wife watched him thinking and buttered her toast twice over again. Constance, he thought, in a panic.

I have known an Alicia and I have known a Margot and I have met a Louise and I once upon a time knew an Allison. But—

Constance?

Never. Not even at the opera. Not even at some tea.

He telephoned Lake Arrowhead five minutes later.

"Put that dumb stupid jerk on!" he said, not thinking.

"Oh, Mr. Junoff? Of course," said a woman's voice as if the description fit.

Junoff came on. "Yess . . . ?" He was one to make two or three syllables out of an affirmative.

"My wife's name is not Constance," said the husband.

"Who ever said it *was*? Who *is* this?"

"Sorry." The husband gave his name. "Look here, just because in a moment of tired blood four years ago I let you rack me on your couch and probe the gumball machine in my head, doesn't give you the right to send me an invitation to your saps-and-boots literary get-together next month. Especially when, at the end you add, 'bring Constance.' That is *not* my wife's name."

There was a long silence. Then the psychologist sighed. "Are you *sure*?"

"Been married to her for twenty years. I should know."

"Perhaps I inadvertently—"

"No, not even that. My mistress, when she was alive, which I some days doubt, was named Deborah."

"Damn," said Junoff.

"Yes. I *am*. And you *did*."

The telephone was dropped and picked up again. The man sounded like he was pouring a stiff drink and giving an easy answer at the same moment.

"What if I wrote Constance a letter—"

"There *is* no Constance! Only my *wife*. Whose name is—" He hesitated.

"What's wrong?"

The husband shut his eyes. "Hold on. Annette. Yes. That's it. Annette. No, that's her mother. Anne. That's better. Write to Anne."

"What shall I say?"

"Apologize for making up Constance. You've got me in a real pickle. She actually thinks the woman was real."

"*Constance* does?"

"Annette. Anne. Anne! I've already said—"

"There *is* no Constance, I get it. Hold on."

He heard more liquid being poured at the far end.

"Are you pouring gin instead of listening to me?"

"How did you know it was gin?"

"Shaken, not stirred."

"Oh. Well. Do I or do I *not* write the letter?"

"What good would it do? My wife would only think you were lying to save my skin."

"Yes, but the truth—"

"Is absolutely worthless with wives!"

There was a long silence from the far end in the villa up by the edge of the lake.

"Well?" said the husband.

"I'm waiting."

"For what, for God's sake?"

"For you to tell me what to do."

"You're the psychologist, you're the expert, you're the adviser, you're the guy who puts together mystical bathe-ins for unwashed minds, you're the chap with gum or something on the bottom of his shoes, *you* think of something!"

"Hold on," said the voice up at Lake Arrowhead.

There was a sound like the snapping of fingers or the adding of more ice.

"Holy Cow," said the psychologist. "I think I've got it. Yes. I *have*! I have. My God, I'm brilliant! Keep your pants on."

"They were never *off*, damn it!"

"Be prepared. I am raising the *Titanic*!"

Click.

There was a sound like more fingers being snapped or more ice added or the phone being hung up.

"Junoff!"

But he was gone.

———

The husband and wife battled through the morning, yelled at lunch, shrieked over coffee, took the fight to the pool around two, napped briefly at four to waken fresh with vitriol and drinks at four thirty, and at five minutes to five, there was an imperious ring of the front doorbell. Both of them trapped their mouths, she on her righteous indignation, he on his now increasingly maddened denials.

They both stared from the bar to the front door.

The royal ring came again. Something mighty and majestic leaned against the bell not caring if it rang forever to call an entire peasant countryside to kneel. They had never heard such a discourteous ring before. Which meant it could be a lout messenger who knew nothing, or a person of such grandiosity as to be forever important.

Husband and wife marched toward the door.

"Where are you going?" cried the wife.

"To answer it, of course."

"Oh, *no* you don't! And cover up!"

"Cover *what* up?"

"Liar! Gangway!"

And she left him in her dust. He went back to the bar and drank heavily for thirty seconds.

Only to see her standing in the doorway at the end of thirty-one seconds. She seemed stunned or frozen or both. With her back to the door, she summoned one hand to gesture strangely toward the entranceway. He stared.

"It's *Constance*," she said.

"Who?" he shouted.

"Constance, of course!" a voice whooped.

And the tallest and most beautiful woman he had ever seen charged into the room, looked around as if evaluating everything, and loped at a good pace to squeeze his elbows, grab his shoulders, and plant a kiss in the middle of his brow, which grew an extra eye immediately.

She stood off and looked him up and down as if he were not a man but an athletic team and she was here to aware medals.

He looked into her great bright face and whispered:

"Constance?"

"You're damn *tootin'*!"

The tall woman spun about to give a similar regard to the

wife, and the wife, if not an athletic team of winners, was at least a mob of admirers come along for the game.

"So this is——?" she asked.

"Annette," said the husband.

"Anne," said the wife.

"Yeah, that's it," said the husband. "Anne."

"Anne! What a great name. May I have a drink, Anne?"

The tall and beautiful woman with the huge halo of blond hair and the steady early morning fog gray eyes and the marching stride and the dancer's arms and hands, folded herself neatly into a chair and stretched out her from-here-to-there-and-happily-back-again legs.

"My God, I'm martini famished. Can it be *possible*?"

The husband stirred but his wife cried, "Don't *move*!"

The husband froze.

The wife leaned forward to gauge this creature, top to bottom, even as the creature had gauged her.

"Well?"

"Well, what?"

"What are you doing here—ah—"

"Constance!"

The wife looked at the husband. "So there's *no* Constance, *eh*?"

The tall woman blinked at the husband. "What *have* you been telling Anne?"

"Nothing." And that was the truth.

"Well, she must know *everything*. I leave tonight on the jet to New York and then tomorrow on the *Concorde* to Paris. I heard there was a misunderstanding—"

"Sure as hell has been—" said the husband.

"And I thought I'd just race over and clear things up before I was gone forever."

"Okay," said the wife. *"Clear."*

"First, do I get a drink?"

The husband stirred.

"Don't move," said the wife, with a deadly coldness in her voice.

"Well, then," said the lady as long as the lovely rivers of France and as beautiful as all of its towers and castles, "here goes. What an incredible *woman* you are!"

"Me?" said the wife.

"Your husband speaks of nothing else."

"Him!?" cried the wife.

"Goes on and on. Drives me wild. Makes me mad with jealousy. How you met, how you courted, where you dined, what your favorite food is, the name of your perfume, Countessa, your favorite book, *War and Peace*, which you've read seven times—"

"Only six—" said the wife.

"But you're on your *way* through seven!"

"True," admitted the wife.

"Your favorite films, *Pinocchio* and *Citizen Kane*—"

The wife glanced at the husband, who shrugged sheepishly.

"Your favorite sport, tennis, and mighty good at it, beat the hell out of him. Good at bridge and poker, beat him again, four times out of five. Were the bright whirl at high school proms, in college, and on board the United States ship for England on your honeymoon and last year on a Caribbean cruise. How you won a Charleston contest on board the *Queen Elizabeth II* coming home from France the year before. Your love of Emily Dickinson and Robert Frost. Your playing Desdemona in a little theater group eight years ago to great reviews. Your tender loving care when he was in the hospital five years back. Your treating his mother as if she were fine Dresden china. Your placing flowers on his father's grave at least four times a year. Your resisting buying two-thousand-dollar Dior dresses in Paris. Your dinner with Fellini in Rome when Federico fell in love with

you and almost carried you off. Your second honeymoon in
Florence where it poured for a week but you didn't care, for
you never went out. The short story you published in the *Ohio
State Monthly*; superb . . ."

The husband was leaning forward now, entranced.

And the wife had grown immensely quiet.

"On and on," said the woman whose name had caused
all the commotion. "Babble babble. How he fell in love with
you when you were twelve. How you helped him with algebra
when you were fourteen. How you decorated this place from
parquetry to chandeliers, from bathroom to back porch, and
loomed the rug in the front hall and made the pottery on the
sideboard. My God, dear Lord, would he *never* stop! Gibber-
gibber. I wonder—"

The tall, the long, the lovely lady paused.

"Does he ever talk about *me* this way, when he's with you?"

"Never," said the wife.

"I sometimes feel," said the beautiful woman, "that I do not
exist when I am with him. That he is with *you!*"

"I—" said the husband.

"Be still," said the wife.

He was still.

"Continue." The wife leaned forward.

"No time. Must go. May I have that drink?"

The wife went and mixed a martini and came back as if
bringing a blue ribbon to best cat of the show.

The beautiful woman sipped it and said, "That's the best
damned martini I ever had. Do you fail at *nothing*?"

"Let me think." The wife sat down slowly and eyed her
competition. "So he *speaks* of me, does he?"

"That's why it's all over," said the lovely lady. "I can't stand
it anymore. If you are so crazy for her, if you love her so much,
I said, for God's sake, what are you doing with *me*! Get. Go!

Vamoose. One more day of The Greatest Wife that God Ever Created will drive me absolutely bonkers. Scram!"

The lovely woman finished her drink, closed her eyes on the savor, nodded, and arose, story after story, lovely battlement after battlement. She stood above them, like a summer cloud, motioning them not to get up.

"Now it's scram for me, too. I'm off to the airport. But I had to come clear up a few things. It's not fair to ruin lives and not rebuild. It's been fun, George—"

"My name is Bill."

"Oops. Dear Bill, much thanks. And Annette—"

"Anne."

"Anne, you've won. I'll be gone four months. When I'm back, don't call me, I'll call you. So long, good wife. So long, Charlie." She winked and charged for the door, where she turned.

"Thanks for listening. Have a great life."

The front door slammed. The taxi, out front, could be heard motoring away.

There was a long silence. At last the wife said, "What was *that*?"

"One of those hurricanes," said the husband, "that they name for women."

He wandered off toward the bedroom where she found him packing a suitcase.

"What do you think *you're* doing?" she said, in the doorway.

"Well, after all this, I thought you'd want me to get out—"

"What, and move into a hotel?"

"Maybe—"

"Where *she* could come get her hooks into you?"

"I just imagined—"

"You think I'm going to let you run free in a world where people like that are lying in wait? Why, you poor custard—"

"You can't get hooks into a custard."

"But she's got a big spoon! Take those shirts out of the suit-cases. Now put those ties over there, and put those shoes under the bed, and come out and have a drink, dammit, and sit down and eat any damn dinner I make for you."

"But—"

"You're a beast and a rat and a bum," she said. "But—"

Tears ran down her cheeks.

"I love you! God help me. I do."

And she ran out of the room.

He heard her fiercely rattling ice into a shaker, as he dialed the phone.

"Put the stupid son of a bitch on," he said.

"Junoff here. Well?"

"Junoff, you brilliant mastermind, you incredibly inventive helpmate friend! Who *is* she? How did you do it?"

"She? Who?" said the voice from Lake Arrowhead.

"How did you remember so much from my sessions with you years ago? How could you tell *her*? What theater group is she from and is she a fast learner and quick read?"

"Haven't the faintest idea what you're talking about. Who *is* this?"

"Liar!"

"Is your wife there? What's her name?"

"Annette. No. Anne."

"Put her on!"

"But—"

"*Get* her!"

He walked out to the bar and picked up the extension phone and handed it to his wife.

"Hello," said Junoff's voice, one hundred miles away on top of a mountain near a lake.

His voice was so loud his wife had to hold the phone an inch away from her ear. Junoff shouted:

"Anne? I'm giving a party up here next weekend!"

And then:

"Come. And bring *Constance!*"

JUNIOR

It was on the morning of October 1 that Albert Beam, aged eighty-two, woke to find an incredible thing had happened, if not in the night, miraculously at dawn.

He witnessed a warm and peculiar rise two-thirds of the way down the bed, under the covers. At first he thought he had drawn up one knee to ease a cramp, but then, blinking, he realized—

It was his old friend: Albert, Junior.

Or just Junior, as some frolicsome girl had dubbed it, how long, oh God . . . some sixty years ago!

And Junior was alive, well, and freshly alert.

Hallo, thought Albert Beam, Senior, to the scene, that's the first time he's waked before me since July, 1970.

July, 1970!

He stared. And the more he stared and mused, the more Junior blushed unseen; all resolute, a true beauty.

Well, thought Albert Beam, I'll just wait for him to go away.

He shut his eyes and waited, but nothing happened. Or rather, it *continued* to happen. Junior did not go away. He lingered, hopeful for some new life.

Hold on! thought Albert Beam. It *can't* be.

He sat bolt upright, his eyes popped wide, his breath like a fever in his mouth.

"Are you going to *stay*?" he cried down at his old and now bravely obedient friend.

Yes! he thought he heard a small voice say.

For as a young man, he and his trampoline companions had often enjoyed Charlie McCarthy talks with Junior, who was garrulous and piped up with outrageously witty things. Ventriloquism, amidst Phys Ed. II, was one of Albert Beam's most engaging talents.

Which meant that Junior was talented, too.

Yes! the small voice seemed to whisper. *Yes!*

Albert Beam bolted from bed. He was halfway through his personal phonebook when he realized all the old numbers still drifted behind his left ear. He dialed three of them, furiously, voice cracking.

"Hello."

"Hello!"

"Hello!"

From this island of old age now he called across a cold sea toward a summer shore. There, three women answered. Still reasonably young, trapped between fifty and sixty, they gasped, crowed, and hooted when Albert Beam stunned them with the news:

"Emily, you won't believe—"

"Cora, a *miracle!*"

"Elizabeth, Junior's back."

"Lazarus has returned!"

"Drop everything!"

"Hurry over!"

"Goodbye, goodbye, *goodbye!*"

He dropped the phone, suddenly fearful that after all the

alarums and excursions, this Most Precious Member of the Hot-Dog Midnight Dancing-Under-the-Table Club might dismantle. He shuddered to think that Cape Canaveral's rockets would fall apart before the admiring crowd could arrive to gape in awe.

Such was not the case.

Junior, steadfast, stayed on, frightful in demeanor, a wonder to behold.

Albert Beam, ninety-five percent mummy, five percent jaunty peacock lad, raced about his mansion in his starkers, drinking coffee to give Junior courage and shock himself awake, and when he heard the various cars careen up the drive, threw on a hasty robe. With hair in wild disarray he rushed to let in three girls who were not girls, nor maids, and almost ladies.

But before he could throw the door wide, they were storming it with jackhammers, or so it seemed, their enthusiasm was so maniac.

They burst through, almost heaving him to the floor, and waltzed him backwards into the parlor.

One had once been a redhead, the next a blonde, the third a brunette. Now, with various rinses and tints obscuring past colors false and real, each a bit more out of breath than the next, they laughed and giggled as they carried Albert Beam along through his house. And whether they were flushed with merriment or blushed at the thought of the antique miracle they were about to witness, who could say? They were scarcely dressed themselves, having hurled themselves into dressing-gowns in order to race here and confront Lazarus triumphant in the tomb!

"Albert, is it *true*?"

"No *joke*?"

"You once pinched our legs, now are you *pulling* them?!"

"Chums!"

Albert Beam shook his head and smiled a great warm smile,

sensing a similar smile on the hidden countenance of his Pet, his
Pal, his Buddy, his Friend. Lazarus, impatient, jogged in place.

"No jokes. No lies. Ladies, sit!"

The women rushed to collapse in chairs and turn their rosy
faces and July Fourth eyes full on the old moon rocket expert,
waiting for countdown.

Albert Beam took hold of the edges of his now purposely
elusive bathrobe, while his eyes moved tenderly from face to
face.

"Emily, Cora, Elizabeth," he said, gently, "how special you
were, are, and will *always* be."

"Albert, dear Albert, we're dying with curiosity!"

"A moment, please," he murmured. "I need to—*remember.*"

And in the quiet moment, each gazed at the other, and suddenly saw the obvious; something never spoken of in their early
afternoon lives, but which now loomed with the passing years.

The simple fact was that none of them had ever grown up.

They had used each other to stay in kindergarten, or at the
most, fourth grade, forever.

Which meant endless champagne noon lunches, and prolonged late-night foxtrot/waltzes that sank down in nibblings of
ears and founderings in grass.

None had ever married, none had ever conceived of the
notion of children much less conceived them, so none had
raised any family save the one gathered here, and they had not
so much raised each other as prolonged an infancy and lingered
an adolescence. They had responded only to the jolly or wild
weathers of their souls and their genetic dispositions.

"Ladies, dear, dear, ladies," whispered Albert Beam.

They continued to stare at each other's masks with a sort of
fevered benevolence. For it had suddenly struck them that while
they had been busy making each other happy they had made no
one else *un*happy!

It was something to sense that by some miracle they'd given each other only minor wounds and those long since healed, for here they were, forty years on, still friends in remembrance of three loves.

"Friends," thought Albert Beam aloud. "*That's* what we are. *Friends!*"

Because, many years ago, as each beauty departed his life on good terms, another had arrived on better. It was the exquisite precision with which he had clocked them through his existence that made them aware of their specialness as women unafraid and so never jealous.

They beamed at one another.

What a thoughtful and ingenious man, to have made them absolutely and completely happy before he sailed on to founder in old age.

"Come, Albert, my dear," said Cora.

"The matinee crowd's here," said Emily.

"Where's Hamlet?"

"Ready?" said Albert Beam. "Get set?"

He hesitated in the final moment, since it was to be his last annunciation or manifestation or whatever before he vanished into the halls of history.

With trembling fingers that tried to remember the difference between zippers and buttons, he took hold of the bathrobe curtains on the theater, as 'twere.

At which instant a most peculiar loud hum bumbled beneath his pressed lips.

The ladies popped their eyes and smartened up, leaning forward.

For it was that grand moment when the Warner Brothers logo vanished from the screen and the names and titles flashed forth in a fountain of brass and strings by Steiner or Korngold.

Was it a symphonic surge from *Dark Victory* or *The Adventures of Robin Hood* that trembled the old man's lips?

Was it the score from *Elizabeth and Essex, Now, Voyager*, or *Petrified Forest*?

Petrified forest!? Albert Beam's lips cracked with the joke of it. How fitting for him, for Junior!

The music rose high, higher, highest, and exploded from his mouth.

"Ta-*tah*!" sang Albert Beam.

He flung wide the curtain.

The ladies cried out in sweet alarms.

For there, starring in the last act of Revelations, was Albert Beam the Second.

Or perhaps, justifiably proud, Junior!

Unseen in years, he was an orchard of beauty and sweet Eden's Garden, all to himself.

Was he both Apple *and* Snake?

He *was*.

Scenes from *Krakatoa, the Explosion That Rocked the World* teemed through the ladies' sugar-plum minds. Lines like "Only God Can Make a Tree" leaped forth from old poems. Cora seemed to recall the score from *Last Days of Pompeii*, Elizabeth the music from *Rise and Fall of the Roman Empire*. Emily, suddenly shocked back into 1927, babbled the inane words to "Lucky Lindy . . . Spirit of St. Louis, high, stay aloft . . . we're *with* you . . . !"

The musical trio quieted into a sort of twilight-in-mid-morning-holy-hour, a time for veneration and loving regard. It almost seemed that a wondrous illumination sprang forth from the Source, the Shrine at which they gathered as motionless worshippers, praying that the moment would be prolonged by their silent alleluias.

And it was prolonged.

Albert Beam and Junior stood as one before the throng, a large smile on the old man's face, a smaller one on Junior's.

Time-travel shadowed the ladies' faces.

Each remembered Monte Carlo or Paris or Rome or splash-dancing in the Plaza Hotel fount that night centuries ago with Scott and Zelda. Suns and moons rose and set in their eyes and there was no jealousy, only lives long lost but brought back and encircled in this moment.

"Well," everyone whispered, at last.

One by one, each of the three pal-friends stepped forward to kiss Albert Beam lightly on the cheek and smile up at him and then down at the Royal Son, that most Precious Member who deserved to be patted, but was not, in this moment, touched.

The three Grecian maids, the retired Furies, the ancient vest porch goddesses, stepped back a way to line up for a final view-halloo.

And the weeping began.

First Emily, then Cora, then Elizabeth, as all summoned back some midnight collision of young fools who somehow survived the crash.

Albert Beam stood amidst the rising salt sea, until the tears also ran free from his eyes.

And whether they were tears of somber remembrance for a past that was now a golden pavane, or celebratory wails for a present most salubrious and enchanting, none could say. They wept and stood about, not knowing what to do with their hands.

Until at last, like small children peering in mirrors to catch the strangeness and mystery of weeping, they ducked under to look at each other's sobs.

They saw each other's eyeglasses spattered with wet salt stars from the tips of their eyelashes.

"Oh, *hah!*"

And the whole damned popcorn machine exploded into wild laughter.

"Oh, *heee!*"

They turned in circles with the bends. They stomped their feet to get the barks and hoots of hilarity out. They became weak as children at four o'clock tea, that silly hour when anything said is the funniest crack in all the world and the bones collapse and you wander in dazed circles to fall and writhe in ecstasies of mirth on the floor.

Which is what now happened. The ladies let gravity yank them down to flag their hair on the parquetry, their last tears flung like bright comets from their eyes as they rolled and gasped, stranded on a morning beach.

"Gods! Oh! Ah!" The old man could not stand it. Their earthquake shook and broke him. He saw, in this final moment, that his pal, his dear and precious Junior, had at last in all the shouts and snorts and happy cries melted away like a snow memory and was now a ghost.

And Albert Beam grabbed his knees, sneezed out a great laugh of recognition at the general shape, size, and ridiculousness of birthday-suit humans on an indecipherable earth, and fell.

He squirmed amidst the ladies, chuckling, flailing for air. They dared not look at each other for fear of merciless heart attacks from the seal barks and elephant trumpetings that echoed from their lips.

Waiting for their mirth to let go, they at last sat up to rearrange their hair, their smiles, their breathing, and their glances.

"Dear me, oh, dear, dear," moaned the old man, with a last gasp of relief. "Wasn't that the best ever, the finest, the loveliest time we have ever had anytime, anywhere, in all the great years?"

All nodded "yes."

"But," said practical Emily, straightening her face, "drama's done. Tea's cold. Time to go."

And they gathered to lift the old tentbones of the ancient warrior, and he stood amongst his dear ones in a glorious warm silence as they clothed him in his robe and guided him to the front door.

"Why," wondered the old man. "Why? Why did Junior return on *this* day?"

"Silly!" cried Emily. "It's your birthday!"

"Well, happy *me*! Yes, yes." He mused. "Well, do you imagine, maybe, next year, and the next, will I be gifted the *same*?"

"Well," said Cora.

"We—"

"Not in this lifetime," said Emily, tenderly.

"Goodbye, dear Albert, fine Junior," said each.

"Thanks for all of my life," said the old man.

He waved and they were gone, down the drive and off into the fine fair morning.

He waited for a long while and then addressed himself to his old pal, his good friend, his now sleeping forever companion.

"Come on, Fido, here, boy, time for our pre-lunch nap. And, who knows, with luck we may dream wild dreams until tea!"

And, my God, he thought he heard the small voice cry, *then won't we be famished!?*

"We *will*!"

And the old man, half-asleep on his feet, and Junior already dreaming, fell flat forward into a bed with three warm and laughing ghosts. . . .

And so slept.

THE TOMBSTONE

Well, first of all there was the long trip, and the dust poking up inside her thin nostrils, and Walter, her Oklahoma husband, swaying his lean carcass in their model-T Ford, so sure of himself it made her want to spit; then they got into this big brick town that was strange as old sin, and hunted up a landlord. The landlord took them to a small room and unlocked the door.

There in the middle of the simple room sat the tombstone.

Leota's eyes got a wise look, and immediately she pretended to gasp, and thoughts skipped through her mind in devilish quickness. Her superstitions were something Walter had never been able to touch or take away from her. She gasped, drew back, and Walter stared at her with his droopy eyelids hanging over his shiny gray eyes.

"No, no," cried Leota, definitely. "I'm not moving in any room with any dead man!"

"Leota!" said her husband.

"What do you mean?" wondered the landlord. "Madam, you don't—"

Leota smiled inwardly. Of course she didn't really believe, but this was her only weapon against her Oklahoma man, so—"I mean that I won't sleep in no room with no corpse. Get him out of here!"

Walter gazed at the sagging bed wearily, and this gave Leota pleasure, to be able to frustrate him. Yes, indeed, superstitions were handy things. She heard the landlord saying, "This tombstone is the very finest gray marble. It belongs to Mr. Whetmore."

"The name carved on the stone is WHITE," observed Leota coldly.

"Certainly. That's the man's name for whom the stone was carved."

"And is he dead?" asked Leota, waiting.

The landlord nodded.

"There, you *see!*" cried Leota. Walter groaned a groan that meant he was not stirring another inch looking for a room. "It smells like a cemetery in here," said Leota, watching Walter's eyes get hot and flinty. The landlord explained:

"Mr. Whetmore, the former tenant of this room, was an apprentice marble-cutter, this was his first job, he used to tap on it with a chisel every night from seven until ten."

"Well—" Leota glanced swiftly around to find Mr. Whetmore. "Where is he? Did he die, too?" She enjoyed this game.

"No, he discouraged himself and quit cutting this stone to work in an envelope factory."

"Why?"

"He made a mistake." The landlord tapped the marble lettering. "WHITE is the name here. Spelled wrong. Should be WHYTE, with a Y instead of an I. Poor Mr. Whetmore. Inferiority complex. Gave up at the least little mistake and scuttled off."

"I'll be damned," said Walter, shuffling into the room and unpacking the rusty brown suitcases, his back to Leota. The landlord liked to tell the rest of the story:

"Yes, Mr. Whetmore gave up easily. To show you how

touchy he was, he'd percolate coffee mornings, and if he spilled a teaspoonful it was a catastrophe—he'd throw it all away and not drink coffee for days! Think of that! He got very sad when he made errors. If he put his left shoe on first, instead of his right, he'd quit trying and walk barefooted for ten or twelve hours, on cold mornings, even. Or if someone spelled his name wrong on his letters, he'd replace them in the mailbox marked NO SUCH PERSON LIVING HERE. Oh, he was a great one, was Mr. Whetmore!"

"That don't paddle us no further up-crick," pursued Leota grimly. "Walter, what're you commencing?"

"Hanging your silk dress in this closet; the red one."

"Stop hanging, we're not staying."

The landlord blew out his breath, not understanding how a woman could grow so dumb. "I'll explain once more. Mr. Whetmore did his homework here; he hired a truck that carried this tombstone here one day while I was out shopping for a turkey at the grocery, and when I walked back—tap-tap-tap—I heard it all the way downstairs—Mr. Whetmore had started chipping the marble. And he was so proud I didn't dare complain. But he was so awful proud he made a spelling mistake and now he ran off without a word, his rent is paid all the way till Tuesday, but he didn't want a refund, and now I've got some truckers with a hoist who'll come up first thing in the morning. You won't mind sleeping here one night with it, now will you? Of course not."

The husband nodded. "You understand, Leota? Ain't no dead man under that rug." He sounded so superior, she wanted to kick him.

She didn't believe him, and she stiffened. She poked a finger at the landlord. "*You* want your money. And you, Walter, you want a bed to drop your bones on. Both of you are lying from the word go!"

The Oklahoma man paid the landlord his money tiredly, with Leota tonguing him. The landlord ignored her as if she were invisible, said good night and she cried "Liar!" after him as he shut the door and left them alone. Her husband undressed and got in bed and said, "Don't stand there staring at the tombstone, turn out the light. We been traveling four days and I'm bushed."

Her tight crisscrossed arms began to quiver over her thin breasts. "None of the three of us," she said, nodding at the stone, "will get any sleep."

Twenty minutes later, disturbed by the various sounds and movements, the Oklahoma man unveiled his vulture's face from the bedsheets, blinking stupidly. "Leota, you still up? I said, a long time ago, for you to switch off the light and come to sleep! What are you doing there?"

It was quite evident what she was about. Crawling on rough hands and knees, she placed a jar of fresh-cut red, white, and pink geraniums beside the headstone, and another tin can of new-cut roses at the foot of the imagined grave. A pair of shears lay on the floor, dewy with having snipped flowers in the night outside a moment before.

Now she briskly whisked the colorful linoleum and the worn rug with a midget whisk broom, praying so her husband couldn't hear the words, but just the murmur. When she rose up, she stepped across the grave carefully so as not to defile the buried one, and in crossing the room she skirted far around the spot, saying, "There, that's done," as she darkened the room and laid herself out on the whining springs that sang in turn with her husband who now asked, "What in the Lord's name!" and she replied, looking at the dark around her, "No man's going to rest easy with strangers sleeping right atop him. I made amends with him, flowered his bed so he won't stand around rubbing his bones together late tonight."

Her husband looked at the place she occupied in the dark, and couldn't think of anything good enough to say, so he just swore, groaned, and sank down into sleeping.

Not half an hour later, she grabbed his elbow and turned him so she could whisper swiftly, fearfully, into one of his ears, like a person calling into a cave: "Walter!" she cried. "Wake up, wake up!" She intended doing this all night, if need be, to spoil his superior kind of slumber.

He struggled with her. "What's wrong?"

"Mr. White! Mr. White! He's starting to haunt us!"

"Oh, go to sleep!"

"I'm not fibbing! Listen to him!"

The Oklahoma man listened. From under the linoleum, sounding about six feet or so down, muffled, came a man's sorrowful talking. Not a word came through clearly, just a sort of sad mourning.

The Oklahoma man sat up in bed. Feeling his movement, Leota hissed, "You heard, you heard?" excitedly. The Oklahoma man put his feet on the cold linoleum. The voice below changed into a falsetto. Leota began to sob. "Shut up, so I can hear," demanded her husband, angrily. Then, in the heart-beating quiet, he bent his ear to the floor and Leota cried, "Don't tip over the flowers!" and he cried, "Shut up!" and again listened, tensed. Then he spat out an oath and rolled back under the covers. "It's only the man downstairs," he muttered.

"That's what I mean. Mr. White!"

"No, not Mr. White. We're on the second floor of an apartment house, and we got neighbors down under. Listen." The falsetto downstairs talked. "That's the man's wife. She's probably telling him not to look at another man's wife! Both of them probably drunk."

"You're lying!" insisted Leota. "Acting brave when you're really trembling fit to shake the bed down. It's a haunt, I tell you, and he's talking in voices, like Gran'ma Hanlon used to do, rising up in her church pew and making queer tongues all mixed, like a black man, an Irishman, two women, and tree frogs, caught in her craw! That dead man, Mr. White, hates us for moving in with him tonight, I tell you! Listen!"

As if to back her up, the voices downstairs talked louder. The Oklahoma man lay on his elbows, shaking his head hopelessly, wanting to laugh, but too tired.

Something crashed.

"He's stirring in his coffin!" shrieked Leota. "He's mad! We got to move outa here, Walter, or we'll be found dead tomorrow!"

More crashes, more bangs, more voices. Then, silence. Followed by a movement of feet in the air over their heads.

Leota whimpered. "He's free of his tomb! Forced his way out and he's tromping the air over our heads!"

By this time, the Oklahoma man had his clothing on. Beside the bed, he put on his boots. "This building's three floors high," he said, tucking in his shirt. "We got neighbors overhead who just come home." To Leota's weeping he had this to say, "Come on. I'm taking you upstairs to meet them people. That'll prove who they are. Then we'll walk downstairs to the first floor and talk to that drunkard and his wife. Get up, Leota."

Someone knocked on the door.

Leota squealed and rolled over and over, making a quilted mummy of herself. "He's in his tomb again, rapping to get out!"

The Oklahoma man switched on the lights and unlocked the door. A very jubilant little man in a dark suit, with wild blue eyes, wrinkles, gray hair, and thick glasses danced in.

"Sorry, sorry," declared the little man. "I'm Mr. Whetmore. I went away. Now I'm back. I've had the most astonishing stroke of luck. Yes, I have. Is my tombstone still here?" He looked at the stone a moment before he saw it. "Ah, yes, yes, it is! Oh, hello." He saw Leota peering from many layers of blanket. "I've some men with a roller-truck, and, if you don't mind, we'll move the tombstone out of here, this very moment. It'll only take a minute."

The husband laughed with gratitude. "Glad to get rid of the damned thing. Wheel her out!"

Mr. Whetmore directed two brawny workmen into the room. He was almost breathless with anticipation. "The most amazing thing. This morning I was lost, beaten, dejected—but a miracle happened." The tombstone was loaded onto a small coaster truck. "Just an hour ago, I heard, by chance, of a Mr. White who had just died of pneumonia. A Mr. White, mind you, who spells his name with an I instead of a Y. I have just contacted his wife, and she is delighted that the stone is all prepared. And Mr. White not cold more than sixty minutes, and spelling his name with an I, just think of it. Oh, I'm so happy!"

The tombstone, on its truck, rolled from the room, while Mr. Whetmore and the Oklahoma man laughed, shook hands, and Leota watched with suspicion as the commotion came to an end. "Well, that's now all over," grinned her husband as he closed the door on Mr. Whetmore, and began throwing the canned flowers into the sink and dropping the tin cans into a waste-basket. In the dark, he climbed into bed again, oblivious to her deep and solemn silence. She said not a word for a long while, but just lay there, alone-feeling. She felt him adjust the blankets with a sigh. "Now we can sleep. The damn old thing's took away. It's only ten thirty. Plenty of time for sleep." How he enjoyed spoiling her fun.

Leota was about to speak when a rapping came from down below again. "There! There!" she cried, triumphantly, holding her husband. "There it is again, the noises, like I said. Hear them!"

Her husband knotted his fists and clenched his teeth. "How many times must I explain. Do I have to kick you in the head to make you understand, woman! Let me alone. There's nothing—"

"Listen, listen, oh, listen," she begged in a whisper.

They listened in the square darkness.

A rapping on a door came from downstairs.

A door opened. Muffled and distant and faint, a woman's voice said, sadly, "Oh, it's you, Mr. Whetmore."

And deep down in the darkness underneath the suddenly shivering bed of Leota and her Oklahoma husband, Mr. Whetmore's voice replied: "Good evening again, Mrs. White. Here. I brought the stone."

THE THING AT THE TOP OF THE STAIRS

He was between trains.

He had got off in Chicago only to find that there was a four-hour waitover.

He thought about heading for the museum; the Renoirs and Monets had always held his eyes and touched his mind. But he was restless. The taxicab line outside the station made him blink.

Why not? he thought, grab a cab and taxi thirty miles north, spend an hour in his old hometown, then bid it farewell for the second time in his life, and ease back south to train out for New York, happier and perhaps wiser?

Much money for a few hours' whim, but what the hell. He opened a cab door, slung his suitcase in, and said:

"Green Town and return!"

The driver broke into a splendid smile and flipped the meter-flag, even as Emil Cramer leaped into the back seat and slammed the door.

Green Town, he thought, and—

The Thing at the top of the stairs.

What?

My God, he thought, what made me remember *that* on a fine spring afternoon?

And they drove north, with clouds that followed, to stop on Green Town's Main Street at three o'clock. He got out, gave the taxi driver fifty dollars as security, told him to wait, and looked up.

The marquee on the old Genesee Theater, in blood red letters, said: TWO CHILLERS. MANIAC HOUSE. DOCTOR DEATH. COME IN. BUT DON'T TRY TO LEAVE.

No, no, thought Cramer. The Phantom was better. When I was six, all he had to do was stiffen, whirl, gape, and point down into the camera with his ghastly face. *That* was terror!

I wonder, he thought, was it the Phantom then, plus the Hunchback, plus the Bat that made all of my childhood nights miserable?

And, walking through the town, he gave a quiet laugh of remembrance. . . .

How his mother would give him a look over the morning cornflakes: What *happened* during the night? Did you *see* it? Was it *there*, up in the *dark*? How *tall*, what *color*? How did you manage not to scream *this* time, to wake your father: what, *what*?

While his father, from around the cliff of his newspaper, eyed them both, and glanced at the leather strop hung near the kitchen washstand, itching to be used.

And he, Emil Cramer, six years old, would sit there, remembering the stabbing pain in his small crayfish loins if he did not make it upstairs in time, past the Monster Beast lurking in the attic midnight of the house, shrieking at the last instant to fall back down like a panicked dog or scorched cat, to lie crushed and blind at the bottom of the stairs, wailing:

Why? Why is it there? Why am I being punished? What have I done?

And crawling, creeping away in the dark hall to fumble back to bed and lie in agonies of bursting fluid, praying for dawn, when the Thing might stop waiting for him and sift into the stained wallpaper or suck into the cracks under the attic door.

Once he had tried to hide a chamberpot under the bed. Discovered, it was thrown and shattered. Once, he had run water in the kitchen sink, and tried to use it, but his father's radio ears, tuned, heard, and he rose in a shouting fury.

Yes, yes, he said, and he walked through the town on a day becoming storm colored. He reached the street on which he had once lived. The sun turned off. The sky was all winter dusk. He gasped.

For a single drop of cold rain struck his nose.

"Lord!" he laughed. "There it *is*. My house!"

And it was empty and a FOR SALE sign stood out by the sidewalk.

There was the white clapboard front, with a large porch to one side and a smaller one out front. There was the front door and, beyond, the parlor where he had lain on the foldout bed with his brother, sweating the night hours, as everyone else slept and dreamed. And to the right, the dining room and the door that led to the hall and the stairs that moved up into eternal night.

He moved up the walk toward the side porch door.

The Thing, now, what shape had it been, and color and size? Did it have a smoking face, and grotto teeth and hellfire-burning Baskerville eyes? Did it ever whisper or murmur or moan—?

He shook his head.

After all, the Thing had never really existed, *had* it?

Which was exactly why his father's teeth had splintered every time he stared at his gutless wonder of a son! Couldn't the child see that the hall was empty, *empty*!? Didn't the damned boy know that it was his own nightmare movie machine, locked in his head, that flashed those snowfalls of dread up through the night to melt on the terrible air?

Thump-*whack!* His father's knuckles cracked his brow to exorcise the ghost. Whack-*thump!*

Emil Cramer snapped his eyes wide, surprised to find he had shut them. He stepped up on the small porch.

He touched the doorknob.

My God! he thought.

For the door, unlocked, was drifting quietly open.

The house and the dark hall lay empty and waiting.

He pushed. The door drifted further in, with the merest sigh of its hinges.

The same night that had hung there like funeral-parlor curtains, still filled the coffin-narrow hall. It smelled with rains from other years, and was filled with twilights that had come to visit and never gone away. . . .

He stepped in.

Instantly, outside, rain fell. The downpour shut off the world. The downpour drenched the porch floorboards and drowned his breathing.

He took another step into complete night.

No light burned at the far end of the hall, three steps up—

Yes! That had been the problem!

To save money, the damned bulb was *never* left burning!

In order to scare the Thing off, you had to run, leap up, grab the chain and yank the light *on!*

So, blind and battering walls, you jumped. But could *never find the chain!*

Don't look up! you thought. If you see *It*, and it sees *You!* No. No!

But then your head jerked. You looked. You screamed!

For the dark Thing was lurching out on the air to slam flat down like a tomb lid on your scream!

"Anyone *home* . . . ?" he called, softly.

A damp wind blew from above. A smell of cellar earths and attic dusts touched his cheeks.

"Ready or not," he whispered. "Here I *come*."

Behind him, slowly, softly, the front door drifted, hushed, and slid itself *shut*.

He froze.

Then he forced himself to take another step and another.

And, Christ! it seemed he felt himself . . . shrinking. Melting an inch at a time, sinking into smallness, even as the flesh on his face diminished, and his suit and shoes became too large. . . .

What am I *doing* here? he thought. What do I *need*?

Answers. Yes. That was it. Answers.

His right shoe touched. . . .

The bottom of the stairs.

He gasped. His foot jerked back. Then, slowly, he forced it to touch the step again.

Easy. Just don't look up, he thought.

Fool! he thought, that's why you're here. The stairs. And the top of the stairs. That's *it*!

Now. . . .

Very quietly, he lifted his head.

To stare at the dark light bulb sunk in its dead white socket, six feet above his head.

It was as far off as the moon.

His fingers twitched.

Somewhere in the walls of the house, his mother turned in her sleep, his brother lay strewn in pale winding sheets, his father stopped up his snores to—*listen*.

Quick! Before he *wakes*. Jump!

With a terrible grunt he flung himself up. His foot struck

the third step. His hand seized out to yank the light-chain *there*. *Yank!* And there *again*.

Dead! Oh, Christ. No light. Dead! Like all the lost years.

The chain snaked from his fingers. His hand fell.

Night. Dark.

Outside, cold rain fell behind a shut mine-door.

He blinked his eyes open, shut, open, shut, as if the blink might yank the chain, pull the light *on*! His heart banged not only in his chest, but hammered under his arms and in his aching groin.

He swayed. He toppled.

No, he cried silently. Free yourself. Look! *See!*

And at last he turned his head to look up and up at darkness shelved on darkness.

"Thing . . . ?" he whispered. "*Are* you there?"

The house shifted like an immense scale, under his weight.

High in the midnight air a black flag, a dark banner furled, unfurled its funeral skirts, its whispering crepe.

Outside, he thought, *remember*! it is a *spring* day.

Rain tapped the door behind him, quietly.

"Now," he whispered.

And balanced between the cold, sweating stairwell walls, he began to climb.

"I'm at the fourth step," he whispered.

"Now I'm at the fifth. . . ."

"Sixth! You *hear*, up there?"

Silence. Darkness.

Christ! he thought, run, jump, fall out in the rain, the light—! No!

"Seventh! Eighth."

The hearts throbbed under his arms, between his legs.

"Tenth—"

His voice trembled. He took a deep breath and—

Laughed! God, yes! *Laughed!*

It was like smashing glass. His fear shattered, fell away.

"Eleven!" he cried. "Twelve!" he shouted. "Thirteen!!" he hooted. "Damn you! Hell, oh God, hell, yes, hell! And fourteen!"

Why hadn't he thought of this before, age six? Just leap up, shouting laughs, to kill that Thing forever!?

"Fifteen!" he snorted, and almost brayed with delight.

A final wondrous jump.

"Sixteen!"

He landed. He could not stop laughing.

He thrust his fist straight out in the solid dark cold air.

The laughter froze, his shout choked in his throat.

He sucked in winter night.

Why? a child's voice echoed from far off below in another time. *Why* am I being punished? What have I *done?*

His heart stopped, then let go.

His groin convulsed. A gunshot of scalding water burst forth to stream hot and shocking down his legs.

"No!" he shrieked.

For his fingers had touched something. . . .

It was the Thing at the top of the stairs.

It was wondering where he had been.

It had been waiting all these long years. . . .

For him to come home.

COLONEL STONESTEEL'S GENUINE HOME-MADE TRULY EGYPTIAN MUMMY

That was the autumn they found the genuine Egyptian mummy out past Loon Lake.

How the mummy got there, and how long it had been there, no one knew. But there it was, all wrapped up in its creosote rags, looking a bit spoiled by time, and just waiting to be found.

The day before, it was just another autumn day with the trees blazing and letting down their burnt-looking leaves and a sharp smell of pepper in the air when Charlie Flagstaff, aged twelve, stepped out and stood in the middle of a pretty empty street, hoping for something big and special and exciting to happen.

"Okay," said Charlie to the sky, the horizon, the whole world. "I'm waiting. Come *on!*"

Nothing happened. So Charlie kicked the leaves ahead of him across town until he came to the tallest house on the greatest street, the house where everyone in Green Town came with troubles. Charlie scowled and fidgeted. He had troubles, all right, but just couldn't lay his hand on their shape or size. So he shut his eyes and just yelled at the big house windows:

"Colonel Stonesteel!"

The front door flashed open, as if the old man had been waiting there, like Charlie, for something incredible to happen.

"Charlie," called Colonel Stonesteel, "you're old enough to rap. What is there about boys makes them shout around houses? Try again."

The door shut.

Charlie sighed, walked up, knocked softly.

"Charlie Flagstaff, is that you?" The door opened again, the colonel squinted out and down. "I thought I told you to *yell* around the house!"

"Heck," sighed Charlie, in despair.

"Look at that weather. Hell's bells!" The colonel strode forth to hone his fine hatchet nose on the cool wind. "Don't you love autumn, boy? Fine, fine day! Right?"

He turned to look down into the boy's pale face.

"Why, son, you look as if your last friend left and your dog died. What's wrong? School starts next week?"

"Yep."

"Halloween not coming fast enough?"

"Still six weeks off. Might as well be a year. You ever notice, colonel. . . ." The boy heaved an even greater sigh, staring out at the autumn town. "Not much ever happens around here?"

"Why, it's Labor Day tomorrow, big parade, seven cars, the mayor, maybe fireworks—er." The colonel came to a dead stop, not impressed with his grocery list. "How old are you, Charlie?"

"Thirteen, almost."

"Things do tend to run down, come thirteen." The colonel rolled his eyes inward on the rickety data inside his skull. "Come to a dead halt when you're fourteen. Might as well die, sixteen. End of the world, seventeen. Things only start up again, come twenty or beyond. Meanwhile, Charlie, what do we do to survive until noon this very morn before Labor Day?"

"If anyone knows, it's you, colonel," said Charlie.

"Charlie," said the old man, flinching from the boy's clear stare, "I can move politicians big as prize hogs, shake the Town Hall skeletons, make locomotives run backward uphill. But small boys on long autumn weekends, glue in their head, and a bad case of Desperate Empties? Well. . . ."

Colonel Stonesteel eyed the clouds, gauged the future.

"Charlie," he said, at last. "I am moved by your condition, touched by your lying there on the railroad tracks waiting for a train that will never come. How's this? I'll bet you six Baby Ruth candy bars against your mowing my lawn, that Green Town, upper Illinois, population five thousand sixty-two people, one thousand dogs, will be changed forever, changed for the best, by God, some time in the next miraculous twenty-four hours. That sound good? A bet?"

"Gosh!" Charlie, riven, seized the old man's hand and pumped it. "A bet! Colonel Stonesteel, I knew you could do it!"

"It ain't done yet, son. But look there. The town's the Red Sea. I order it to *part*. Gangway!"

———

The colonel marched, Charlie ran, into the house.

"Here we are, Charles, the junkyard or the graveyard. Which?"

The colonel sniffed at one door leading down to raw basement earth, another leading up to dry timber attic.

"Well—"

The attic ached with a sudden flood of wind, like an old man dying in his sleep. The colonel yanked the door wide on autumn whispers, high storms trapped and shivering in the beams.

"Hear that, Charlie? What's it say?"

"Well—"

A gust of wind blew the colonel up the dark stairs like so much flimsy chaff.

"Time, mostly, it says, and oldness and memory, lots of things. Dust, and maybe pain. Listen to those beams! Let the wind shift the timber skeleton on a fine fall day, and you truly got time-talk. Burnings and ashes, Bombay snuffs, tomb-yard flowers gone to ghost—"

"Boy, colonel," gasped Charlie, climbing, "you oughta write for *Top Notch Story Magazine*!"

"Did once! Got rejected. Here we are!"

And there indeed they were, in a place with no calendar, no month, no days, no year, but only vast spider shadows and glints of light from collapsed chandeliers lying about like great tears in the dust.

"Boy!" cried Charlie, scared, and glad *of* it.

"Chuck!" said the colonel. "You ready for me to birth you a real, live, half-dead sockdolager, on-the-spot mystery?"

"Ready!"

The colonel swept charts, maps, agate marbles, glass eyes, cobwebs, and sneezes of dust off a table, then rolled up his sleeves.

"Great thing about midwifing mysteries is, you don't have to boil water or wash up. Hand me that papyrus scroll over there, boy, that darning needle just beyond, that old diploma on the shelf, that wad of cannonball cotton on the floor. Jump!"

"I'm jumping." Charlie ran and fetched, fetched and ran.

Bundles of dry twigs, clutches of pussy willow and cattails flew. The colonel's sixteen hands were wild in the air, holding sixteen bright needles, flakes of leather, rustlings of meadow grass, flickers of owl feather, glares of bright yellow fox-eye. The colonel hummed and snorted as his miraculous eight sets of arms and hands swooped and prowled, stitched and danced.

"There!" he cried, and pointed with a chop of his nose. "Half-done. Shaping up. Peel an eye, boy. What's it commence to start to resemble?"

Charlie circled the table, eyes stretched so wide it gaped his mouth. "Why—why—" he gasped.

"Yes?"

"It looks like—"

"Yes, yes?"

"A mummy! *Can't* be!"

"Is! Bull's-eye on, boy! *Is!*"

The colonel leaned down on the long-strewn object. Wrist deep in his creation, he listened to its reeds and thistles and dry flowers whisper.

"Now, you may well ask, why would anyone *build* a mummy in the first place? You, you inspired this, Charlie. You put me up to it. Go look out the attic window there."

Charlie spat on the dusty window, wiped a clear viewing spot, peered out.

"Well," said the colonel. "What do you see? Anything happening out there in the town, boy? Any murders being transacted?"

"Heck, no—"

"Anyone falling off church steeples or being run down by a maniac lawnmower?"

"Nope."

"Any *Monitors* or *Merrimacs* sailing up the lake, dirigibles falling on the Masonic Temple and squashing six thousand Masons at a time?"

"Heck, colonel, there's only five thousand people *in* Green Town!"

"Spy, boy. Look. Stare. Report!"

Charlie stared out at a very flat town.

"No dirigibles. No squashed Masonic Temples."

"Right!" The colonel ran over to join Charlie, surveying the territory. He pointed with his hand, he pointed with his nose. "In all Green Town, in all your life, not one murder, one orphanage fire, one mad fiend carving his name on librarian ladies' wooden legs! Face it, boy, Green Town, Upper Illinois, is the most common mean ordinary plain old bore of a town in the eternal history of the Roman, German, Russian, English, American empires! If Napoleon had been born here, he would've committed hara-kiri by the age of nine. Boredom. If Julius Caesar had been raised here, he'd have got himself in the Roman Forum, aged ten, and shoved in his own dagger—"

"Boredom," said Charlie.

"Kee-rect! Keep staring out that window while I work, son." Colonel Stonesteel went back to flailing and shoving and pushing a strange growing shape around on the creaking table. "Boredom by the pound and ton. Boredom by the doomsday yard and the funeral mile. Lawns, homes, fur on the dogs, hair on the people, suits in the dusty store windows, all cut from the same cloth. . . ."

"Boredom," said Charlie, on cue.

"And what do you do when you're bored, son?"

"Er—break a window in a haunted house?"

"Good grief, we got no haunted houses in Green Town, boy!"

"Used to be. Old Higley place. Torn down."

"See my *point*? Now what *else* do we do so's not to be bored?"

"Hold a massacre?"

"No massacres here in dogs' years. Lord, even our police chief's honest! Mayor—not corrupt! Madness. Whole town faced with stark staring ennuis and lulls! Last chance, Charlie, what do we *do*?"

"Build a mummy?" Charlie smiled.

"Bulldogs in the belfry! Watch my dust!"

The old man, cackling, grabbed bits of stuffed owl and bent lizard tail and old nicotine bandages left over from a skiing fall that had busted his ankle and broken a romance in 1895, and some patches from a 1922 Kissel Kar inner tube, and some burnt-out sparklers from the last peaceful summer of 1913, and all of it weaving, shuttling together under his brittle insect-jumping fingers.

"*Voila!* There, Charlie! Finished!"

"Oh, colonel." The boy stared and gasped. "Can I make him a crown?"

"Make him a crown, boy. Make him a crown."

———

The sun was going down when the colonel and Charlie and their Egyptian friend came down the dusky backstairs of the old man's house, two of them walking iron-heavy, the third floating light as toasted cornflakes on the autumn air.

"Colonel," wondered Charlie. "What we going to do with this mummy, now we *got* him? It ain't as if he could talk much, or walk around—"

"No need, boy. Let folks talk, let folks run. Look there!"

They cracked the door and peered out at a town smothered in peace and ruined with nothing-to-do.

"Ain't enough, is it, son, you've recovered from your almost fatal seizure of Desperate Empties. Whole town out there is up to their earlobes in watchsprings, no hands on the clocks, afraid to get up every morning and find it's always and forever Sunday! Who'll offer salvation, boy?"

"Amon Bubastis Rameses Ra the Third, just arrived on the four o'clock limited?"

"God loves you, boy, yes. What we got here is a giant seed. Seed's no good unless you do *what* with it?"

"Why," said Charlie, one eye shut. "Plant it?"

"Plant! Then watch it grow! Then what? Harvest time. Harvest! Come on, boy. Er—bring your friend."

The colonel crept out into the first nightfall.

The mummy came soon after, helped by Charlie.

———

Labor Day at high noon, Osiris Bubastis Rameses Amon-Ra-Tut arrived from the Land of the Dead.

An autumn wind stirred the land and flapped doors wide not with the sound of the usual Labor Day Parade, seven tour cars, a fife and drum corps, and the mayor, but a mob that grew as it flowed the streets and fell in a tide to inundate the lawn out front of Colonel Stonesteel's house. The colonel and Charlie were sitting on the front porch, had been sitting there for some hours waiting for the conniption fits to arrive, the storming of the Bastille to occur. Now with dogs going mad and biting boys' ankles and boys dancing around the fringes of the mob, the colonel gazed down upon the Creation (his and Charlie's) and gave his secret smile.

"Well, Charlie . . . do I win my bet?"

"You sure do, colonel!"

"Come on."

Phones rang all across town and lunches burned on stoves, as the colonel strode forth to give the parade his papal blessings.

At the center of the mob was a horse-drawn wagon. On top of the wagon, his eyes wild with discovery, was Tom Tuppen, owner of a half-dead farm just beyond town. Tom was babbling, and the crowd was babbling, because in the back of the wagon was the special harvest delivered out of four thousand lost years of time.

"Well, flood the Nile and plant the Delta," gasped the

colonel, eyes wide, staring. "Is or is not that a genuine ole Egyptian mummy lying there in its original papyrus and coal-tar wrappings?"

"Sure is!" cried Charlie.

"Sure is!" yelled everyone.

"I was plowing the field this morning," said Tom Tuppen. "Plowing, just plowing! and—bang! Plow turned this up, right *before* me! Like to had a stroke! Think! The Egyptians must've marched through Illinois three thousand years ago and no one knew! Revelations, I call it! Outa the way, kids! I'm taking this find to the post office lobby. Set it up on display! Giddap, now, git!"

The horse, the wagon, the mummy, the crowd, moved away, leaving the colonel behind, his eyes still pretend-wide, his mouth open.

"Hot dog," whispered the colonel, "we did it, Charles. This uproar, babble, talk, and hysterical gossip will last for a thousand days or Armageddon, whichever comes first!"

"Yes, *sir*, colonel!"

"Michelangelo couldn't've done better. Boy David's a cast-away-lost-and-forgotten wonder compared to our Egyptian surprise and—"

The colonel stopped as the mayor rushed by.

"Colonel, Charlie, howdy! Just phoned Chicago. News folks here tomorrow breakfast! Museum folks by lunch! Glory Hallelujah for the Green Town Chamber of Commerce!"

The mayor ran off after the mob.

An autumn cloud crossed the colonel's face and settled around his mouth.

"End of Act One, Charlie. Start thinking fast. Act Two coming up. We *do* want this commotion to last forever, don't we?"

"Yes, sir—"

"Crack your brain, boy. What does Uncle Wiggily say?"

"Uncle Wiggily says—ah—go *back* two hops?"

"Give the boy an A-plus, a gold star, and a brownie! The Lord giveth and the Lord taketh away, eh?"

Charlie looked into the old man's face and saw visitations of plagues there. "Yes, sir."

The colonel watched the mob milling around the Post Office two blocks away. The fife-and-drum corps arrived and played some tune vaguely inclined toward the Egyptian.

"Sundown, Charlie," whispered the colonel, eyes shut. "We make our final move."

————

What a day it was! Years later people said: That was a day! The mayor went home and got dressed up and came back and made three speeches and held two parades, one going up Main Street toward the end of the trolley line, the other coming back, and Osiris Bubastis Rameses Amon-Ra-Tut at the center of both, smiling now to the right as gravity shifted his flimsy weight, and now to the left as they rounded a corner. The fife-and-drum corps, now heavily implemented by accumulated brass, had spent an hour drinking beer and learning the triumphal march from *Aïda* and this they played so many times that mothers took their screaming babies into the house, and men retired to bars to soothe their nerves. There was talk of a third parade and a fourth speech, but sunset took the town unawares, and everyone, including Charlie, went home to a dinner mostly talk and short on eats.

By eight o'clock, Charlie and the colonel were driving along the leafy streets in the fine darkness, taking the air in the old man's 1924 Moon, a car that took up trembling where the colonel left off.

"Where we going, colonel?"

"Well," mused the colonel, steering at ten philosophical miles per hour, nice and easy, "everyone, including your folks, is out at Grossett's Meadow right now, right? Final Labor Day speeches. Someone'll light the gasbag mayor and he'll go up about forty feet, kee-rect? Fire department'll be setting off the big skyrockets. Which means the post office, plus the mummy, plus the police chief sitting there with him, will be empty and vulnerable. Then, the miracle will happen, Charlie. It *has* to. Ask me why."

"Why?"

"Glad you asked. Well, boy, folks from Chicago'll be jumping off the train steps tomorrow hot and fresh as pancakes, with their pointy noses and glass eyes and microscopes. Those museum snoopers, plus the Associated Press, will rummage our Egyptian Pharaoh seven ways from Christmas and blow their fuse-boxes. That being so, Charles—"

"We're on our way to mess around."

"You put it indelicately, boy, but truth is at the core. Look at it this way, child, life is a magic show, or *should* be if people didn't go to sleep on each other. Always leave folks with a bit of mystery, son. Now, before people get used to our ancient friend, before he wears out the wrong bath towel, like any smart weekend guest he should grab the next scheduled camel west. There!"

The post office stood silent, with one light shining in the foyer. Through the great window, they could see the sheriff seated alongside the mummy-on-display, neither of them talking, abandoned by the mobs that had gone for suppers and fireworks.

"Charlie." The colonel brought forth a brown bag in which a mysterious liquid gurgled. "Give me thirty-five minutes to mellow the sheriff down. Then you creep in, listen, follow my cues, and work the miracle. Here goes nothing!"

And the colonel stole away.

Beyond town, the mayor sat down and the fireworks went up.

Charlie stood on top of the Moon and watched them for half an hour. Then, figuring the mellowing time was over, dog-trotted across the street and moused himself into the post office to stand in the shadows.

"Well, now," the colonel was saying, seated between the Egyptian Pharaoh and the sheriff, "why don't you just finish that bottle, sir?"

"It's finished," said the sheriff, and obeyed.

The colonel leaned forward in the half-light and peered at the gold amulet on the mummy's breast.

"You believe them old sayings?"

"What old sayings?" asked the sheriff.

"If you read them hieroglyphics out loud, the mummy comes alive and walks."

"Horse radish," said the sheriff.

"Just look at all those fancy Egyptian symbols!" the colonel pursued.

"Someone stole my glasses. You read that stuff to me," said the sheriff. "Make the fool mummy walk."

Charlie took this as a signal to move, himself, and sidled around through the shadows, closer to the Egyptian king.

"Here goes." The colonel bent even closer to the Pharaoh's amulet, meanwhile slipping the sheriff's glasses out of his cupped hand into his side-pocket. "First symbol on here is a hawk. Second one's a jackal. That third's an owl. Fourth's a yellow fox-eye—"

"Continue," said the sheriff.

The colonel did so, and his voice rose and fell, and the sheriff's head nodded, and all the Egyptian pictures and words flowed and touched around the mummy until at last the colonel gave a great gasp.

"Good grief, sheriff, look!"

The sheriff blinked both eyes wide.

"The mummy," said the colonel. "It's going for a walk!"

"Can't be!" cried the sheriff. "Can't be!"

"Is," said a voice, somewhere, maybe the Pharaoh under his breath.

And the mummy lifted up, suspended, and drifted toward the door.

"Why," cried the sheriff, tears in his eyes. "I think he might just—*fly*!"

"I'd better follow and bring him back," said the colonel.

"*Do* that!" said the sheriff.

The mummy was gone. The colonel ran. The door slammed.

"Oh, dear." The sheriff lifted and shook the bottle. "Empty."

———

They steamed to a halt out front of Charlie's house.

"Your folks ever go up in your attic, boy?"

"Too small. They poke me up to rummage."

"Good. Hoist our ancient Egyptian friend out of the back seat there, don't weigh much, twenty pounds at the most, you carried him fine, Charlie. Oh, that was a sight. You running out of the post office, making the mummy walk. You shoulda seen the sheriff's face!"

"I hope he don't get in trouble because of this."

"Oh, he'll bump his head and make up a fine story. Can't very well admit he saw the mummy go for a walk, can he? He'll think of something, organize a posse, you'll see. But right now, son, get our ancient friend here up, hide him good, visit him weekly. Feed him night talk. Then, thirty, forty years from now—"

"What?" asked Charlie.

"In a bad year so brimmed up with boredom it drips out your ears, when the town's long forgotten this first arrival and departure, on a morning, I say, when you lie in bed and don't want to get up, don't even want to twitch your ears or blink, you're so damned bored. . . . Well, on *that* morning, Charlie, you just climb up in your rummage-sale attic and shake this mummy out of bed, toss him in a cornfield and watch new hellfire mobs break loose. Life starts over that hour, that day, for you, the town, everyone. Now grab git, and hide, boy!"

"I hate for the night to be over," said Charlie, very quietly. "Can't we go around a few blocks and finish off some lemonade on your porch. And have *him* come, too."

"Lemonade it is." Colonel Stonesteel banged his heel on the car-floor. The car exploded into life. "For the lost king and the Pharaoh's son!"

———

It was late on Labor Day evening, and the two of them sat on the colonel's front porch again, rocking up a fair breeze, lemonades in hand, ice in mouth, sucking the sweet savor of the night's incredible adventures.

"Boy," said Charlie. "I can just see tomorrow's *Clarion* headlines: PRICELESS MUMMY KIDNAPPED. RAMESES–TUT VANISHES. GREAT FIND GONE. REWARD OFFERED. SHERIFF NONPLUSSED. BLACK-MAIL EXPECTED."

"Talk on, boy. You *do* have a way with words."

"Learned from you, colonel. Now it's your turn."

"What do you want me to say, boy?"

"About the mummy. What he really is. What he's truly made of. Where he came from. What's he *mean* . . . ?"

"Why, boy, you were there, you helped, you *saw*—"

Charles looked at the old man steadily.

"No." A long breath. "Tell me, colonel."

The old man rose to stand in the shadows between the two rocking chairs. He reached out to touch their ancient harvest-tobacco dried-up-Nile-River-bottom old-time masterpiece, which leaned against the porch slattings.

The last Labor Day fireworks were dying in the sky. Their light died in the lapis lazuli eyes of the mummy, which watched Colonel Stonesteel, even as did the boy, waiting.

"You want to know who he *truly* was, once upon a time?"

The colonel gathered a handful of dust in his lungs and softly let it forth.

"He was everyone, no one, someone." A quiet pause. "You. Me."

"Go on," whispered Charlie.

Continue, said the mummy's eyes.

"He was, he is," murmured the colonel, "a bundle of old Sunday comic pages stashed in the attic to spontaneously combust from all those forgotten notions and stuffs. He's a stand of papyrus left in an autumn field long before Moses, a papier-mâché tumbleweed blown out of time, this way long-gone dusk, that way at come-again dawn . . . maybe a nightmare scrap of nicotine/dogtail flag up a pole high-noon, promising something, everything . . . a chart-map of Siam, Blue River Nile source, hot desert dust-devil, all the confetti of lost trolley transfers, dried-up yellow cross-country road maps petering off in sand dunes, journey aborted, wild jaunts yet to night-dream and commence. His body? . . . Mmmm . . . made of . . . all the crushed flowers from brand-new weddings, dreadful old funerals, ticker-tapes unraveled from gone-off-forever parades to Far Rockaway, punched tickets for sleepless Egyptian Pharaoh midnight trains. Written promises, worthless stocks, crumpled deeds. Circus posters—see there? Part of his paper-wrapped rib-cage? Posters torn off seedbarns in North Storm, Ohio, shuttled south toward Fulfillment, Texas, or Promised Land, Calif-orn-I-aye! Commencement proclamations, wedding notices, birth announcements . . . all things that were once need, hope, first nickel in the pocket, framed dollar on the café wall. Wallpaper scorched by the burning look, the blueprint etched there by the hot eyes of boys, girls, failed old men, time-orphaned women, saying: Tomorrow! Yes! *It* will happen! Tomorrow! Everything that died so many nights and was born again, glory human spirit, so many rare new daybreaks! All the dumb strange shadows you ever thought, boy, or I ever inked out inside my head at three a.m. All, crushed, stashed, and now shaped into one form under our hands and here in our gaze. That, that is what old King Pharaoh Seventh Dynasty Holy Dust Himself *is.*"

"Wow," whispered Charlie.

The colonel sat back down to travel again in his rocker, eyes shut, smiling.

"Colonel." Charlie gazed off into the future. "What if, even in my old age, I don't ever *need* my own particular mummy?"

"Eh?"

"What if I have a life chock full of things, never bored, find what I want to do, *do* it, make every day count, every night swell, sleep tight, wake up yelling, laugh lots, grow old still running fast, what *then,* colonel?"

"Why then, boy, you'll be one of God's luckiest people!"

"For you see, colonel." Charlie looked at him with pure round, unblinking eyes. "I made up my mind. I'm going to be the greatest writer that ever lived."

The colonel braked his rocker and searched the innocent fire in that small face.

"Lord, I *see* it. Yes. You *will*! Well, then Charles, when you are very old, you must find some lad, not as lucky as you, to give Osiris-Ra to. Your life may be full, but others, lost on the road, will need our Egyptian friend. Agreed? Agreed."

The last fireworks were gone, the last fire balloons were sailing out among the gentle stars. Cars and people were driving or walking home, some fathers or mothers carrying their tired and already sleeping children. As the quiet parade passed Colonel Stonesteel's porch, some folks glanced in and waved at the old man and the boy and the tall dim-shadowed servant who stood between. The night was over forever. Charlie said:

"Say some more, colonel."

"No. I'm shut. Listen to what he has to say now. Let him tell your future, Charlie. Let him start you on stories. Ready . . . ?"

A wind came up and blew in the dry papyrus and sifted the ancient wrappings and trembled the curious hands and softly twitched the lips of their old/new four-thousand-year nighttime visitor, whispering.

"What's he saying, Charles?"

Charlie shut his eyes, waited, listened, nodded, let a single tear slide down his cheek, and at last said:

"Everything. Just everything. Everything I always wanted to *hear.*"